To all friends, past and present. You matter.

I Claim This Land for Spain

I'VE BEEN LOSING MYSELF for years, and I'm not even that old. I was never good at denial, and that's never helped me much. Let's see if I'm any good at running. Well, that's already happening. This never prevented me from thinking too much. I'm good at that. Thinking, it's what's for breakfast; not to mention every other meal. Despite being out and about under a silver morning sky, I find myself wired as all hell and wish I had any time for even some bad coffee to settle the well-deserved hangover I'm trying to ignore. It's remarkable what we don't know if we simply don't want to know it. I woke up this early because I was too afraid to say goodbye and be done with it. I thought I wouldn't get

NEVER GOING HOME

Jeff Marlowe

Never Going Home

Copyright © 2020 Jeff Marlowe
All Rights Reserved

www.jeffmarlowebooks.com

Library of Congress Control Number: 2020919369
ISBN: 978-1-7358917-0-5 (paperback)
ISBN: 978-1-7358917-1-2 (eBook)

Capablanca Books
Philadelphia, PA

past the front door, yet somehow here I am. Here and now I know there's no good to come from it, and the here and now comes down to two empty milk crates resting on the street.

I've seen these things just about every day before now; in the morning usually, or on a day off, when I come home, sometimes even late at night. I live in the hybrid suburbia/city section of my town. It's old and the parking is abysmal in my neighborhood, abysmal being too kind a word for it. I can try to imagine how better it was before every household had a car for every person of driving age some thirty years ago perhaps. I would like having a car parked right outside my home just like anyone else but here there really are no driveways, garages few and far between, and I accept the fact that parking is left up to the street alone, or high-priced paid lots just as far; so I park only as close as I'm able, and never taking any thought to the fact I do not own the pavement.

This particular daybreak has at least lent the opportunity to solve a grandiose mystery for the ages. I hate my own keen sense of observation. When I first saw these milk crates some time ago, I thought someone had thrown them away. Obviously, if they are left on or off the curb, they wanted the garbage men to take them off to the landfill. So, if I or anyone else needed these things, we could just take them, similar to how some people take couches from the curb if they are decent. Hell, my friends and I did that once or twice in college. It's not as if we could buy one back then.

The crates are not here for that purpose today. I find myself more and more appalled by the behavior of the human species, and that's in no small part to my own naivety and apparent underestimation of such a state of ignorance. Ignoring it was easier, but I'm not good at easy either.

Maybe I just never wanted it to register but in the short time I realize these orange (with a strong tinge of dirty brown) milk crates are my neighbor's way of reserving her own parking spot on a public street. Yes, I've seen the crates many times before but have never witnessed anyone actually doing this, like they were ninjas or something, never to be seen, they just sort of magically appear there on a daily basis, even on weekends when it suits them. Yet this morning as I walk down the hill towards the corner home, I see her, not only that but I see her working her magic, pulling the two putrid milk crates from the back of her aging SUV and placing them just far enough apart enough to reserve her own space for whenever she gets home tonight. Why do I doubt my own revulsion with it? I simply don't believe it, almost horrified at witnessing a crime.

For the first time since living in this neighborhood I see her, in growing daylight, straight ahead and in the act. It's all a tad epic, honestly. I am not sure what to do about it; indeed, what really could be done? I walk slower, uncontrollably giving her a look of disapproval, slightly shaking my head. Not sure how I could be happy with this person. She's intruding on her own neighborhood, breaking the law and just all around being rude. Though make no mistake about it, she's unbelievably pissed off at me.

Her aging, melty eyes bore into me enough to make me believe for nearly half a minute that I've really done something wrong here. Not only is she so disappointed in me; I can almost feel the tension rise from her, the wrath festering all the more for what I have done to her. I don't believe in spirits or astrological energy but the Force is disturbed here, and it is terrifying. Her frown is bending so profoundly it makes me feel like an obnoxious intruder, a jackass who makes her ashamed to be my neighbor and remembering a better time when usurpers like me didn't live here. It is really me who is the antagonist in our newfound duo, and the question our story leaves the two of us is: what the living hell is wrong with me? I think this girl's head is about to fall off her shoulders based on it not being able to ever stop shaking. She's like a scowling, selfish old bobble head doll. She's shaking her head so much that I would be surprised if she doesn't have a headache before she drives off; not that this would ever stop her.

By this reaction, she's become a victim somewhere within the past minute. She does not deserve to be treated this way. Hasn't she had enough? If I am gaining anything at all here from my own disapproval, it's that she is threatened; she is oppressed, and it does not matter if I have no idea why.

Never speaking, the neighbor rolls her eyes and works her art of the smirk in extreme disappointment as she continues to break the law and take possession of public property as if she bought and paid for her section of the street as an extension of her home and therefore of herself. I continue to walk in my direction, albeit slowly. I can't take my eyes off of her as she finishes spacing her milk crates, and justifying to herself how much of a prick I am. It's all half-tough, but she's getting her point across: I'm the bad guy here. I just wish I really knew why, and I'm sorry but when I get to her age, I will still not approve of this. That's likely a problem too.

Looking at her closely now, she's really not exceptionally old, yet definitely aging, perhaps in the late 40's or early 50's, not overweight but positively getting there. She's wearing tight blue jeans stretched around her inflated backside. I can see a bit too much eye makeup on her, somewhat distracting attention from her flabby neck and squinted, lazy right eye. I can't look at her too long. This is not due to her appearance but what she's really doing. She's reserving a spot on our damned public street and clearly thinks I am in the wrong for disagreeing with it.

I'm not sure if it's this crime, or that I'm expected to not care about this that gets to me. This neighbor is astounding because after making me feel at least briefly guilty, she has me feeling really alone, and I keep walking.

I imagine the fact that I took direct notice of her and involuntarily scowled and snorted at the sight of it was enough to so profoundly offend her and draw such extreme, albeit silent vitriol. There's some role I'm not filling here, some sort of don't ask, don't tell policy with the parking arrangements that I am not accommodating, and to be honest, I just don't see a need to.

She slams her door just hard enough to get her point across. She's not looking at the road, but out into disappointed space. Her tires screech just a little, an exclamation point on the silent tongue lashing she has just given me. This girl didn't wake up this morning and go about her day just to be troubled by the likes of me. She was not supposed to get caught; and challenging her on it was an injustice thrown upon her against her will. None of this was ever meant to go down. I spoil it all for her today. There's no way in hell she is changing, that would demand maturity that is just not there, even given whatever our age difference.

I'm glad she's leaving, but we are not as different as she likes to believe. She misses the days when every neighbor knew each other and did not violate their (perceived) property and personal space; and she misses the community that once existed right here in our little part of town. I miss it too. I just never got an opportunity to actually experience it. I never had what she is pining for, and wishes people like me didn't take away from her, or at least imply it. I may flatter myself to think she drove off discerning about what the incursion my generation is, and how I do not understand anything. How could I? I'm younger than her, after all. I overestimate the prospect of her understanding my own appreciation of certain griefs with time here. She's far from interested. What is hers is hers, and there should be no question. It's alright. I don't want her to like me anyway.

Anyway, she's gone. I've never met this neighbor and know nothing about her but I know she's been living here much longer than I have, probably longer than anyone still here from her time. It's not enough I let her drive off in a huff and don't touch the milk crates. The fact that I showed such dissent, even if only through body language, is enough to know what I'm dealing with. It's not sufficient for this friendly neighbor to do this on a daily basis, and it's not enough to get away with it just as much. I haven't succeeded in stopping any of it today yet there is clearly something else she wanted (if not needed) that's not being rewarded to her. Sorry, my dear, we can't always win, though we can evidently always deny.

Maybe it's not pure arrogance. Time is on her side; at least it is as far as of any real concern. Milk crate girl's family probably bought and paid off their house thirty years ago, back when almost everyone could pay off their homes before their youngest child was five years old. No such option will I ever have. She's far less concerned about that turn of events but I can't help but wonder if she likes it.

Parking in this area was probably quite manageable then, less population, families with only one car, not one car for each of the four or five people living in each house. I wish I had known those days as she did. I still would not drop milk crates on the street today, yet it would have all been so nice to have. This neighborhood was somehow more than what we have today, not less. I was not there; I just try to remember anyway. Again, just can't ignore it, it seems; and I'm not entirely sure why I should.

Back to the present now, unpleasant as it may be. Milk crate girl could leave at any time in the morning and come back any time later, no burden of walking more than ten steps to the front door. By any means necessary. I wonder if anyone besides me even notices the parking reservation toys. Either they are flat out ignorant like her or in denial. Perhaps too afraid of the consequences or trouble if they spoke up even slightly. She does not just want her own way, she gets it too, and that demands no one, certainly not me, expressing dissent. It's obvious the wrong people benefit from this state of affairs. I would love to not care, but I do. Am I wrong here? No one around to tell me. Sadly, I don't know if many would care if I actually asked.

If I can say it, I get it; the parking in this town sucks. I don't like it any more than anyone else does. For being my charming neighbor, perhaps you feel you deserve something more because you have lived here for so long. You do not. Reality is not evidently what the cool kids are into these days but the street, even the street right in front of your door, is community property. Maybe she has a bad knee, some effects from a hip surgery, but if that is the case; why not at least get a handicap parking decal or something to that effect? I do not see a limp; and by her visceral attitude toward me; I can surmise she's just fine. The parking sucks, and this is her solution. She's gotten away with it; and I'll bet she knows why.

We can't own this, and we should know we can't have what we want every day just because it's convenient. We can't exist together if you can't get over yourself. Milk crates. You really do have nerve.

I wish I was living in this neighborhood some fifty or sixty years ago, and that is all the more sad as my neighbors of this bygone era are the ones breaking my heart today with a couple of frigging milk crates. She probably still hates me for it. The damage is done even if I never wanted it.

I don't accept it as an excuse but my delightful neighbor is not the only perpetrator in this city to have done this. She is quite consistent with her daily routine, but I have seen others on different streets, in front of different front doors' exercising the same perceived right. It was just two winters ago a series of heavy snow storms hit and beyond the salting and overcrowded supermarkets, the general hysteria included more of the milk crate miracles, mostly in the form of orange cones, trash cans, and metal chairs with large rocks resting on them; all of these placed into dug out parking spots on the street, juxtaposed with snow-covered cars bumper to bumper along the ancient streets. Lovely winter wonderland insanity.

Incidentally, there was some local media backlash regarding these exquisite reservations. A young just-out-of-college girl was leaving her apartment for work on one of the snowy days that winter and passed two fairly decent looking chairs resting on a cleared-out parking spot on the snowy road. She had just moved to the area and needed a couple of chairs for at least the interim at her apartment. Not too far removed from the college years, she knew a good "dumpster-diving" deal when she saw one. Students would leave everything from bookcases to couches (and nice ones too) outside their dorm or campus apartments when the school year ran out. This young student and her friends would often take advantage of the discarded furniture which was great on a college student's income. This happens more often than I thought, apparently.

If the owners do not want the chairs, she was going to happily take them. What is more, they were nice enough to leave heavy rocks on each of these chairs, so as they will not blow away in the wind. How kind of them. The young resident removed the rocks, took the chairs, placed them in the trunk of her car and drove off to work happily, having her home seating issue taken care of at least for now.

What she did not know is that not so long after removing the chairs, a local Jetta owner pulled in to the conveniently vacant parking spot and left for the train station some blocks down the street. When the Jetta's owner came home after work that evening, he found all four of his tires slashed, and a note on the windshield stating, "Don't ever park here again!" Police were summoned, the Jetta was towed, and according to the legend, a man yelled out of a window next to the notorious parking spot something along the lines of "serves you right!" as the car was being towed. Of course, the disgruntled home owner was not charged with vandalizing the tires due to lack of any material evidence. This incident did make local headlines.

On the news, the mayor was asked to comment on this and similar instances. He said that it was absolutely illegal to hold public street spaces for parking, however, he asked that we all understand that we have a "culture" of small streets and row homes in this city, and we should respect that in times of severe weather, reserving parking spaces can be common and should not be hindered until the weather danger has sufficiently passed. Yes, the mayor said all that; this trusted adult charged with the responsibility of running the city. So much for the maturity of leadership. He seemed rather annoyed at even having to address the issue. Can I ask why this is such an issue to begin with? Why all the sensitivity? Should such concerns not be discussed at all?

On the other hand, the mayor is older like the new neighbor friend I made this morning. We can't have the newcomers ever thinking that they can share the place, can we? That might be a stretch, but then again so is reserving public parking. I don't even dislike the local politicians that much, but Miss Milk Crate was given a stamp of approval with all this, not that she ever needed it. She doesn't have to make sense, and neither do those in power. So much for looking up.

I remember thinking then, and now for that matter, reserving public property is illegal and I can't see how it's tolerated, bad snow storms or not. I know this city has other problems, but are we really going to just shut all eyes to this when it's clear and presently a crime? What else can I get away with if it snows?

Incidentally, to our favorite milk-crate neighbor, it's now late April! There isn't a flake of snow on the ground. The parking is still difficult, and I have seen this type of thing all year round. She's not the only one. Others in town use cones, trash cans, even large rocks, impractical as that seems. Never once has the Mayor, the police, the parking ticket agents, or any type of official authority done any one thing about it, rain or shine. It's actually interesting if one can give any thought to it. After all, what can the police or parking ticket agents do?

They have no problem at all ticketing or towing any car that runs a minute over the parking meter time, or parked within an inch of regulation space from a fire hydrant. However, what would be the point of ticketing a chair? One can't ticket that or milk crate reserving a space. After all, those in authority could never know who the perpetrators actually were so no ticket would be justified, and no towing because there is no actual car there.

Though this begs the question that if the police and parking authority are going to be an "authority," the why do they not take charge in simply removing these placeholders as they find them illegally marking a parking space? People would know it is the duty of those charged with public enforcement to remove them, they won't get ticketed but the action itself is not tolerated, snow or sunny weather. Yet there is no money in that. So here we are. If this is even a crime (and it is), it's the perfect crime as one cannot really get caught; or even investigated for the crime. Win-win I presume. Brilliant, and now pointless. She's gone now, leaving no one here but me.

As I ponder all this (the pondering an apparent sin unto itself); this isn't at all how I assumed my day would begin. Last night I was afraid to sleep for fear of waking up so the next day would begin. I know I can't turn this off. It's time to go. There is the matter of that letter is on my desk, if it is still my desk. I could have emailed it last night if I ever hit that send button, and I could have slept through this majestic encounter and the milk crates would still not go away.

Be that as it may, it's not right. Not at all. The only thing I feel some shame for is yielding the milk crates to their resting place on the street as I leave; and not any less irritated because of it. I didn't take them away. They are still resting there. Maybe I'm letting it get to me for no good reason; more truthfully, I'm not doing enough about it. Maybe I care too much. Maybe I was born too late. Maybe I am right. Maybe I can't deal with it now.

It's still very early in the morning; the silver sky is just pale enough to make me believe I have some benefit of time over everyone. I may just have enough time to undo the damage I almost did. I am not ashamed of it, yet on approximately an hour's rest I start walking faster, near running to erase one of the most terrifying stunts I've attempted in recent memory. Time is even less of a friend than that aging narcissist who just drove off. Sad that I've been up all night with barely any sleep only to find I'm not brave enough to challenge two milk crates; and far less of the courage to follow through with quitting my job.

Chapter Two

King of the All-Nighters

I'M NOT A GOOD liar, so I might as well confess to this now. Yesterday, I quit my job. It's true, though I'm not sure if anyone besides me actually knows this yet. At its face value, that may sound as a bad enough a sin, but as it turns out, I have actually provided two sins for everyone to glare at me all the more in addition to just resigning employment. The first of these unabashed sins is that I quit my job without notice. I just wrote a letter of resignation and left. Who knows if anyone has read it yet, and that's why I'm practically running out of breath to the office now.

The letter alone could raise a number of eyebrows. I can see why this is taboo and almost thought twice about it, but it's not as if employers are in the habit of giving notice when they fire or lay off anyone. No one ever seems to frown upon employers for doing this to their underlings. When do we ever really think upon it? There is a reason for this.

Yet worse than any of this, the second of these sins is my attempt to leave my job was done with the full knowledge and embrace of any and all consequences of the fact that I did not have another job lined up at all to replace it. I put myself out of work with nothing after the fact. That's just unforgivable. Even if I have my own reasons, they're not good enough, not by a long shot. I am not proud of it, but this is where I am in life this lovely morning.

I've been at this working world thing for over ten years, or so I tell myself. When I was a kid, they used to call it the "real world" yet for the life of me I cannot find anything terribly real about it. Wish someone would have told me that then (they wouldn't have indulged even if I asked). I can't recall having been given one sentence of genuine honesty from anyone in quite some time. Though, who am I kidding; it's going to get pretty obvious very soon that I am not as audacious as I assumed to be. I am disgusted with myself for it, though I expect am a permissible coward in this case. It all depends on how this goes.

Maybe I wanted too much. Though likely I was never told enough, and with good reasons (for "them" anyway). I remember not just thinking of myself so much. I was raised on the idea that working hard, sacrificing, and learn-ing everything I could, would be a benefit not just to me, but to society at large. The generation I grew up in would only do better than our parents had before us, and maybe even become the world's new "Greatest Generation." We would reverse all that was wrong with the world and make it better for everyone. We could do this and wanted to. Or if not, at least we wanted a level playing field in which to act on these opportunities. Now that was wishful thinking.

It's amazing really, working hard (though hardly working as of late) to move up a ladder that's no longer there. I'm starting to think "they" never wanted it there to begin with and simply figured out that it's not in their interest to share and thus they don't have to. I always wanted to have a job and work, just more on the work to live and less the live to work angle. I think I would still be here either way. I often daydream of traveling through time, going into my fourth or fifth grade elementary school classroom, and denounce to all of us sitting there (in front of the egotistical, immature, and ancient witch of a teacher) that we should congratulate ourselves; for we will be the first generation in modern history that will not do as well financially (and I say culturally) than the generations that have come before us.

We have already been outperformed otherwise, and by the time we are all our parents' age, we will have not at all reached the same level of prosperity, not by a mile, and it keeps going, and kids, you all will likely reach a point in your life where you accept that this is where it is all going. So, please ask yourselves how it feels to be on the decline of a civilization. At least some such guidance with this epidemic would have gone a long way for us, but it was never there. Never once.

Up until yesterday, I was actually not out of work and had a job to speak of, such as it was. That all said, I am not at all in a good work situation and my options are growing ever thinner as the days and weeks go by. The fact that I have (well, almost) quit my job now is actually nothing unique when viewed though our current lenses; or the "these days" factor. Most jobs these days don't last more than five years or so for one reason or another; and we often have at least ten jobs by the time we reach our mid or late thirties era. As such, it is practically of no consequence that I'm leaving. Though in my case, there is that second sin.

If I was to base my career, for whatever it was, upon my own father's for example, I would have likely had one job in life that would have lasted decades, not just around eighteen months. Moreover, I could have been far more dedicated to my job, (as my employers could have been to me to me), if I only held one, perhaps two jobs throughout my entire adult life. But this isn't the case for me, and surely not so many others, let alone the generations to follow us.

Baby Boomers, my parents' generation, respected authority a hell of a lot more because it all worked for them, all the more reason to conform in their cause. What would be the point of challenging the bosses or evidently just as worse: thinking of it? Yet those who have up to ten or so jobs by mid-life will likely not have the inflated sense of self-esteem that seems to come from the other experience. If our jobs do not last more than a few years, or maybe half a decade with luck; and if we can be let go at any given time during our tenure, and often are; then the results can often be disastrous by comparison, and not just in a monetary value.

We often dismiss those whom have lost a home in which they never really had in the first place. Can the experience of ten jobs in less than twenty years be accepted into any home? Not based on our predecessors' standards, absolutely not. There are a lot of old values lingering in modern times. I tried to somehow run away from it last night; and the sad truth of it is, I don't know how to leave home, notwithstanding I know "home" is not there. I don't know how to leave at all.

I ended my work day yesterday with my desk cleared, my cubicle door unlocked, and a signed letter on my desk, and lord knows if anyone has read it since the milk crate incident this morning. I didn't talk to a soul on the way out of that office. What I remember of the trip back was that I was in fact too petrified to remember a thing and equally horrified to go to sleep last night, lest I have to wake up to meet a day I did not want to see. Last night was not by any means the only "all-nighter" I have ever had in my semi-longish life. I've spent a few, some even recently, strictly at home but this wasn't going to happen this time. I didn't want to tell anyone about my two dreadful sins; but I wasn't going to get anywhere by staying in, so well after nightfall I was taking my trepidation out on myself, and taking anyone I could find at all along with me for the ride.

It's predominantly row homes where I live. I wanted to get lost in some mountains, never to be found again, but there are none. Nowhere to go and at the time, no job. There is a main street not far with more expensive apartments and a good number of bars and restaurants that my friends and I like to frequent. We can even take a train into the downtown area for more yet last night, I didn't even know what to do with myself, let alone where to go. Hard to be out about town when one is by himself. I look at people wandering around, spending time with friends, herding kids, holding hands, just talking to other human beings. It all makes me feel all the more alone. I wanted to jump into someone else's party, some other group's night. There were plenty of people around, yet even if it was twice the population out it would not matter. I was alone, and I expect I deserved it.

Something else worth saying which I hadn't and won't tell anyone was that wandering around the streets last night, I actually saw a couple having sex in their bedroom window. Disturbing at first glance, I did not want to hang out and stare for too long but it was like looking at a train wreck, I just couldn't turn away from it. The window itself was foggy enough, but to be sure, a young, slender, girl was bent over in front of the glass, palms pressed against the pane, head turning and nodding about while her boyfriend (so I could assume) thrusted behind her, occasionally groping her neck but mostly staying away from the window himself, just could not get much of a look at him, not that I was trying.

I could not help but laugh under my breath, and was rather pleased no one else was around watching this as I wasn't interested in being part of a peanut gallery audience sharing comments. Just let these people do their thing. The girl getting her handprints all over the window was certainly enjoying it. I can't hear them, not that I was listening for sounds, yet nonetheless it seems rather intense in there. Who knows why they had sex in front of a window. Indeed, why does sex have to be so "traditional?" No need to always be in bed or anywhere practical for that matter. I wanted to keep moving on, and they are still going at it judging by the shadows through the thickening fog.

It's amazing what can get us excited. We often need that extra something to make life interesting, a break from the routine, and these two were taking care of that in spades. I could see from where I stood then that the girl in the window was a brunette with long and curly hair (and likely sweaty through the misty looks of it). Her hair was whipping and bobbing around, and she was quite the feast to look at, considering she was stark naked. I never had any kind of preference for hair color, and it's mostly beyond me how some men have a tendency to state a preference.

I suppose this goes along with the "to each and their own" theme going on through the window frame right then.

Wanting to close this particular part of my evening a bit more rapidly, I remember a long time ago when I might have turned my head away in some degree of disgust at these two screwing each other in the window for potential onlookers to catch a glimpse at them, which is, in their defense, kind of the whole idea. But I just walked away right then, because despite the show, it's not my place to watch and hardly to judge, and not one to window and tell. To be honest, I have been in the window myself once or twice in my lifetime, so I don't blame them. All the same I've been trying to put this out of my mind, mildly amusing as it was. I never spoke about the window scene to anyone, though the image isn't leaving my mind any time soon. Treasure your memories.

After quitting (in a manner of speaking) my job I did make it back to my place, leaving my small box of what-ever personal stuff I took away with me by the door. I can't remember much else in between then and the window exhibition but I just could not stay home. Maybe I couldn't stop feeling I was losing my mind considering what I had just done. I never had the answer to that arbitrary ques-tion we are sometimes asked, as to what super power we could have if we ever had the choice. For me, it was never super strength or speed or even flying like some of my old favorite heroes. What I wanted was the power to time travel, or at the very least to slow time before it hit me that my bosses were actually reading the letter that I left on my so soon to be former desk.

I thought to myself maybe I could drink all the thoughts and problems away, at least for a little while. That was to no avail and I didn't try. While drinking was a new and fun activity in college, I take little interest these days. Maybe it's a sign of getting older and more aware. Maybe that's why many drink even more. I'm not even sure what the definition of "too much" is in these times anyway. I suppose even a little can be enough to offend more than just one person. Hard to believe it at this point in my life but I used to smoke. I was never once addicted to it, and I stopped with no personal resistance at all some point in my early twenties, probably when the aforementioned alcohol interest came about. Cigarettes were just something I smoked socially with my friends. I was never too cool to smoke in the high school bathroom, and I never cared to.

I think what prompted this nonchalance with smoking was an absurd, however common, conversation I had with a fellow fifteen-year-old back then. All the guys liked to play fight or wrestle around in the gym or sometimes in the halls if we could get away with it; and martial arts films were still cool even through the 80's and early 90's so I "play punched" Mark Burbine during gym period one day; by that I mean I tapped him in slow motion in the chest with my fist. Mark quickly defended himself by holding up his hand and boasting "Don't smoke, man. I need to quit smoking, don't ever start the habit." Ridiculous. He was fifteen, and younger than me by a few months (a time frame which matters to teenagers much more). and just trying and outright failing to be cool by appearing "older," and somehow more experienced. Nonsense. It didn't work on me so I never really got into the habit despite the acceptable smoking era, however bygone.

Cigarettes were so few and far between after college, I haven't bought a pack of smokes in I don't know how long and they are ridiculously overpriced now so that was not going to happen last night. I can't believe they were around seventy cents a pack or some thirty years ago. The post millennium. What an era to live in. Unhealthy habit, but there is something to smoking I think we have lost in the subsequent decades, something of our culture has died off even as we did, and I can't see it coming back. Hence, one of the reasons I bought a cigar last night and enjoyed lighting up after it was completely dark.

I don't want to start the habit. After the "last day" at work debacle, I just wanted something real. Cigarettes weren't going to cut it so a cigar it was. That cigar was harsh, and was challenging to smoke at first but I finished it. It hurt me. It was bad for me. It harkened back to a time where more than just one nervy, wayward soul walking the streets was smoking, however unhealthy. These are all reasons I actually enjoyed it.

When I was a kid, I liked old black and white movies. I would watch *The Three Stooges* on our rabbit ear antennae TV. I got a kick out of them then (still do) because I watched them with my grandfather an uncle whenever I would visit them. That's not all we watched. I loved Bela Lugosi's *Dracula*, all the old monster movies, really. My grandfather held the likes of Clark Gable, Bing Crosby, Gary Grant and Katherine Hepburn in the highest esteem, among some of the other greats. But to him, my uncle, and myself included, no one could rise above one Humphry Bogart. I was never sure what resonated with him to my grandfather or myself, but the way Bogey wore those suits and hats, his bad ass attitude and command of all his scenes, the sarcasm and quick comebacks to everyone except the dames who took his heart; he was simply the best. He was a man's man and even the man I looked up to, my horseback cop grandfather, knew it was so.

This is all notwithstanding the smoking. Bogey was a smoker. I expect almost everyone was in his time. I don't admire him for that. I know it probably killed off more actors and actresses over the years it was more socially conventional; but it was ubiquitous to that culture, to our culture. There was something there. Why the hell were Bogart, Bacall, and Bing Crosby, etc. even something to begin with? To any number of reasons, I'm sure, but the film noir, swing, jazz, detective novels, all of it; it was new to people back then. I didn't live during this time, that window has passed. The thirties and forties and beyond were likely not easy, but they all had something that's lacking in more recent decades. Life began imitating art for real. I have been mostly waiting around for that to happen again, and often questioning why it doesn't.

It's hard to find "new" any longer. We are living in the era of cultural stagnation. America has lost its cultural product; finding those yet to be discovered shores has become a superficial knowledge at best. No cultural creation today, and I doubt there really are any, of certainly the post millennium that can even compare to what we fashioned in those days. My cigar burned out before long, and we all burned out a long time ago; I just wish it were not so.

Smoking that cigar didn't make me Bogart. It didn't kill me, and I'm still not taking up the habit though I admit I would like to smoke one again soon. Maybe I just wanted to be part of the old world of my grandfather or Bogey somehow, even for just a short while. I even wore my black fedora hat. Yet even that I had to buy online. Days gone by. Maybe I wanted to reverse time, however brief, and however alone. To concede, it was rather fun, I just wish it didn't make me feel even more out of place. There are not too many cops riding around on horses either. It's all gone away.

I remembered thinking that maybe all that time alone wasn't really the best course of action. I wasn't willing to tell anyone I knew about quitting the job but the lonely, brooding Bogart effort only got me so far, as if I even knew then or now where I was supposed to be going. Maybe putting out the bat-signal would do something for someone; me specifically, but there was no way I was discussing current events with any of my people.

I don't remember a single phone number. I realized this sad fact standing there on the street last night while, for whatever reason, looking for a phone booth. I have a cell phone, of course, I can't remember not having one or what I would do without it. We used to live without them. Yet as I result, I can't remember a single number. I want to step into a phone booth, briefly cut myself off from the pedestrian bubble and talk to a friend and have him join me on the out and about; or change into Superman and fly off if I could, to at least be part of the past. The phone booths aren't coming back either. I could not even tell my friends what happened with my job, and certainly was not in the mood to explain it to them. It's a moot point considering none of my friends even answer the phone much anyway. So I went for the text. There are generally always results.

Out of fairly limited options, I always start my text messages with Chris Allen. Somewhat ironic as of all my friends, I've known him for the least amount of time. Even if he is not working on his latest heart attack (I'm starting to realize with good reason), I know what answer I will get but I tried him anyway.

I waited in my imaginary phone booth, wondering how long until I was reminded, I was on my own out there. His reply was heartfelt, however predictable.

Why did he have to remind me that we work together? I won't even see that staff meeting. This was freaking me the hell out, I hate this mounting fear, it's making my stomach sick, and there is no known cure either. Of course, he is with his girlfriend. Nice gal, but she altogether supersedes my usefulness as a friend more often than not, and I needed something better than that just then. It was best to let him go, not pushing the texts any more than I have with him. So, I tried plan B: Dave Huston, who is single. Well, most of the time he is. He's complicated, but really not. I baited my best hook.

A blatant lie. Dave knows (and on occasion from what I can tell, likes) that I don't have a girlfriend and knows it's unlikely on a Tuesday night that the bars would be all that lively, but telling Huston that there may be girls for him to lie to is like asking a dog if he likes bacon; he usually loses interest in anything else surrounding him. He never sent a response. He's not a responding kind of guy, too cool for that most of the time, too in demand, or so he wants everyone to believe. He does crack me up though. He's otherwise occupied, obviously; can't imagine why; but the answer is likely he's busy with his pillow pal, Lisa Otts.

Lisa has always been interesting to me as she is a gal well into her thirties who manages to be "single" at all times in that she is never in a relationship. The girls at my job would hate her for this very reason. Still, she and Dave have that physical or friends with benefits thing going on, I can't imagine Dave is her only beneficiary and Dave seems not to care, so good for them. I never really understood it. That sort of thing was just not for me.

Just as well, neither of these guys would appreciate my present predicament, no sense in indulging them to understand or even be sympathetic, and Chris probably has it worse than me at work. I doubt me quitting would help his own cause very much. As if he's not guilted enough there already, he's my friend and there is that guilt by association, and ultimately that one less fish to fry could make someone next on the menu. He could very well be on his own, and I hate cutting him loose that way by leaving. Again, I was really trying to freeze time last night, and stop that sun from rising for everyone to discover what I had done when they came to work the following day, Chris included. No one knows. I rather liked it that way, but there's not an atheist's chance in heaven for that to last.

All the sadder, I ran out of friends to text. I have more than just two pals to connect with. There is Hal, and Joey at the forefront in life lately but the former is too much of an asshole, and the latter too old. I could reach out to older friends but that was not the time to do so, it's not as if anyone else would accept what I did anyway. It is something, how Dave is all about the girls all the time. He wouldn't believe, or maybe even like the fact, that I met a girl last night as well despite all the brooding. A break from the routine and making life interesting can easily come about when we don't have anything else to lose. I walked into a bar alone, somehow managed to get her attention without really trying, and after a while I told this complete, and frankly cute, stranger everything I both could and would not tell any other living soul.

Chapter Three

The Maple Leaf

I HATE DRINKING ALONE. I have done so from time to time at home yet if in a bar or restaurant (hate eating alone too), it just doesn't make sense or feel right to be in such a social situation alone. I can't say if I feel like a loser or a creep doing so but overall it takes little time for me to feel like someone or everyone is watching me, and I will play on my phone or fake a call to make it look like I'm just killing time or waiting on someone who is running late and will join me soon. The charade never lasts, and I would just as soon ask for the check and bail out as soon as possible. Last night I didn't care.

I dropped in on some random bar. Somewhat crowded, not over-packed, dimly lit, but yet not a dive were the only requirements I had. This one was good enough, typical weekday night crowd, cute waitresses, a bartender not so busy to forget I was there, random televisions, mostly playing the hockey games, and some distracted by video poker. None of them knew me.

Often, I would be out with Dave, Hal, and maybe Chris (if his girlfriend allowed him), but regardless, the first and last thing on Dave's mind would be scoping out the female scene and seeing where and how he could get lucky. With him engaged in other activities at that point, the noise of Dave's never-ending game to pick up girls was lessened enough for me to simply order a drink and strike up a conversation with a Canadian transplant returned home.

That was Sara. Dave would be so proud but why tell him? If she told me her last name I forget and at this point could not care less to remember. I knew the Canada thing as soon as I saw her; it was the red maple leaf tattoo. Of course, it was showing on her lower back. Where else could it have possibly been? Not sure why that area developed into the tattoo trend it did but she wanted me or anyone to see it so I looked. I took her for a Canadian or at least a huge hockey fan but she was only so much of either.

I only half remember how I approached her, yet I did sit right next to her. She was with two friends who very much appeared to be a couple. They were a couple well engaged into each other; both decent looking and well kept; the gal almost as cute as Sara.

If anything, they encouraged her to talk to me. One smile was all I needed when normally I would have spent all night analyzing the situation. Frankly, I was just happy that the more typical situation of five or so guys surrounding the evidently single girl was not playing out as usual. Minor miracles. All I knew then was that I didn't want to go home and sleep, that would bring tomorrow on far too easily and that was no good for anyone.

I remember saying, or slightly shouting over the music: "Enjoying yourself tonight?" She seemed delighted to talk to someone. I suppose her being a third wheel is what turned her on to talking to anyone. I hoped she would not figure out that misery loves company yet not much else. Conveniently for her, hockey was playing on one of the bar TVs so I had enough hooks to make a least a conversation work, and better still I had nothing to lose.

"I'm Sara, I'm here with my friend and his girlfriend we are celebrating my return I guess." She was friendly enough and quite pretty. In addition, the red maple leaf tattoo feature, Sara was tallish, thin, somewhat younger than me, maybe in her late twenties and noticeably blonde. She looked like she was poured into those low-rise jeans, exposing the maple leaf I could in such a way I think she wanted everyone to see. Me as well?

Yet I digress. To what would be Dave's disappointment, I was in no mood nor within capability to pick up a girl last night so this was just going perfectly well, and probably for that reason. She had an intelligent, sexy, and honestly lonely feel about her as she sipped her cherry vodka. Just to talk to her was a small victory, at least for not really trying anyway.

I told all three of my temporary new friends my name. "Din Swift" raised some eyebrows; I never met another human being on earth with the name. The couple Sara was with, Michael and Teresa, shook hands with me and seemed pleased to go about their own date and let their friend cease being the third wheel for a little while. As I had guessed, Sara had recently moved back to the states after an extended stay in Canada, very proud of her life living abroad in the northlands.

"Well, welcome home," I said clinking her glass with my beer. "I've been to Canada before, just for a trip to Niagara Falls and a couple days in Toronto, which is like the U.S., I know. I've never lived in another country though." This lit Sara's pride beams a bit, after all, she was more than a tourist up there.

"It's a different experience with another culture when you live somewhere as opposed to just visiting," she says. "I have seen Niagara Falls, sure, but it was all just tourists there, not the real Canada. Did you stay on the New York or Canadian side of the falls?"

I winced as I knew exactly what was coming out of this girl in return. "I stayed on the Canadian side when I was there," I tell her, "then in just downtown Toronto, not too far of a drive, relatively."

Her pride bright again, her response was infallibly, "The Canadian side has a better view, can't see anything in that U.S. view. It's just better in Canada."

She was right of course, about the view at least. No, probably all of it. I have no idea if life is any better in Canada or not, and I stayed on the Canadian side of the falls on that trip because I was told the view was better and it was. Still, it seems everything is an indicator or at the very least at this point, a reminder that the U.S. just isn't as good, as attractive, or as "in" as it once was in the world. The lame view from the New York side of the falls is no exception. I'm not from New York, but its country of origin is my own. In this experience, I don't feel like part of a losing team or anything, but I can't help shaking the idea I'm in the wrong time and maybe even in the wrong country. Sara's somewhat justified ego isn't helping much.

For all the rare joy one can feel over spending a brief part of a single evening with a single girl, Sara did play into a couple of my own suspicions. Not the least of which was when I asked her why she moved to Canada in the first place.

"A guy," she said to my nonchalant eyebrow raise. Yes, it's almost always a guy, it seems. I wish it were otherwise and I often do, but I've done dumb things for romance myself so who am I to judge? Can't blame her for trying, and moving to another county or anywhere for a relationship is never easy and equally difficult to leave and return home after its failure. Nevertheless, it doesn't help anyone talking about past relationships so I was glad she was forthright enough to change the subject and nice enough to not have the entire conversation about her adventure in Canada in asking what I do for a living.

Sara worked in Canada and evidently now works as an accountant for an investment company. Lucky her to move home from abroad and still have a job. I wondered if that is because she's pretty. All I could do was go into my dime tour description of what I do and hope she didn't pick up on what is happening too much.

"I work for a nonprofit organization that helps students, mostly kids, with learning disabilities. I'm on the marketing end, which is cute code for saying I prop up the fundraising department for donations. They make special books and sponsor programs to help kids with reading in general and any special needs in studying, listening, and any psychological issues they may have."

"Sounds complicated, so you work fundraising for a charity then?" That was another requested explanation that I expected entirely before meeting this girl. I ordered us another couple of drinks and went on.

"For my part, I tend to downplay that I really work for an arm of an organization that begs for donations from foundations, or more often, directly from rich people, but what I do ultimately does strengthen that effort by writing various articles and putting together marketing brochures for people to read through, or for fundraisers just to have in their hand, honestly. It's to get the word out, and to make it all appear professional for lack of a better word for it. The real game is with the direct fundraisers; they go out and ask for money, so they have a measurable input to provide so that's good for them. I just support them, however indirectly."

"So, you'd rather be a fundraiser? I don't get the impression you like the work too much," she replied, again with that aura of pride she can't seem to tame. Her friends Michael and Theresa continued to whisper apparently sweet things to each other. I wondered if it has anything to do with a hotel window in the near future.

"No, I can't be a salesman," I replied, finishing my drink way faster than her; had to order another one if I was to stay.

"There are no real sales in nonprofit organizations, what was your major in college anyway, Din?" This was going great.

"English," I replied to her veiled smirk. "And you might be surprised as to how much nonprofit organizations behave like greedy, no limit corporations. They very much have the same mindset and methods, especially in regard to disposable employees."

"You feel disposable? That isn't good." Sara's eyes drifted back to acknowledge her friends again. She spent notice-ably more time staring at the television.

"Sadly, we are all disposable. I'm obviously not too happy with it but it is my job, for however long it is mine. I just wish I had more say in the matter. I'm also a rather honest person; another reason I'm not with the program, such as it is."

"You are honest," she said with a cringe that I really could not tell if she was serious or not. "That's not good either, even worse. English graduates don't make much either so I'm not surprised by the nonprofit gig, they pay less."

It's amazing how this girl went from a rare and charming encounter with an intriguing stranger with a faux Canadian heritage, to a gal I could not keep my eyes off in the pipe dream of a maple leaf tattoo; until becoming someone whose head I could pour my beer over, and several times for that particular insult, however common it is.

"Thank you for your input there," I said clinking her glass again. This time, she didn't raise it back. "I might be leaving the job anyway."

"Oh, you have another job lined up?" There she went with the predictable million-dollar question, one of two in this case.

I smiled at her. "It would be nice if we could have the opportunities available to the post-college working types some fifty or so years ago. I could open up a bookstore or something."

"Well it's not the 50s or 60s and you can't do that." Sara was almost rolling her eyes. This has more than one purpose. Yet for the 1950's point, she was right but not so right as she thinks.

"I'm aware it's not the golden years anymore. Apparently, I won't get those. None of us will. But something we had then has become lost to us now and I don't think it should have gone away. For instance, Elvis Presley doesn't have to have relevance to kids now but why do we have rap artists all over the top 40 records in America? Rap may be fun for some people; yet why is it near everything? It's almost as if any other genre of music is disparaged by comparison, and it's not changing. It's the entire culture, it's all clearly become something less than before. Dare I mention we pay a lot more for even less altogether."

"What do you mean?"

I could have gone on and on with Sara, but I don't think she wanted to listen, not that this could ever stop me. People could go into a manufacturing job in those years, they could open a bookstore if they wanted. They could try to do the same today but with fewer chances of succeeding and less relevance to the times at large. Is this reality? Sure. Is it fair, or right? Absolutely not. The movies today suck too. There were all kinds of B-movies in the 50's and 60's but when was the last really successful movie in terms of box office sales that really left the audience dumbstruck with relevance and emotion? I can't think of too many at all; and the ones I can have conspicuous strings attached. It's all gone away, and I want it back, not just for me at all; for the sake of the world if the cliché be forgiven. Somehow, I doubted Sara was so concerned.

"The opportunities are not all there, and they should be," is all I said to her to underscore my own point. "The generations before us, hell, our own parents had better opportunities; it should be the other way around."

"I know" she said. "It sucks that it's not the same as what they had. Still, I don't think you are serious about opening up a bookstore and to just quit your job now would be crazy."

I laughed without making the noise. "I wish I was crazy but I'm not. I consciously quit my job and left without having another one lined up."

Sara's eyebrows rose above the top of her forehead, I was still admiring her golden, maybe dyed, hair though with the cat out of the bag, it was a pointless effort by then. I just put it all out there before she could reply or offer any amount of protest.

"Maybe American culture has been going away over the past ten years or so, and very quickly at that. I know the economy is bad, and even if it was good, there is no guarantee of finding another job any time soon to make this financially viable. Sorry to drag you through this, remember, I am a bad liar. My job was unstable even before tonight, and yes, I quit today. I've had enough of going into work every day trying to make people who can never be happy in their lives, well, happy; and then having them upset all the time because of this culture of failure. Something had to be done, one way or the other.

"I didn't even give them notice that I left. That was my first sin. I know we are supposed to give two weeks or so of notice but then again, people on my team of coworkers have been fired or laid off without such a generous notice, usually they get less than two minutes for notice of that, but no one ever seems to ask why it is acceptable on the other side of the fence, or in this case, at the other end of the totem pole. My second sin is that, yes, I didn't even have another job lined up to replace this one. I just left at the end of the day today and that was it, I haven't told anyone, until you."

Sara visibly swallowed air. "Wow, that's heavy. Do you have a girlfriend?"

Of all the questions she could have asked following that tirade, this is what she comes up with? Easier subject to deal with, I guess. Whatever makes her more comfortable.

"No, I'm single;" I replied knowing such an admission can be worse than being unemployed, especially to the certain type of girl.

"I guess that's good, a girlfriend would be so pissed at you if you had one."

I needed another drink, in fact I needed two or three more. "You're single," I said into my drink, yet to her.

"Well, not officially," she replied gripping her purse handle while turning towards Mike and Theresa, whom by now seemed to be getting wind that Sara and I were talking about something she was just not interested in talking about. She's probably never been officially "single," since she was twelve, and somehow I wasn't' surprised. She changed the subject back to the more uncomfortable matter at hand.

"There is nothing wrong with being unhappy at your job; lots of people are these days. But you might be seen as a flight risk for other employers, and it will be tougher to climb the ladder somewhere else too."

"What's the ladder? I could be considered a flight risk but who isn't? Is there necessarily a set of opportunities ahead of us? Older generations seem to like to look down upon those who are younger than they are, thinking Gen X or Millennials are slackers, not working as hard as they apparently did. Without any rungs on your 'ladder,' there is a lot of flight risk. I just happen to be actually flying. Not to mention, it's not like our 'superiors' are flying anywhere either. There is a big wall of managers, most of them baby boomers. They are not inclined to go anywhere, or find another job. I don't get the impression they want to share 'even' space in their game with the generations younger than them, let alone share the distribution of income.

"Should I not mention the loans and debt that eat up most of the younger salary, and by younger, I don't really mean right out of college? How is this any different than someone in their thirties? On top of this; and to be candid, often because of this, many people hope to leave their jobs within three years or less if they are in the thirty or even forty something age bracket. Thus, we are all flight risks, just with little to nowhere to fly. I get the sincere impression that 'ladder' of yours is gone, in fact long gone."

"But they leave when they have something else; and Din, don't you have college debt to? You must have been really frustrated to leave."

I just nodded. I get it. It's amazing, really. I'm well out of college and still in debt, and that is me and many. Kids in or right out of college now have expenses four or more times higher than our boomer forbearers decades before us; and they didn't have to go to college, necessarily. We don't talk about it enough, yet many begin their careers in an environment of companies and lovely nonprofits like mine cutting back on health care benefits, cutting if not disregarding pensions, all while the boomer's children are actually more educated and tech savvy, though does it matter when you are obviously not welcome in the current economy that's too old for its own good?

"It was different for workers in Canada," Sara said. "There is a bit more of a social safety net when it comes to life as a whole. But in America, no one trusts the government so it's safe to say no one is going to trust their employers to take care of them either so you are a lot more on your own."

"Born too late and in the wrong county too, that's just great," I replied, again she just can't get that Canadian chip off her shoulder and at least for her last point, I can't blame her. I gave her one last diatribe.

"Time and place. I really believe that's when American culture started to die; all in the span of about twenty or so years. Think about music, movies, books, and economy more so; these things either shrank in significance to their former existence or were stagnated altogether. There are no more Sinatras, Marlon Brandos, even Madonnas when you think about. No new artist or innovation has captured the hearts and minds of Americans the way they have been captured in the past. No young people even care about Sinatra or his successors if they existed. No one cares for the talent of Fred Astaire even if some artist like him could exist in the main stream today. I ask again, why did it have to go away? The 90's have little and the 00's all but have no flavor of their own. It's like a taste of a soda from a can left out in the sun."

"Doom and gloom," Sara said as she picked up her purse as if to leave."

"Well, it's not all doom and gloom, there is some hope."

Sara looked genuinely surprised again. "Really? How so?"

"I never sent anyone my resignation letter at work."

"What do you mean?"

"The letter is just sitting there on my desk at work, and no one will see it until tomorrow morning. Not only this, I did write up an electronic version but never actually hit the send button."

"So, you never actually resigned?"

"No, I suppose not. Not yet, anyway. That's why I'm out here, alone with you and your friends. I couldn't sleep if

I wanted to and don't mind telling a complete stranger, if you still are a stranger."

"A stranger probably wouldn't know half as much as you have told me. It's kind of weird. But we all have to go now; it was nice talking to you, Din." She stood up and her friends waved and smiled me goodbye. I told them to enjoy their window and that just got me a couple of looks like I was from Mars.

I didn't ask nor wanted to ask for her number or anything. Dave would probably crucify me for not getting at least that far with her. Michael and Theresa were out of the door by now; Sara didn't hug me but gently touched my elbow.

"Good luck with the job search, Din. That must have been one hell of a resignation letter. Hope it at least pisses them off somewhat." With that, she left after her friends and was gone; no worse for wear but something told me happy to be moving on to whatever was next for her. She's just back from Canada, with no definitive future for her other than not really being single any time soon. I expect she does not want that pointed out either.

After finishing another beer, I wandered off alone. I wish I had another cigar or something to smoke but then again, my clothes would stink and the nostalgic mood had all but left me after Sara and I parted ways. She was right though. It was one hell of a letter. By far one of my better writing pieces though I doubt its intended audience would agree too much.

It's a shame Sara was not really single, but that was too much to hope for. I was in no mood to find a new girlfriend either, yet I always wanted to be married before the age of 30 but that time had come and gone well enough before now. Sara seemed uncomfortable anyway, and I can somewhat see why. It is true, single people have their issues too. We seldom care to take notice of it. Hierarchies indeed. There should be a science for what we choose not to think about.

But with her gone, it was time to intercept that letter before anyone could read it, no one can read it. That way I will still have a job. I didn't actually tell Sara everything; at least in that I was too scared to live without a job at all. This is also why I didn't really sleep before my encounter with the queen of the milk crates. I needed to use what little time frame I had to save myself, to get to the office before anyone was gone. Luckily, the main doors are open early, and I don't actually have an office at work (not important enough for that); so I was able to get in and remove that letter from my desk.

That perfect letter. It will have to wait for another time to shine on so. It's all surreal enough and one day I want to comprehend how it all came to this and why life got so far away. I quit my job, went out drinking all night, confessed it all to a girl I never knew before or since and she didn't seem to want to talk about it; and then chickened out to save myself from unemployment. This makes sense enough. I made it to my office before anyone was there.

I've grabbed the letter of resignation I left there from exactly where it was on my desk and placed some personal items back where they look like someone still works here; had just enough time to send a fake "out sick today" email to one of the floor managers who deals with that, avoided running into anyone else somehow; and hallelujah, mission accomplished, I still have a job, and I got it all done before eight in the morning.

I had to have today off as there was something else I never mentioned. My first interview in the new job search turns out to be this morning; and I'm doing so with barely any sleep and regretting not eradicating those milkcrates. When resetting my office space, I had a suit on under my jacket the entire morning. I have until tomorrow to really recover the treacherous fumble of life and work here. So I'm not down and out, and I still have an income, for what it's worth. I have friends at my job and won't give up for their sakes, at least not yet.

Maybe I have missed the sail, maybe I was born too late for this world; but I'm not done trying. If I missed the sail then I have to go for another one. I jumped into the ocean and rescued myself for fear of drowning alone. I can see what's wrong here but oddly enough, I just do not feel bad about it at all. Though this would change for the worse; along with other things.

Chapter Four

It's Going Out of Style

Searching for a job is a job in and of itself. I would go so far to say that not only is it a job, it's an art form. Something I can't shake and is on my mind right now: I feel guilty for "leaving" my job the way I did though I'm pretty sure no one will catch on. I even feel guilty for missing a day. I find it painstakingly ironic that I decided to leave my job, (well, almost), and feel such guilt for nearly leaving my responsibilities with no one to take care of them, even though more than half of them hardly notice more than half the time. No one will significantly challenge me on the out sick excuse for missing a day but anything negative is anyone's chance to notice these days.

It's not an option to be honest and say I have a job interview; on top of this, I can't tell my new potential employer why I'm really leaving my job, outside of bullshitting the "seeking new opportunities" story I have no choice but to offer. You can't tell your current boss that you are seeking new opportunities. It would be too much of a problem to speak of it out loud, even if I get the damn job, and not just for the sake of gossip. An employee wanting to leave is an employee with some kind of problem or grievance to some degree or another. That's something negative on them, there are no two ways around it; and they don't like that, how could they?

It's not like I can just walk into this meeting and say, "I hate my job, it pays far less than the crap I have to put up with and the boss is a megalomaniac whose sights are going to be set on me sooner or later, if they haven't already." Everything has to be amicable, nothing negative. Some might actually understand the plight of the job seeker, but that's becoming all the more rare in and of itself.

After all, why would an employer want to hire someone who is into trouble or has problems with the boss in any way shape or the form? They could be willfully inheriting someone else's problem and that's not going to happen. They want their cake and want to eat it too and far too often than not; they get it that way. So, it's best not to upset the applecart too much, at least not so directly.

Interviews are just about what not to say as it is answering questions; and not only what to say, but how. It's a game. It shouldn't be, but it is. There is too much one can't say.

Such a list of way too many items to count include: You can't say your boss is a jerk or a bitch. You can't say you didn't get that promotion and you are pissed off. You can't say you work with a bunch of idiots or drama queens. You can't say you are sick of hearing them talk about their boyfriends and want to avoid the day they come in with a damn rock on their finger. You can't even say the commute is too far. Nothing selfish. Above all, you can't say you want more money. That is a serious no-no.

As I sit here in the waiting room of this new office, I'm not actually pondering these things as much as a nervous person about to be interviewed. They managed to get under my skin already by giving me a pen and clip board to fill out a job application which I absolutely cannot stand. The small problem with this is that they already have my resume which answers about ninety nine percent of the questions on this form. I sent them my resume when I applied online and even brought extra copies of said resume as well as that is still the accepted etiquette.

More so the problem is revealing my horrible hand-writing. It's bad, and I make no excuses or apologies for it. I never had good penmanship and can remember back to when I was a little kid that I could read and write just fine at an early age but never was able to impress or avoid judgement from teachers, along with teacher's aides and even my parents; all of whom referred to my handwriting as "chicken scratch" without offering any type of solution to this problem. It's as if they felt simply telling me and humiliating a child, they would improve my skills in some way. It never happened. So here I am today, potentially being judged solely on my lack of pretty handwriting skills and not my actual skills or experience at all. Please just read the resume, it's there for you.

Seriously, they want everything handwritten out on this form. Ironic for a company that makes an online (formerly print) magazine. I have to write out my job history with a brief description of my responsibilities at each and include any and all details with my education background; another opportunity to be judged unfairly because I went to a smaller, rinky-dink college that most people never heard of, not the U of this or that State which probably had simi-lar curricula anyway. Another opportunity to feel inferior before I even really get in the door here. So much fun, I can't wait for the secretary to roll her eyes at me when I give her back this clip board, and how the more irritated I get the worse my handwriting will be. She will notice.

Not to mention, I am still running on next to no sleep after my wonderful evening of meandering around town being terrified of the next morning and confessing it all to the Maple Leaf. Maybe I should mention all that in this interview, but I'll keep it professional. I know how to act. That is a valuable skill, yes?

The manager finally comes to collect me (making a stern face when she is given the clip board, good grief) and she takes me down to the meeting room; arms folded the entire time for some reason. She less walks me there as wobbles as this manager is noticeably pregnant. She's older than me, but not by much. She has a wedding ring on, a simple business suit, and shoulder length brown hair, nothing too remarkable outside the pregnancy. She doesn't ever smile, at least not to me.

The office building isn't that inviting to begin with. It's remarkably quiet with not many phones ringing, no one talking from what I could hear; all around stale. It was simply not welcoming at all. The manager fits right in. For myself, I like to think I don't give off the worst personality but she doesn't want to be here, and that's not good for me. It could be she is having a bad day and this is bad timing but I sense something from the aloof attitude that it's not so simple.

"I plan on going on maternity leave soon, that's why we are interviewing and hiring for this position now," she begins.

I actually like kids, so I smile. "Congratulations," I say. "Are you expecting a girl or a boy?"

She half smiles, once more, aloof. "A boy," she replies. "First off, do you have any questions for me?"

I'm somewhat uncomfortable as I was not expecting this question right off the bat. "Can you tell me more about the position," was all I could come up with.

"Well, Din, the purpose of this position is to write, re-write, and proofread a variety of different documents and articles that will ultimately go up on our digital website. The company started out as a print only magazine over fifty years ago, but we are excited now to be digital only, so we are looking for someone just as excited and ready to go in that direction.

"You will also have to do some database entry and maintenance along with various other document management tasks in addition to the production or editing. It's a very hands-on position and you will be expected to work under minimal supervision and be a self-starter."

"Sounds great," I say, lying through my teeth because it is kind of a shame. Does she not feel like supervising though that is her job? Or is this a situation where she wants the hiring piece done and over with and that will be it for her?

I like print media. I get a headache enough as it is staring at computer screens all day and like to read physical books and even magazines when I get the time. I know the economy and the world is moving elsewhere but I would categorize my own attitude towards that as something much less than excited. I'm not proud of the fact that everything is heading in a digital direction for the sake of it; there is still peace to be found in having something real to hold; and we're letting it all go. I hope she doesn't pick up that I am such an old soul.

She goes into more of a spiel about the company and the position in general, nothing too new from what I gathered from the job description and just general research I did on this company. Apparently not in the mood for small talk, she eventually gets around to fingering through the copy of my resume she has and picks out random things to talk about.

"What is IT Corporation? You have experience in IT?"

Of course, she had to pick that one to ask about. It was some eight or nine years ago that I got my first job out of college. The name was so stupid, as the company had merged so much during its history that it changed names about a dozen times at least before I walked through the door.

At the time, they had just settled on the name IT as the company's original name was "Industrial Tank" and they decided to shorten this to "IT" for some reason, not real- izing that using an acronym that doesn't mean anything is confusing, not to mention the confusion that "IT" implies a tech company and the end result is I ended up having to explain this to everyone including an overly-reserved, somewhat cranky pregnant manager years after that company sold itself again.

I explained to her that it was actually an environmental remediation firm, that bid on contracts to clean up and close out landfills that were no longer in use, or remove remnants of gas stations that had closed anywhere on the earth. I worked with the team who wrote up business proposals to get the contracts for those types of projects, and writing up and editing material for that company.

"Landfill closings? That seems like an odd field to get into, are you an engineer? Why did you choose to work there?"

With that my respect level just dropped about a millionth. As common as it is to presume so, I didn't choose to work there. We do not actually choose where we work. Where I work is ultimately up to managers such as this one. They decide. I "chose" to work for the environmental company not because I like working with construction workers, not because I like living in a clean environment, but because they had a job opening, I applied and interviewed, and one way or another, I was given the job. I had to pay my rent, food is not free and I like to eat, so I took the offer.

Sadly, the key word there was "give," but I needed to work just like anyone else, and they gave me a job to work at and subsequently collect a paycheck. It almost feels like I was benefiting from a very bad charity that I worked for, feels that way for every job, honestly. At IT, I was later laid off with hundreds of others during the bankruptcy and merger with the next company; and I have no idea what they are called now.

This is a problem I can see right here in this interview. The manager is acting like she is doing me a favor for even granting me the time of day but simultaneously acting as if I have a clear choice in what I'm doing for work, what I have done, and what I can do. Sure, there are places I want to work but if up to me, I would not be here at your excitable online magazine. Not to mention that I was nearly almost out of work entirely until I chickened out on that plan. Yes, that's my own doing but I had to apply for other jobs if I ever expected to live long enough without one.

"It was an interesting opportunity, and it was near my home at the time, so it was convenient," giving her my standard go-to answer for that question.

"Do you have any questions for me?" she asks again. I feel a bit lost here and also get the impression she doesn't like interviewing or asking questions in general, and if she is not into this then how can I be into it more? We go back and forth on this for a while. She actually asks the "have any questions for me" question twice more before the interview is over. I don't know what kind of employee she's looking for, but it's becoming a bit of a long shot that it's me.

I will never forget two other distinct questions I was asked here today. One of these was "What can you accomplish at this company that someone else could not?" I have heard of questions like this before. How in the living hell am I supposed to know what someone else would or could have accomplished? That's on them. Was she trying to dig up dirt on me? The references I provided won't do that for her if this gets to that point. Everyone has someone in their past (though we seldom admit it) who could bad mouth them, or say something negative. Are these the people hiring managers really want to talk to? I'm starting to think they do not even know what they want, and there is no way they are taking responsibility for themselves.

The other ridiculous question, however common, I was asked was "What are your weaknesses?" This is asked a lot in interviews, and no one is honest with this and if they were, well, they would never be hired so why ask? Did she want me to say something along the lines of "I treat people like shit and am addicted to downloading porn?" Perhaps if these managers would start asking more intelligent and original questions, then the prospective employee would not be forced to lie when approached with this nonsense.

Eventually we get to the dreaded salary expectation. I never know how to say what I want to be paid, it would be nice if they just stated what the job pays and leave it at that. But no, it's to their advantage to make a game out of it so they do. I could quote a number and if it's too high, I just killed myself in this interview because they won't pay it; if it's too low I lose as I will never know if I would have been paid more and will have to suffer the day to day of this job not knowing I could have at least been compensated more. If I say the exact price, then they can feign budget problems and low ball the salary in turn which is exactly what she does.

Honestly, she seems annoyed with the subject of salary which is an interesting phenomenon on its own. All companies care about is money. This is true of a "magazine" business such as this or nonprofit organizations like the one

I still miraculously work for. If this is true, and it is, then why are they across the board sensitive to the subject of money in regards to salary? If it's all we care about, why are we so uncomfortable really talking about it?

We can talk about revenue or fundraising goals, sure. We can talk about the value of a contract, or and individual donation to a charity; but "on the ground" we do not seem at all to like to speak about an employee's ability to live, or take a vacation, or pay off a debt, or take care of their kids; hell, life in general. We don't find any comfort talking about this at all. Indeed, during this very interview, we talked about my background, the job, what drives us in the workplace for a place to (allegedly) enjoy working for, but the conversation concerning salary for me and expense for them is reduced to a rushed afterthought which frankly fewer than two minutes of time was granted to discussing said concern. We're not talking about money at all.

I tell her I am negotiable and quote a salary range I'm comfortable (not really) with. She makes a note of it and frowns, again annoyed with her own question and more than seemingly annoyed with me. This concludes the brief interview and she escorts me back to the front desk. She walks with her arms folded again; and me not removing the idea she just does not like to interview. Maybe it is just me? I hope so. For the second time today I have to ask myself if I am wrong, imagining all of this somehow, and it's becoming a habit.

I am not sure what her problem really is. She's in her own world and likes it there. If anything, shouldn't she be excited for the prospect of a new employee? This is a chance to meet your new team member, someone you will interact with every day and, like it or not, be a second family as we probably spend more time in life at work than we do at home. It's a much as a part of our lives as a spouse or children, and needs our attention and responsibility. In this case, we should be far more interested in the hiring process than this manager is, even as an expecting mother.

Then again, maybe that's the notion. If hired, we are going to have to see each other and interact with one another on a daily basis as part of each other's lives. No matter what an applicant's skills, no matter their education or experience; this means nothing when considering the time we are going to have to share in the long run. You have to see this person every single day, maybe even on weekends. In that case, I'm not entirely sure why she made the stink she did on my handwriting, my past jobs, or even the schools I attended. None of that mattered which is, to say the least, unsettling. I could have gone to Harvard and had over ten years direct online magazine experience and she may still very well have acted like this. It was likely all decided before now.

It's possible. Why bother with any of this if the hiring is already decided? Of course, there may be requirements in some companies to interview more than one candidate for a position, but don't drag all this out if internal candidates or perhaps even nepotism have already decided the outcome. I have been in other interviews, and spent a good amount of time and effort pursuing them, that were already wrapped up and the job doesn't really exist as the internal hire (or even worse, the boss' friend) was hired long before the damn position was even posted. Can you not tell this to someone up front? It would save a lot of time and anguish.

If it's such a burden to hire, I don't know why I'm here today. Unfortunately, none of this is ever in the job description. As to place an exclamation point on the whole ordeal, I am given one of the weakest and briefest handshakes I remember getting, as if she hated the idea of touching another person; a handshake that basically says "get out now, I have better things to do" though she really doesn't.

Then I leave. It's not even noon yet. Like anyone else, I leave thinking about what I could have done better in that interview. I could have talked myself up some more, tried to figure out a way to match my past skills into this new job somehow. That said, I am not really sure it would have worked. If she noticed the handwriting and the "small" school background but I cannot change what those things are. Speaking of college, I didn't go to school and study the art of making cranky managers happy, I wish they had a course in that; several courses now that I think of it.

It gets harder when I consider I have been working for over ten years, just counting post-college jobs alone, and it never seems to get any better. That interview was no better than the ones I had when I was twenty-three and eventually got hired at the infamous IT Corporation, and I didn't choose to work at an online magazine either but thought the experience might be good and lest we forget, I needed a damn job anyway. I may not have actually quit Learning Tools (the nonprofit I nearly quit yet still work at) but I nearly did and I still need a new job one way or the other. This is untenable.

I know I am asking for more than what is available these days. I want a level playing field but no one else seems to want one, especially if they and theirs are even remotely threatened say, by a new hire to work with every day. I know I'm presuming I deserve a job but is keeping me out of work or in a precarious work environment helping anyone at all outside of hurting me?

I did go to college after all; even have a master's degree. It's all in English writing and Literature and thus it's an education, and one that I have made practical use of in my three or so jobs I've had since graduating. I like being smart, if I am at all. It seems I could be happier by not thinking at all, or so implied the Maple Leaf. I enjoy reading and getting into character and story; after all, are we not on this earth to figure things out? We learn something new every day, so it is said. I learned less about this potential new job than I did about the motivations, or lack thereof, of the manager responsible for (evidently) hiring someone.

Again, untenable; but she does not seem to care about me, if this is the end of our business relationship, it's probably for the better. I would expect some sort of decision from her one way or the other. Yet I may not even get that much.

Getting a new job is not going to solve all of my problems. Nevertheless, it's no small need and will have a determining factor on where my life goes from this point to the next so I have a clear and vested interest. I love this bold new era; this living generation is unique in that they have numerous new elements to fear. Modern employees (more so the younger ones) live with the constant threat of being laid off. True, layoffs were common in the 30's 50's, etc. yet the idea that one can work without fear of this today is absurd, and worse yet, more socially acceptable and a simple business operating procedure almost everywhere.

Simple business operating procedure, while a threat to me to be sure, isn't really the problem I have anyway. It's only noon but it feels much later. It's cold outside yet I keep sweating; and too much has happened. I may have called out sick but I'm going back into work today anyway. Now is not the time to go home and waste time not wanting to go back to work. I could probably catch up on some sleep but I'm too wired for that as it is.

Part of it is the guilt. I can't stand my job, that's true. Yet I took off today to make time for myself and therefore less for them. That's all topical enough to the point, but every damn time I take time off (for legitimate reasons or not, whatever legitimate is) something comes up that has to be taken care of and they never miss you when you are in, only when you are gone. So I'm going back into work today. Fear.

I also get to check in on the current love of my life, a girl who is so unattainable I may as well be trying to date Scarlett Johansen. Despite that bit of drama and fun, I need to check in on work with Joey and get back to Chris, the only actual friend of mine that works at my office, and see how life is treating him. I need to check and see how the latest of his obligations to former pet doggie visitation rights saga unfolds.

Chapter Five

Machinations

I GET CONFUSED ON THIS subject just as much as anyone. That subject being my good friend Chris Allen's apparent need to travel some two hundred miles south to Virginia once a month to collect his girlfriend's ex-boyfriend's pit bull terriers and take them back home for a couple of weeks. I don't even know why I'm thinking about it. Chris is a friend, and I stick by him; yet at odd times, his own dealings in life can extend even beyond my own, which is saying something; perhaps a bit too much in his case.

I need to break it down even for myself. Despite his major issues at work, Chris is quite happy (arguably just a bit too happy) with his live-in girlfriend Christina; a fairly attractive girl who works mostly the graveyard shift as a nurse at one of the university hospitals. It looks like it's all going well until once a month I (and evidently, Chris) am reminded that Tina used to live with a former boyfriend to whom she was engaged. This man drug her all the way down to backwoods Virginia for a job of his and the only thing that kept her happy there was Cooper and Shirley; their two loveable pit bull terriers which the sun rose and set upon.

Break-ups happen more frequently than we are all willing to admit; and for any reason. For whatever her explanations, she broke up with this fellow and moved back up here. Shortly thereafter she met Chris and they began dating some two years ago. Chris however, actually never objects to the bi-monthly exchanges Tina and her ex make with the dogs; because she wants to see them. It's like they are children with visitation rights. I have to admit I questioned this of Chris more than once; and he always shrugs and asks me what the problem with this is. In this regard I may be out of touch as well, though I wonder.

He just drove down there again this past Sunday; I still can't help but to at least imply something is wrong, or something terribly off with these transactions. He doesn't seem to mind. Somehow, getting back into work today, I doubt Chris is going to want to talk about the doggie drama, as he will be working on yet another conniption fit over his problems with his job and more specifically, his boss. Well, our boss to be even more accurate. I just hope it hasn't gotten worse. It is far more real than the dogs.

I came in late with only a few hours in the day to go;

amazingly sharp with my story that I simply didn't sleep well and called out sick even though I barely slept at all after my night out on the town before the interview. I manage to set up my office again with the few calendars and decorations I had ripped down and none were the wiser for my quitting game now in the "could have been" folder.

I've been here for almost three years. Learning Tools is a nonprofit organization that provides in-class mentors and books specializing in helping children and college adults with learning disabilities in and out of the classroom. It relies nearly entirely on donations and some government funding to exist. I work with the fundraising department to support their efforts. It's a nonprofit, an office environment like any other, one floor, bad coffee, and a lot of guilt. I even get my own cubicle, as the more important people have their offices. It's a business. It's significant to remind everyone of that here too; it's beyond me why so many people assume it's otherwise. Maybe the taxes are filed differently, but that's as far as it goes.

I actually do precious little of what my education and experience (which they apparently hired me for) qualifies me to do. It didn't take them long at all to realize I was younger than most of the staff here, and since I was not a direct fundraiser like Chris or the rather detestable Nicole Ramos, what I wanted to do mattered very little to anyone so I ended up as a database coordinator, helping them organize all of the various gifts or donations that come through and helping track different fundraising initiatives that they have by entering information and running reports. One has to be proud.

This came about around a month after I was hired and not only realizing that I was youngish, the baby boomer population that has been working here the past twenty years or so simply do not want to learn new technologies. The long term, older, employees are only doing what they have been doing for years, and don't have to change, because they are older. That makes perfect sense. I just happened to come about not as a technological guru, but I caught on quick to new software we have for everything, and thus ended up in the database position with no room to object if I was interested in keeping my job for any length of time. I hate myself for rolling over but the new kid in town doesn't ask many questions, neither do the older kids here for indisputably sad reasons.

I am hardly a representation of my entire generation, but it would seem to me the next generation of leaders would want their needs or initiatives to be nurtured if companies had any real interest in retaining them. This company, and yes, I openly refer to this nonprofit organization as a company, seems only interested in its own needs. Why be concerned with the needs of employees, or other expenses?

In the meantime, boomers get to remain perpetually in charge of a whole generation's lives while enjoying the comfy chairs at the top. This nonprofit I'm still somehow a part of has only a few baby boomers really in charge, at least in my own department. Yet our leader, for lack of a better word, is not part of the Senior Leadership Team that runs this company as a whole outside of the board of trustees. Though by the amount of time she spends with her nose up their respective rectums, one would think she's an official member.

We have a larger team but most of my day if I interact with anyone is with only about a handful of, and by that, I mean maybe five, people or so on a day to day basis. Chris Allen is one of the direct "frontline" fundraisers, going out and asking rich donors for more money, or approaching charitable foundations when deemed to do so. I like working with a friend; though he feels, and may very well be right, that his time here is coming to an end as he is constantly butting heads with the boss whenever she has time for him, and she's making too much of that sadly.

One of the other main fundraisers is Nicole Ramos. She thinks I'm gay. Seriously, she is quite convinced of it to the point I am always extremely uncomfortable around her. Nicole is one of many, by which I mean all, younger staff girls that live with their boyfriends. Since we have been working together, I have dated girls but by and large have been single as a dollar bill for the stretch of it, and still am. This has not gone beyond Nicole's notice; given that Chris has a girlfriend and relationships are all that anyone can seem to talk about here.

A year or so back, having taken notice that I was single, Nicole had no qualms about asking me why this is, and not taking any satisfaction in my answer that I just happen to be single now and some people are really not in a relationship for a certain percentage of their lives; Nicole actually accused me of being gay. Not only did she think I was gay and "in the closet" for not talking about my alleged sexuality, she said that I have "nothing to be ashamed about" for apparently being gay, and that my denial of this wasn't necessary, and even a bit homophobic for not coming out for being what I was not.

I don't think everyone believes I'm gay yet no one really takes any time to challenge her on it, which is in itself suspicious. Was Nicole ever single? She has us all believing it was never so; I wish she would have spent less time deciphering, beyond incorrectly, that I'm gay and sticking to her own perceptions and maybe introducing an available coworker to one of her single friends; but of course she has none, why would she?

Of no wonder is that Nicole's best friend at work is the more respectful, and by leaps and bounds prettier, Cathy Hill; my own particular obsession for the past year or however long she has worked here. Cathy is an events coordinator, working for the director of events when that director is not ploughing the hell out of her boyfriend who happens to be a donor and also happens to be not her husband. We have everything here.

Cathy is amazing; perfect smile, perfect body, perfect voice and friendly as all anything. Cathy is someone I can't take my eyes or mind off for any good length of time. Cathy has somehow gotten the sun to shine on her perfect skin at her own direction. Cathy has the look of the super-model and the girl next door look combined perfectly at all times. Cathy is unbelievably sexy. Cathy is oblivious to my feelings for her. Cathy has a boyfriend, and Cathy will never shut up about him.

Anyone would think that the presence of an established relationship would sway me against any feelings I could have for this girl. They would be wrong. Still, it's absolutely uncanny how a girl can work in the words "my boyfriend" into any subject of conversation, business or otherwise, anytime and anywhere. She's there to remind us that she does in fact have a boyfriend, and woe to those who ever forget it.

Of course her office space has to be directly next to mine so not only do I have to hear her talk about her boyfriend, Ryan, all the time; she more than too often confides in me as to the latest in "I have a boyfriend" world, and she never lets up. To be sure, Cathy was the first person I ran into when I got back into the office today.

"Hi, Din! How are you feeling?" she asks. She actually seems less than her normal cheery self for some reason today.

"I'm okay; I didn't get much sleep last night and thought I needed the whole day to catch up. It was not so bad, so I decided to come back into work anyway."

"My boyfriend is like that, always tossing and turning at night. I keep telling him he's setting himself up for the vicious cycle of being tired all day, taking naps after work and then not sleeping at night."

Never fails. "It's something like that," is all I say to her in return.

Cathy doesn't give up though. "Din, I never told you, last night Ryan was out and I was all alone in the house. I went to bed around eleven and I heard someone outside. I was so scared and then I heard the door open. I almost screamed! I thought it was a robber but it was my boyfriend's dad, he came by to drop something off at eleven at night, I didn't even know he had a key. I'm so mad at them right now."

This is actually interesting. "What did you say to them?" I ask.

"I just said I was pissed he came by so late at night and that I should have been told his dad had a key. I don't think I can deal with that happening again. I'm actually thinking of moving out."

"Will you?"

She doesn't even look at me. There was a long silence, it got uncomfortable; not milk crates on the street uncomfortable per se but it was there. "I don't know" was all she said, barely audible under her breath.

Heaven forbid. I have no idea how to react to this other than fighting back a huge killer smile from spreading across my face. She's so terrified of her damn boyfriend's father, who knows what other problems, and also so equally terrified to be alone. She can't just have a boyfriend but complicates it more by living with him; this makes it especially difficult for her ever to become single again and thus difficult for me to be sure.

This inability to be alone among the younger girls here is in noteworthy contrast to their older bosses. Take Cathy's direct supervisor. She's on her way back to the office now, given the time. She's older, somewhere in the early fifties I guess and she has been married for twenty years or so. This has little bearing on the nearly daily affair she conducts with a representative of one of the foundations that provides this organization funding. Around this time of day, Elizabeth Tavel, Director of Events, comes back into the office with her hair a bit too disheveled for anyone not to notice that she was "out for lunch" just a bit too long downtown. Apparently, the boyfriend bliss is not meant to last forever.

I am saved from addressing Cathy any more than I have to, given the delicious turn of events in her life by Elizabeth returning almost on cue, walking along with Nicole in tow, approaching Cathy for something that has probably nothing to do with me whatsoever. I'm reminded again of where my place is at this office.

Elizabeth is older, but still maintains a pretty mane of long blonde hair that covers up her smoker's wrinkles very well; even when tousled about from her afternoon activities. She's tall and thin for her age. The skin around her neck is red from either sunburn or other reasons, I cannot tell but she's often in this state so I have begun not to notice, or at least not care as much when I do.

Nicole, much taller, has bronze skin all around, her features highlighted by her long, black and curly hair. She does not have the face that Cathy has, not even close, only just enough to place her in that league of always having a boyfriend; apparently that's easy enough. I just really hope she does not suggest another gay boyfriend for me today.

Cathy never speaks to me about that issue; she is far too busy talking about her boyfriend twenty-four hours a day to really care; though she has never once one hundred percent denied it either. I do wonder if she's happy that I am single though. It must matter somehow, and it must have some affect in some way, I just don't know what.

As my rare luck would have it, it isn't mentioned. This is likely because Nicole is walking along with Elizabeth, who while a Senior Manager, might as well be the boss; as she is best friends with our Director, Miriam Gaw; who I am beyond happy is nowhere to be seen today. Miriam is probably glad-handling the Senior Leadership team in some benign meeting or another. Otherwise she would effortlessly be making at least one of our lives hell, and probably Chris.

Brushing her mussed hair back, Elizabeth says, "Jodi Molano will be at next week's event, she's bringing in some marketing materials her company printed up; Din, can you and Chris help her and Cathy with setting up the table at the entrance so we can give those out? Thanks."

I simply nod. I sometimes work events, mostly as a token male helping to move around the heavy stuff; boxes and display tables or what have they. I actually don't even mind them other than far too often being reminded of how unimportant I am when compared to management, or pretty girls who will openly discuss their boyfriends with random rich people.

I actually never met Jodi Molano. This company loves to hire its consultants to make it seem more realistic and often farms out a lot of work to independent vendors, not the least of which is Molano's independent nonprofit consulting business. I can't wait to hear about her boyfriend or husband. Elizabeth closes the door of her office across the hall. She and the girls obviously have something important to talk about or at least want everyone else to think so. It's not all of that flavor here, as we do employ some old men. Strange as it may be, I consider at least one of them a friend; though half the time I really don't know why.

Joey LeMari, Elizabeth's next-door office neighbor is much older than me, early sixties, I think. His office is empty, nobody home. He's probably out at an interview of some donor or another for his writings. I was actually hired to work with Joey a hell of a lot more than I presently do. He needed assistance writing up his articles, which I did for a while until they figured out I can work the database, and so my position has been changed ever since, and with little thought or concern from them.

He reads a physical newspaper at lunch every day, I wonder how he would have done on that job interview I had earlier. He's probably only used the internet twice. Like others, he has been here forever and with such seniority comes the inexplicable job security for someone who uses cassette tapes for his donor interviews. I don't want him to be fired or to retire (though one can question); I like Joey at least to talk to on occasion but how he holds on to the dark ages in terms of technology is near supernatural in skill. At least he likes old movies and actors though. Can't have enough of that.

Chris Allen is on the other side of that spectrum entirely, and maybe even more bizarre. Chris can be a bit of a child trapped in a thirty something year old man's body, if that body was very balding to a rim of brown hair flanked by large framed, near coke bottle-esque glasses with skin so pale it would be near impossible to spot him in a winter storm. A short man, hiding in his office near me often, Chris really is a friendly guy for as guarded as he has been lately. He has that "nerdy," overweight reliable quality about him as he scarcely ever hits the gym despite having a membership. He's a good friend, and probably my only selfless reason for not actually quitting this place. I would have felt terrible for him. He doesn't know.

Chris' office is not decorated with books and vintage tape cassettes like Joey, but with Disney and Lord of the Rings posters and toys. Most of these are kid's fast-food meal style toys adorned about his desk, and not the classic Disney stuff, more *Lilo and Stitch*, and *Toy Story* era items. He keeps it modern in that respect. I know he's always been a fan of the Lord of the Rings; I have been myself since I first read the novels in middle school. The Disney stuff I think he gets from his girlfriend. I would be remiss to not mention the pictures of him, Tina, and her part time pit bulls right next to his computer. I am happy he is happy, but he does not help me much with the single guy problem at this office. There is not much that could help. At least he doesn't give me so much shit about it.

He stands and shakes my hand as I come in. Chris is part of my group of hang out guys, that is when Tina allows him out. It's not so bad as she works night shifts most of the time. I must not find Chris so close a pal as I never told him about quitting the job and running out without a new one. That alone flames the pain in my gut, I just wish I could decide if telling him would make me feel any better.

An unfair change of subject could be to ask him more about the doggie visitation rights. It's just not something

I could feel comfortable doing. When I date someone, I generally prefer, in fact entirely prefer, for the ex-boyfriend to be out of the picture. Having him around in any way leaves open the possibility for relapse or at the very least the option for one. What's interesting is that Tina's ex is four hours away at least. It seems like a lot of trouble to go through and above all this, it's for a couple of dogs. It's quite the agreement.

I don't bring this up to Chris as despite the cheery décor in his office; his mood is noticeably on the grim side; not surprising considering who he works for. I should know, I work for her too. Nevertheless, we can sometimes feel the anger and pain of another just by standing in their midst. I thought I was having a bad day; Chris is no exception.

After asking me to close his door (I hate doing that) Chris says "I'm looking for a new job,"

"Really?" I ask with my attention rising to the ceiling in the hopes of not telling him what I only told a stranger.

"I've had it with Miriam. She's crazy, I will never get on the same page with her and I'm sick of her lectures. It's all about money with her, I know raising money is what we do but I can't spend my time trying to make a crazy person content somehow, it's impossible; and on top of that she expects me to work nights and weekends just to prove I'm into this crap like she is, and that's all for the sake of it. We are not even that busy lately. She spends that time doing the job of management, whatever the hell that is."

It's all a lot, and at the same time, not much to take in. I'm not surprised he wants to leave. Some would say Miriam Gaw breathes, eats, and shits fundraising for this company, yet it's all about manipulating her staff and trying, however fruitlessly; to get on that Senior Leadership board she will never get to. If our jobs are trying to make the boss look good, we are failing. This could be one cause of her behavior but there is more. The real problem is that no one ever questions it. There is a reason for that too.

Still, I can't envy a man in Chris' position of having the responsibility of direct fundraising and at the same time having to report to that predictably unpredictable lunatic we all call a boss. Some will actually say he's only there to make Miriam look good. She undoubtedly feels that way. Besides the obvious hubris, that's unthinkable, or certainly unsound. He's doing a job he can't possibly do well, if at all, and exclusively suffering the consequences for it as if there is nothing wrong with this situation to being with. Once we are on that radar, on that downhill slide, well, there is generally only one direction to go.

"She sent me home in tears the other night," he says, not being able to look me in the eyes when he says it though I know it's not because he's lying; he's telling the dead truth. Should I feel less humiliated because Chris is more? I don't. No one should have to suffer that, let alone him.

"Not sure I can take much more of it," he continues. "Tina doesn't want me to be out of work but she's sick of me coming home miserable, so there is that to consider. I took this job thinking it was going to be a job, not making this tyrant happy. It's getting ridiculous. She can't manage this department; she can't manage her way out of a wet paper bag, frankly."

He is in quite the state. The Disney toys don't help his cause much here. He's being pushed around like a little kid by a bully. We can make light and joke of it but it's not a good situation to be in. It's more serious that we give it credit. That's because we are afraid.

"We have to do at least something," I say to his hanging head. "Dave, Hal, and I are hanging out Saturday night; you should come out with us. After that, we can talk about whatever is on your mind over a drink, how is that?" I still feel guilty as hell for quitting and can't tell Chris that now, not with the shape he is in.

"I can do that; Tina is working that night so I'm not doing anything,"

Just like that, permission granted. That's something else I'll probably never bring up in front of him but I always feel weird with him having to check with his girlfriend like he's a kid checking in with his mom. At least I have plans set up for this weekend, there is no way I want to spend another night alone like last night; trying not to remember, but I do. The fact that I still have a job and no one appears to have figured out I quit is a plus.

A conversation about our mutual boss should not have to be so touchy but it will be; it already is. It always is. People can complain about the boss all the live long day, and they probably do more than we think. Yet even the dumbest of us are smart enough to know what that means, and Chris is not a dumb guy. Complaining about the boss runs the risk of said boss hearing about said complaints. If they are watching us enough to have a problem with us, which is clearly the case with Chris, then the fact that we complain places us in a precarious position. Some bosses are better than others, but this is Miriam Gaw, and Chris has every right to be scared, not for his life of course but for his job and therefore his livelihood, which is his life.

I began my day by willfully destroying my own livelihood and ending it by trying to help Chris save his. Somehow, I feel worse for him than I did for myself. Still, I somehow doubt Chris will bring up what no one has brought up here for the past couple of months. As afraid as we are for the boss' wrath and covering our asses, we somehow think we know better than to talk about what crimes have gone on right in our faces; and we refuse to speak of it all the same. I doubt I will make him feel any better. What can I change? Would things be any better if I had actually left?

The truth of the matter at this damn nonprofit organization (corporation) is that not all of us are here that should be. There is another. We don't talk about Brooke Mesa at all. She used to be on our team, but the more "public" circumstances of her departure remain a subject beyond sensitive, instilling fears within the remaining staff like she's some kind of ghost and by not talking about her, that's exactly what she is, an apparition, a spirit to be forgotten. But I remember everything.

Brooke worked on systems here, which basically made her an IT type that fixed all of our tech issues as they came about. This was probably a lot of fun for her considering she worked for an organization where the majority of the "senior" staff hated technology, particularly new technology that screwed up what was theirs, and what was theirs in these cases was their routines, and these are not to be trifled with.

Although I remember it like it just happened yesterday, it was well over six months ago that Miriam held one of her emasculating staff meetings. These things took place about once or maybe twice a month and were her way of letting us know we were not doing well both financially and in day-to-day labor matters as well. It's her sick way of keeping us on our toes, making sure we know she is consistently unhappy with us, and the purpose is to therefore make us do more and better work for her to not like again in turn, and tell us at the following meeting the exact same thing. Consistent failure.

This meeting was different as it was in the news that a major earthquake had struck the country of Haiti and some several hundred thousand people had been killed.

The quake was all over the news and in general conversation around the office. A lot of charitable initiatives came about to help the country from all parts of the US and some of our major donors announced plans for financial and other aid for the people of Haiti.

Our esteemed Director mentioned this in no trivial manner at our meeting and said she is disappointed that our organization would lose donations expected to come in, and they will be lost to the Haiti earthquake effort. Such competition. This made it extremely difficult for me to hide making an exasperated face and shaking my head which is dangerous since Miriam looks out for such things. I was freed from any accusation of disagreement as Brooke took up open opposition to Miriam for this in front of everyone.

They actually fought over it right there at the conference room table with Brooke asserting that people are dying and had lost their homes and did not have access to clean water among other problems a 7.0 magnitude earthquake could cause and that we shouldn't be upset if our bottom line is affected, as those donations were going to a better and more immediate cause. Miriam ripped into her, slapping her forefinger over and over again on her monthly revenue chart saying that the expectations to meet this organization's goals never end and that Senior Leadership and the trustees expect us to meet them no matter what.

I don't remember all that was said but they raised their voices at each other over this for a good ten minutes and of course everyone at the meeting, including myself admittedly, kept their mouths shut as they knew challenging the boss could mean much worse in their own lives than even an earthquake could offer. The meeting ended without much resolution on this conflict.

Some months after, Brooke announced her two weeks' notice when she found another job. I doubt most were very surprised. It all went as normal at first. We even had a farewell lunch for her that Miriam conveniently did not show up for. What's interesting and caused more discomfort than that Haiti discussion ever could was that after Brooke gave her two weeks' notice, she was then fired on day thirteen. She was gone and no one uttered a word about it. Nothing.

The boss really felt in her heart she was right. This alone was enough to make me sick. Miriam fired an employee on her second to last day on the job; this was awkward to say the least because no one knew how to react to it, which I expect was the whole idea. No one even speaks of Brooke to this day and it's an unwritten rule not to even think of her but the message was clear; and it was wrong. Miriam is not going to treat people the way she would be treated; she treated Brooke as she pleased and that is it, and it didn't help anyone individually or as a whole except for the boss' ego; her own self-worth alone. We go along with this to what end?

Miriam has been here for a while. Too long, honestly. Did her "superiors" treat her this way? What's sad being that Miriam's older generation enjoyed affordable housing, well-paying jobs, a relevant social safety net, and just an overall political and work system that actually included them. They probably still think they worked harder for it.

Treating subordinates the way Brooke (and now Chris) were being treated means our skills or lack thereof are centered entirely on our ability to circumnavigate the boss' will. To deal with the ego, everything else is secondary; and we do not question it. If anything, most subordinates emulate such behavior in the hopes to gain favor, or advantage; all the while only behaving this way out of fear alone.

I won't forget any of this which is one of the reasons I left and don't speak of it now, not even to Chris though I am getting close to at least tell him I'm interviewing. Chris is on Miriam's radar now. He has never nearly had the level of public disagreement with the boss that Brooke had but that incident had its effects despite no one ever talking about or even acknowledging that it happened. I suppose I'm doing the same. I made my own statement by quitting, but by backing (chickening) out, am I any better than everyone who ignores Brooke's existence and pretends she never was anything for fear of the boss' reprisal? I can't ignore that. It appears most do not want me to not even think about it. That's not working either.

Chapter Six

Weapons of Mass Agitation

I RECENTLY HAD A DREAM I was back at the Learning Tools office. I was at my desk, everyone between her and I was a blurry field of black, there but not really there. I wish it was Cathy I was watching but our dreams offer us no choices, only windows at best. The figure in the distance was Miriam. She actually is remarkable when you really look at her. She is older than the rest of us, somewhere in her early sixties, I think, could be more. She's noticeably thin. I can't imagine how she keeps in shape other than walking back and forth to meetings all day. I don't want to know what she does in her spare time. Apparently, she is divorced, and just works all the time now. Such a contrast in lifestyle here between the young and the old. What's terrifying is that I think I'm the only one who notices.

In addition to the slender build, she is thin lipped, scaly-skinned, almost as if blood did not circulate, with sharp cheekbones; longish, cropped curly hair that looks as if she was growing pubic hair all over her skull, running a brush through it occasionally if she had to. That head of hair is something I always notice first about her, no matter what. In addition to her cold and prickly personality, it's something that would always grate on my nerves and always will. Disturbing.

In the dream, she walks not past me, but across my path, keeping her distance in line with her aloof attitude she always has with me. She always has something better to do, even when directly engaging me. She is my superior and we are swimming in the soup that will never let me forget that. I expect that's the whole idea of being a superior in its purest form. It's a never-ending flow of stagnant water. She drinks it right from the tap and does it every day.

She gives me an annoyed look and goes into her office and closes the door. She loves that door closed. It's utterly amazing how a closed door can make us feel more important than someone else. It's not about what they know, it's often about keeping you away from the know. Again, how else are we to feel superior? Miriam is something of a master at this, but for all her talent, enough is never enough.

The dream immediately segues to me sitting with Brooke Mesa in her cubicle. It's freezing and snowing hard outside the far window; the snow piling up on the cars parked outside fast. Brooke mentions how hard it is coming down and that it's only getting worse throughout the rest of the day. It's not even noon. Everyone is wondering if they are going to let us out early to beat all the bad and frankly dangerous commuter traffic that's sure to come.

Sooner or later, a preoccupied human resources manager comes by but does not say anything; she is ducking her head into that Senior Leadership meeting Miriam just left which is somehow going on all day without end. Brooke says she can hear what is going on inside somehow. I miss that girl's perception. In my dream, she is blurry, as if I can't see her; yet she was there. Not forgotten.

"If we have to stay, they have to stay," was the commandment coming out of that board room. There is no way they were leaving their precious meeting come rain, sleet, or snow, or even if it began hailing giant meteorites; they wouldn't ever leave. That was the command: "we" and "they." This is not what one should expect from mostly over middle-aged "adults" who are running a professional organization with the safety of employees in mind. This is how children behave, and that's how they like it. Their way. Above us. They just don't like being called "children," or perhaps worse yet, even implying it. Such could lead to Brooke's ultimate fate.

Yet this is what happened. The HR manager eventually announces that we can leave an hour early, around four that afternoon. This doesn't make sense either. Why wait until everything is covered in snow; why not let everyone go now so as to beat the worst of the storm? Brooke points out as to how painfully obvious this is. Letting us out early, even in the face on a dangerous storm is giving the employees, one's inferiors, a day off no matter which way you look at it; and this cannot be tolerated.

It took most people hours to get home that day. Brooke only has a twenty-minute commute but the snow made that day's drive home about two hours because of all the traffic. There were still people speeding past her. I know all this because even though this was a dream, it actually all happened. All of it. There was in fact a snow storm last winter and it fell on an important day for Senior Leadership and I remember shaking my head at the "us and them" mentality they had and wondering why the hell they waited for more snow to accumulate before letting us out. I suppose we should feel guilty if we wanted anything more.

No one really made a fuss. They just grinned and took it all; and more likely convinced even themselves it was acceptable by simply lying to themselves that it was. It's a coping mechanism. It's amazing what we can tolerate (and thus proliferate) in this type of behavior, more so especially when it comes from the bosses. Some of the staff even laugh off the accusation that it's even wrong. It's a type of personality that is becoming far too common. It's a type of personality I cannot seem to digest correctly. It's the type of personality of Dave Huston.

Dave is a friend who I'm reluctant to say is often not a friend. To boil it down, a cruder way of putting it; to reverse the cliché, Dave is very more often than not "hoes before bros." I can't really remember a time when he wasn't this way. It's been over ten years since I first really started hanging out with Dave, I don't always know why I still do. He is not often not shackled down in a relationship like Chris is so at the very least that's good news for me as Dave is often around and available to be the best friend he can be, such as he is, without having to go on bi-monthly doggie trading visits with an ex's ex flame.

In late college I rented out a tiny three-room local townhouse which we managed to pack with a total of seven roommates. I didn't have my own room but at least half of it was mine and I always had to have my DVDs and music CD's on display for some reason. Most people never really took notice of this but on one of our random parties we had at this place, a fellow student I never met and to this day have no idea who invited him, if anyone, wandered into my room and started taking appreciation of my second row of CD's which were the "classics" as I had them, mostly Elvis Presley, the Ramones, Rat Pack mixes, and Johnny Cash among the eclectic collection of others that Dave glossed over.

"The man has good taste," is what Dave said to those in my room by that part of the night, not knowing the man was me so I just smiled and said "Thanks, no one else has noticed." He simply laughed. He loves to laugh. He laughs at literally everything. That's because it's his defense mechanism. Once Dave told me that just keeps him from crying. Once I tried to nickname him Tee Hee after the old James Bond villain from the second Ian Fleming book but it never stuck, unfortunately. No one ever reads.

Dave cared less about the music as "chasing tail" then, which is no different than he is now, but the fact that he took notice in his world meant something. I don't remember if he was at all successful that night with his female ventures, yet mutual appreciation for Cash and Elvis was the extent of our own conversations until I ran into him again a year or so later.

To my honor, he remembered me at a post-graduation gathering, and after that we eventually became friends; or at least mutual wingman buddies that helped each other run their games though Huston was far more interested in his than mine. I honestly think he only kept me around to help him score with girls at bars or parties, or anywhere. I don't remember once ever actually helping him do that and even less for my part even wanting to try. That was not for me, I was never good at pursuing girls so I let things play out as they did. Nevertheless, here we are years later

I don't know if I should laugh or cry for it. It's good to have friends, even batty friends such as Dave.

Something else about Dave: he is always late. I forget this nearly every time but the man has never once showed up when he says he will, or even showing up at decent time at that. He will always keep you waiting. He doesn't entertain any challenge to this behavior and will laugh if he is questioned, laugh if he is nervous, laugh if anyone else is angry, and probably laugh if I was ever run over by a truck. That's Dave: Weapons of Mass Agitation, another nickname I could have given him that probably would never stick. I have long come to the conclusion that Dave is so deliberately late, light-hearted and laughing, and just an all-around flake because he has something to gain from all of this behavior. He does make the laughing work for his denial, sadly. He's all too good at that.

People who are late all the time, and people who are to "busy" all the time (another frequent Dave claim) have something to gain for all their time management or lack thereof. There is a kind of science to these occurrences and Dave does it so much that he very likely does not realize he's doing it but nevertheless, it is a deliberate habit of his in this case. Why would someone be late all of the time? Anyone can be running late, sure, but always? How is this possible?

Poor time management is one explanation but think of the psychological fallout from one who is chronically late.

They are absorbing attention, however negative. We start wondering where they are, when they will get here; and however annoyed with them we may be, our minds are on them; they get something more in terms of attention. This becomes more so in Dave's case who has been late all of the time for years. We all but expect this behavior but as long as he arrives after us, the deed is done. He keeps us agitated.

What of being "busy" all of the time? Our lives and our jobs can be demanding, but it is remarkable in Dave's case as in anyone else's that no one is ever too busy so as not to find the time to let others know that they are busy. Indeed, one may be as busy as they claim (which I claim is highly unlikely, it's just playing games) yet the result, if not the payoff, of this behavior is that Dave and his ilk are "in demand." They want you and everyone else to know how important that they are and they are not going to let anyone forget.

Dave is one thing as a (bad) friend but I have been through worse as I have even dated girls like this. It was always hell and it never lasted very long, particularly if I brought up the time games as an issue even remotely. What is the ultimate purpose of this behavior? We work hard and are busy for a reason, or at least we are supposed to be. To have friends and lovers are what we work for, is it not? I want to be right on this.

That said, I am not going to be with someone who has to pencil me into their schedule for sex and could never compete with their "busy" days so these relationships never worked out. I always wondered if this is why Dave is usually single like me. Probably not, he seems to just like the pursuit of the female sex like the Coyote chasing the Roadrunner, he often doesn't know what to do with himself if not in pursuit mode. That and he has Lisa Otts to play with whenever he has an off season so Dave will take what he can when he can.

Lisa Otts. I'm not even sure how Dave met her. I admit I can have a foul mouth from time to time but Lisa's is a sewer compared to mine with the amount she curses and the depths of taste she has no apparent problem delving into. If Dave really intended me to be his wing man, Lisa is his wing girl as he knows or at least somewhat accurately believes that by having girls around him will attract more to him somehow.

Lisa is at least different from most others in my life in that she is single most of the time and actually seems proud of it. It gets disturbing when she tells us she "fucked some guy last night," I do my best to tune that out, which is probably why she acts that way more around me. Repulsive charm. I curse as much as the next person but Lisa manages to make me uncomfortable nonetheless, and she knows it. That makes her unattractive to me off the bat but Dave likes having her thick-thighed, foul mouthed, squealing voice around for whatever she is.

To any success she brought to Dave, be as it may, she is far more than just company. It took a while, but Dave eventually admitted to a "friends with benefits" status with Lisa to fulfill certain needs or desires they had over the years. I've had sexual relationships with girls who were not officially "girlfriends" but an exclusive friends with benefits arrangement is something I don't really think I could stomach, ultimately. But ultimately, I am not Dave Huston, and feeling a little prouder of that each day as of late.

I openly admit the guy is a bad friend but he is a friend nonetheless, and they are hard to come by, especially as we get older. Despite the fact that he is an old soul like me and appreciates older music and films, Dave has a remarkable insight, however twisted to his own means, into the world and the modern human condition in this country specifically. The man is not half as cynical as I can get but if one peers through his agitations and bullshit, he does on occasion have something honest to say, despite the fact that he enjoys lying so much, particularly lying to girls.

For whatever reason, Dave and I carpool to the supermarket today to get our week's groceries. I guess he just doesn't like shopping alone and he also likes to pretend he eats healthy in front of me so again, I have my purposes. He's late again, of course. Playing off his penchant for gambling, I came up with a game to play at the supermarket which he has taken to. Today will be no different. Dave came by today, his typical unshaven and unkempt look.

The dark hair not combed, as if he just got out of bed. His clothes are noticeably wrinkly as he hates or simply doesn't bother to iron his shirts. He's taller than me but somehow manages to slouch and shrink himself to a more equitable height. Dave's not going to look good unless he has too.

Our sinister game is called *Three out of Five*, the loser must pay for one of the winner's food items. The rules are quite simple: we go about our own ways, shopping separately for whatever we need. Each girl that we come across is a point of contention depending on if she is with a guy or not. It could be her boyfriend (likely), or simply with a friend (friend-zoned), maybe a brother, but if she is with a guy then that's "one for one." If the next gal is alone then we have "one for two." The first person to get to three out of five wins; we have never gone home disappointed.

When we first started playing this game, instead of the sixty percent victory, I proposed that seventy-five or eighty percent of the girls we saw would be with a boyfriend, I still think that's the likely number even if they are shopping solo. Dave never went for such a high percentage but enjoyed playing the game nonetheless. I'm not sure why he likes it as the premise of the game flows against his very interest in life but he plays it all the same. I find it all innocent fun enough unless one starts reading into it which I often do.

"One for one," Dave says as he passes me in the supermarket. We never buy the same items. He can be fair, rare as that may be. The chronic lateness is hardly "fair" but like in everything else, a bad friend such as Dave has his moments, I just wonder if he really appreciates having friends. "Two for two," is all I can say to him as the game continues. Whatever friend he is, Dave keeps things amusing. One would think not so when considering Hal Sutts.

Thankfully Hal is not here with us now but he will be soon. It's one of the trade-offs that come with hanging out with Huston. I don't know how friends form these days; it just seems to happen when fortunate. Dave brings Hal along, I don't really know where he came from, I bring Chris along from time to time and somehow, we become the occasional quartet of friends; sadly, often a trio. It's mostly food, beer, and Dave wanting to chase down girls but we are friends, for what that's worth at this point. It's important to hang out with the guys; at least it is to me. Hal is less (and I mean less) of a bad friend and more someone I tolerate, and even that begrudgingly. Hal is a school music teacher of some kind; though I know he often works for his father's machine parts company when he needs the money.

Friends matter. They matter more than we give it credit for. For better or worse, we are born into our families. That's not a choice. Friends come in and out of our lives for a wide variety of reasons but these are the real people to connect with in this world. They are not our origin in most cases, but those we met along the path, those we chose to become a part of. Friends matter even more than a relationship or a spouse in many respects. This rings especially true if one is not close with family. How much and to whom can we speak to and confide in for relationship problems or worse yet, said relationships' end?

Hal does not deserve that much credit. While I never quarreled with him directly (keeping my mouth shut too often), he is by far and beyond one of the biggest jackasses I have ever been so unprivileged to call "friend." He comes from Dave's world, I have no idea how those two met, just along the way somewhere. I remember distinctively back when Brooke Mesa was fired. I remember explaining the situation to a disinterested Dave and Hal on one of our out drinking nights somewhere.

I explained to them in detail how Brooke did not get along well with her director, Miriam, and that they had a public "tiff" and were basically yelling at each other in a staff meeting, everyone in the room falling silent. It was never resolved and the fight just sort of stopped with awkward stares from Brooke and everyone else all around. Sometime later, Brooke gives her two-week notice and Miriam fired her on day thirteen.

Dave didn't say anything, seemingly disinterested and passive with the entire sociological issue. Hal's exact words were "that was to send a message." He said that with the most confident smirk I can remember seeing; this man really knows his art of ignorance; mostly due to the fact that he thinks he is dead right. He almost seemed confused that I brought this story up in the first place; yet never doubting it was true.

I am unable to really decipher what Hal actually meant by that but to this day, none of my conclusions make my stomach settle. His tone when he made the "send a message" comment was that of agreement. There was the smirk. He liked that Miriam did what she did to Brooke, or at the very least Hal respected it. Why? Hal had nothing to gain from this situation; he and Dave don't even work with us and never met Miriam or Brooke. I think that was it right there, and never trusted or liked Hal ever since, just tolerated him for what it was worth.

Still, he said "send a message" with pride, it's worth checking in as to why. Does he like relishing in the misery of others? Hal certainly fits the type. After all, someone else "failing" has its merits to us, none of which for good reasons. Perhaps Brooke being out of a job and falling before the boss' will is indirectly empowering people like Hal. Someone else having less invariably has at least a psychological effect of another having more by comparison. This is a wealth driven society after all.

I don't even think it's that simple. There is something else. I can't prove it entirely but something in Hal's reaction to the Brooke incident and not to mention his attitude toward the world in general, makes me believe with more than just a little certainty that there is an agenda here with Hal; it's with a lot of people in general, more so these days. Hal never met and could care less about Miriam's management style, or Brooke's possession of a job or not. People lose their jobs somewhere every day; it can't be that relevant to him.

Yet there was something in my telling of that story. Brooke may be just some gal who lost her job but I gave Hal a clear reason for his reaction. She mouthed off to the boss, in public, no less. We just don't do that, and while Hal has nothing to do with Miriam, he knows what authority is. Miriam has an insatiable ego, but such behavior is common. It's obvious that Brooke and Miriam did not get along. It was cruel for Miriam to complain about revenue loss due to an earthquake in Haiti and Brook nailed her on this, thus she more or less embarrassed Miriam. At the very least she undercut her authority. Brooke's finding of another job and giving notice was an obvious reaction to her differences with the boss and Miriam will not even let the implication slide.

Hal likes this ego. After all, it's his ego too. He would not want what little authority he had undercut, certainly not if he was in Miriam's position; and Brooke giving her notice almost cheated Miriam out of her revenge, cheated her out of the spite she had to give in return. So Miriam would not let that happen and fired her before she could officially leave; thus not granting her any kind of victory by leaving. Hal "sides" with the authority because it is in his best interest to do so, however indirectly. To disagree with the situation or to encourage others to make a stand against Miriam is to invite a chaos that is just too threatening for comfort, even someone who does not work in that organization. Sending a message, indeed.

In this at least, Hal is right. Look at how no one at Learning Tools said a word after Brooke was fired, and that name is not even spoken of now. We are all potential victims and to lash out in even an indirect way at the executioner is to invite harm, or at least a hard time which is bad enough. Lovely world we live in; you are so charming, Hal.

"Two for three," Dave says as he passes me by the milk doors with a grandiose smile. Things are going in his direction for all the good it's doing. He's not going to try to pick someone up at a supermarket but likes that the odds could be in his favor. Shortly I see a girl not too far unlike Cathy walking about; more so that she is with a boyfriend so that is three for four.

Nothing happened again until we find another gal in the checkout aisle unpacking groceries with her obvious boyfriend. Four for five with Dave's identification and the game ended up there, disappointingly maybe, yet interesting enough when considering Dave's and my own often disputed odds. Fun while it lasted as we were heading out for drinks soon after and Hal would be meeting up with us. I only shook his hand once in my life to my recollection. Like Dave, Hal largely keeps unshaven but he also keeps a long mane of hair loose and never in a ponytail, as if he is some 60's hippie type (who is actually conservative as hell). He is a bit on the chubby side and never seems to work out in addition to always eating so much more than any of us.

He does have an odd memory for someone who does not seem to care about me (or anyone for that matter besides himself) much. Hal meets us outside Dave's place after we put our weekly grocery affairs aside, and somehow manages to ask me a dead-on target question.

"Any luck with your girl, Kelly?" he asks.

I don't remember ever bringing Cathy up to him before. Maybe he heard about it from Dave or likely he just over-heard Dave and I talking of it. Hal is not as obsessed with picking up girls as Dave. I think he had a girlfriend way back when but Hal just seems generally concerned with antagonizing others and making them feel worse about themselves.

"It's Cathy, Hal," I say for now. This is just another reminder, unfortunately. I can't help but shake the feeling that Hal is just trying to remain relevant among his own friends. I still use the word "friend" loosely with him but such behavior makes me feel like I am less a part of a group of friends and part of a clique instead. Cliques are no good to anyone. If Hal is trying to remain relevant by talking about girls, and more importantly the pursuit thereof, he's not Dave's friend, he is more of a follower. He's trying to get under my skin and what is worse; I'm going to let him.

It's a misconception that guys talk about sports and video games all the time over drinks like we are having now; at a dive bar Dave likes because they have two-dollar roast beef sandwiches. He is so cheap, it shows. The place is near empty most of the time, the music somehow permanently stuck on 80's hits while the place itself so understaffed the chef walks from the kitchen to serve us our food himself. I just enjoy.

I want to talk about Cathy to someone. It's near impossible to talk about any feelings I have to these two goons. That's what friends are for even if they don't realize it or want it. I'm here for them, for what it's worth. Too bad Chris is not here, he might take me more seriously but he and I rarely talk about my little obsession with Cathy since we all work together. Dave and Hal are working with what I have now.

"She told me she got in a bad fight with her boyfriend," I say to them.

"All right!" Dave yells while toasting his beer. "Trouble in paradise!"

I hate myself for agreeing with him. Should I? Is it wrong to be happy that a crush whom is taken by another is going through, or could be going through, a rough patch in their relationship that could end with that crush being single? Am I swimming in someone else's wake or "on the rebound" as it's called? Perhaps so, but how long can a person be single, especially a beautiful girl like Cathy? I can't have her in any context if she is in a relationship, it's no small detail.

"She lives with her boyfriend," I say in recapping the scenario at least to Hal who has not heard this from me before. "I don't get the impression she is entirely happy with the situation and she got real freaked out when her boyfriend's father waltzed into her house late at night, it scared the hell out of her. She got all pissed off at her boyfriend for that happening and I think she really might want to leave."

"You hope so," said Hal. "She won't though. Not a chance." Dave nods in agreement. I could tell he liked that I was getting my hopes up too much.

"What makes you say that, Hal?" I ask, knowing full well exactly why Cathy was never going to move out of her boyfriend's place, not a chance.

"It's an implication that she won't be able to handle," Hal replies. "She doesn't want to break up with this guy, right? We've heard you talk about this girl before, Din. For her, the sun rises and sets in this guy's boxer shorts. She may be pissed at him and she may very well no longer want to live in that house with him and get her own place but therein lies the problem. Moving out from the cohabitation is taking a step back in the relationship. She is not going to do that because of what that means."

"This guy must be getting laid all the time," Dave says, speaking of her boyfriend. Him and his one-track mind.

There are ways to put some cracks in their theories though. I run the risk of spoiling the guys' night out; now it's a good thing Chris is not here yet.

"She's a competent girl," I say. "She could actually break up with this guy and survive on her own. She would just have to be single again."

Dave laughs and Hal smirks. "Not happening," Dave says. "Wishful thinking, at best. I have seen this girl before, she's slamming hot. She could be single but it would not last very long. There's always a fucking boyfriend. She can't live without him. Her relationship is like a drug she's hooked on and can't, and actually won't, get off of. She needs to be in a relationship; at all times. She can't be single."

I ask the worst possible question I could to Dave. "Why?"

He hates that. I know it. "Why" is a dangerous question.

"These are the times," is all Dave says with no subtle element of disgust. Disgust for me? I have to ask again: why?

Yet I don't, lest this evening do down a path I just do not want it to. Just in time a text comes in from Chris which I read aloud to the guys.

Can't make it tonight. Tina's not feeling well. Let's get lunch tomorrow. I desperately need to pick your brain, thanks, man.

I leave that last sentence out, but the guys get the hint. It's just as well, I need to get away from Hal for a bit and Dave is probably meeting up with Lisa anyway. No use for us.

"Chris' wife making him stay home again. No permission." Dave says and Hal agrees without saying anything for a change. I doubt they care that much that Chris can't join us. Would they care if I couldn't make it?

"Is he still letting her do that dog visitation thing?" asks Hal. I just don't want to answer. That's all I need to hear on that matter.

"They are not married but they might as well be, I guess." I say and could explain he's got it bad at work but it's not going to go down well as they care more about a manager that's not even theirs over a friend that apparently is. We have another round of drinks (on me) and we head out for the night. Dave drives, with Hal riding shogun. Along the way out we drive past a wedding or a wedding photo shoot or something along those lines. It looks fun, I just can't see myself in that situation, too many people looking at me and I don't need the attention. They do, perhaps. Good for them. The couple in the tuxedo and wedding dress are too far away to hear Hal yell "Cheat on him!" out the window. I feel bad for not feeling too bad about this; and not to mention for laughing out loud.

Chapter Seven

Working on the Supplantation

FRIENDSHIPS CAN END. I'VE always had more trouble with this than most others. They grow apart, have differences, and paths change direction, anything. It happens a lot more than we admit, and I was never really comfortable with accepting that. It's not for me and never was. There are friends and yes, girlfriends from my past I am currently sharing air on this planet with; they are out there somewhere yet they are gone, buried somewhere in time, as I am to them. I know times change, and needs and circumstances change; and I can even think of some I'm happy I am no longer friends with but it's always unsettling or just plain sad when someone we know becomes someone we knew.

Another damning factor to this is how much more difficult it is to gain and even maintain friends as we get older. Chris Allen can be an overgrown kid at times, but he's probably the closest thing to a best friend I have in this world. I can be a kid too, I admit. It's good for all of us to some degree or another. I grew up reading comic books; which helped me getting into reading books for real as I went on. Chris and I can still talk about old super-hero books or movies which, I maintain is something special as the Dave's and Hal's of the world are too cool, and I use that term extremely loosely, for such conversations.

By contrast, whenever Chris can hang out with the rest of the guys, it's clear (and it's clear why) that he is not a fan of Dave's constant pursuit of girls. Chris has never gone for it, they have never to my recollection butted heads over this issue but like Dave, it's easy to read Chris' expressions. He would always rather be somewhere else than with Dave on the hunt. They don't hate each other. If anything, they can get along with each other more than me; they bond over talking about real estate opportunities (to my knowledge, none of them actually own property) and sometimes the stock market. Another case where money is acceptable. I get the impression they don't like that I take little interest in this. I think I'd rather talk about the girls or the comic books instead.

I meet up with Chris for lunch as planned. We can only meet at the across the street from the office, The White Dog

Café; a semi-swanky place, business crowd by day, drunken college students by night. We can't get too far from the office without notice. I know half the time they don't care but the last thing Chris or I need is bad public relations at this point, and the one time we take even a slightly longish lunch or come in late is the one time we will be chastised. I'm actually surprised Chris is taking even this small risk but we can't talk in his office forever.

I want to, yet I know we are not going to talk about Cathy. Like all my friends, Chris knows I have feelings for her but is far less interested in talking to me about it, despite being a better friend to me than most. He's simply not into the pursuit phase of any given or potential relationship. That and he knows Cathy has a boyfriend, so he identifies the situation as simply not worth talking about; why talk about a potential break up if that could also happen to you?

I dare say that part of the reason he didn't hang out with Dave and myself before was because he knew we would probably play the three out of five game. Not for him at all. There is a reason for this. The reason is Chris has his. He's a fantastic guy and a great friend and I honestly like his girl-friend Tina, but he is so in that world of his own. I suppose even talking about other girls or discussing the possible dissolution of another's relationship could be damming to him, even indirectly. I reluctantly get it but I wish the times were not so. It's not easy being single in a world all about relationships; and less for those without and don't get a lot of love, figuratively speaking. Well, literally speaking too.

It's crowded, so we sit at the bar of The White Dog and have lunch there near the entrance. Any seat is good enough for us and we are only eating sandwiches and fries anyway. I know why we are here; Chris has been far too readable of late. His balding head and glasses somehow highlight his frustration, I know he's not happy at the job because of the damn boss though I still don't tell him that I quit and came back like I did. I wonder if I'll ever tell anyone besides the Maple Leaf, who is long gone anyway.

"Thanks again for listening, Din. I know I've been in the dumps lately and not too fun to be around," he says while munching on his burger, almost nervously. "Sometimes I can't even talk to Tina about this. She knows I don't like my job but losing it is a whole other can of worms with her. She wants to buy a house together, she's already looking; but I know that's not happening with this job. I have to get another one, and soon."

Chris is afraid and I don't blame him. Losing or potentially losing one's job is a scary process, one we think about so less often than we really should. He can't make Miriam happy, that's more than just fairly obvious. This alone should not be an acceptable reason for his potential firing, yet sadly it is the case. It's good for him that he has Tina, but I know he can't talk to her about this situation too much. Touchy subject with one's spouse or potential spouse in Tina's case. The guy let's her go all the way to Virginia to visit the dogs from her previous relationship, he should be able to talk to her about trouble at work or serious matters such as a job loss. Nevertheless, I don't think Chris can ultimately afford to turn his girlfriend off with this subject. I could be wrong, but if I'm not, it's most certainly not a healthy arrangement for them.

Still, while I don't know what will happen to any of us, a good friend is a man who can be relied upon when he can't or won't rely on his family or significant other. Where else is there to go? The friends we really have are the friends we have when we are down. It's not as if I am telling Chris everything going wrong in my life, and there is certainly plenty of that, and it's not a competition; to see whose life sucks more. With coworkers, I have been conspicuously quiet about my opinions of Miriam and the other "authorities" since Brooke was fired; yet Chris probably gets it. I just can't expect him to embrace the truth of it all. We are all in that precarious situation.

He's often the happy fool (when he is happy, anyway) yet I wonder if hanging around me has somehow hurt his moral even more. I hope not. If he has half a brain cell, he can tell I'm at least disillusioned with this place as he is, and not just because of my little useless crush on Cathy. I just hope my own thoughts and feelings are not as dangerous as I think they can be. Nevertheless, today is Chris' day, so I'm not telling him about the next interview I have already lined up. I could use Chris as a reference if it goes well but I won't ask him until it's time, and that time could be coming soon.

To his point, Chris is at an interesting crossroads in his life despite the ridiculous doggie visits. Such "crossroads" in life are important, more so that the Miriam Gaws of the world simply don't care about him, but his house idea caught my eye. I've been renting apartments or crashing with roommates since I was sixteen years old. I probably will be for a lot longer. Chris and I are not even so young. Everyone loves to give Millennials hell for this sort of thing but this is another example of my own generation, Gen X or however we are labeled, being passed over.

Millennials may be graduating college at the wrong time in history but it's hardly any better for us, and just as bad if you really think about it. Chris and Tina could try to buy a house (presumably together), and hope they can make the payments on it, hope they can keep consistent employment (not looking good so far), and hope that they don't have to go back to school or go into any more debt than they may already have; and ultimately hope that said house won't fall below half the value of whatever they were overcharged to buy it to begin with.

Our immediate forbearers didn't suffer this flaring of inequality. They bought their houses and paid them off well before they reached Chris' age, certainly. I wonder how Chris might receive that if spoken aloud. Would he feel even the least bit bad or even to ponder that someone who had better opportunities now lays milk crates on the street to assert her own privilege in the matter? It's mid-day, those crates are on the street right now. Immortal, somehow. Other problems at hand, I know. Chris manages to break my chain of thought in similar way.

"Did you ever see things coming to this?" he asks, "You can call it a mid-life crisis if you want but we are only getting older and it makes one wonder where it's all going. Pretty sick that I want a promotion, I need a raise, yet I go into work every day and feel like a kid just out of college, if not a child outright before an authoritarian parent who is obsessed with me not disagreeing with her. I don't actually disagree with her that much; she just doesn't communicate what she wants, or at least to her underlings, she doesn't know what she wants; she just wants it and wanted it yesterday. It's on me if I can't deliver whatever that is. Does she like playing this game?"

"You work just as hard as she does," I say to him. "Sometimes I get the impression she doesn't even want that. It's kind of like a 'you do what I tell you but don't work so well as to the point you are a threat to my job or standing here. You are not really a threat to her but she does not really see you as much more than a tool to meet whatever her ends are; such as being promoted to the Senior Leadership team, most of whom are a bunch of selfish jackasses anyway."

I may be wrong, but judging by Miriam's ego being so harsh with Chris, along with the Brooke firing, it's not that obtuse to suggest such an idea. It's obtuse to suggest otherwise. The old, throne-sitting, sorry excuse for a director should be happy; despite all of Chris' suffering and subsequent analysis, we are still not even bringing up Brooke's name today, or thinking of it unless in denial, and speaking of it in peril. Chris could be next, hell, I could be next; and somehow it would be our own fault and never Miriam's. Regardless, Chris is still the man who's really on point with these issues over this particular meal.

"I'm thirty-eight and want to move up the ladder," he continues. "Is that a crime? I would not even call it a mid-life crisis; I've been at this working world, or 'real world' thing as you so often put it, Din; for over twenty years. Somehow the means are no longer there and I'm spending all my time worrying about keeping the crappy job I have; let alone how I can work hard enough to move up. I'm not getting younger either.

"I get it that Miriam is trying to 'move up' herself by getting on the Senior Leadership team. They will never let her in because they know she's crazy, and they don't care if her staff suffers that. Miriam is a baby-boomer and they are hardly done with their careers. It's not helping her if anyone below her moves up or apparently even does anything in their job that entails not making her look good somehow. She seems fine in terms of her health, and even if she doesn't; Miriam probably won't retire until she's well into her seventies so that's another reason not to stick around.

"The damn baby boomers just had it way too good and they are not letting go," he continues, "and we have less than those who immediately came before us. Their own parents fought to save the world in the 1940's. Not only were the boomers the first generation to have access to all resources; they are not handing it off to the next generation as their parents did. Indeed, pretty much anyone younger than them is some level of a menace to what they have. What interest have they in some college graduate or anyone younger than them entering their workplace? How could they want that? They will not be supplanted; and here we are. Such a distinct honor, being the first generation in modern history to have less than their parents had."

Chris has apparently been reading my mind every so often. Not sure if I should laugh or cry. "The upper crust is still moving," I say. "It favors no one except themselves. The fact that Miriam is not moving even further up shows how little those upper echelon boards just don't care about the troops on the ground if you will. Their noses are just too far up in the air to smell the shit. They probably forget what shit smells like and that's the way they want it. How could they possibly be concerned with you or me if it's all about themselves?"

Chris' face lights up in agreement. Misery loves company. It does feel good once in a while to have your crazy ideas verified by someone so as to in turn verify you are, in fact, not crazy. We are just so often sensitive of what we speak of and when. I'm still not bringing up my quitting adventure or Brooke, sadly.

"There is nothing inherently wrong with wanting more," I continue. "We're not just fresh out of college and we've been at the game for a while. People like Joey and Elizabeth are older; they don't seem to be gunning for promotions like Miriam but they have it fairly well off regardless, and Elizabeth and Miriam are actually friends so that's something. So Tavel gets paid a lot while doing relatively little, she has Cathy to do all of her leg work. In the meantime, Elizabeth has her own legs way up in the air from banging that donor she met a while back. What's his name anyway?"

Chris squirms without actually really moving. He looks at me but not in the eye; as if taken aback with the conversation changing to Elizabeth's extramarital affairs. Again, it's outside his comfort zone for any given number of reasons. So much we can't say, even away from the office. Exposing Elizabeth's affair would not affect Chris or myself in any direct way, but that whole thing with her being the boss' friend unfortunately matters more than we often ever say.

"His name's Michael Gogol. We don't know that they are actually having an affair unless you somehow caught them in the act of doing so. Gogol is actually going to be at that event that you are supposed to be helping Jodi Molano out with, might not be a good idea to bring it up."

"I never met Molano. Is she the sensitive type?" Chris sighs a heavy breath, getting redder in the face. Is he mad at me? I hope not. It's not as if I'm talking about Tina running around and screwing a rich nonprofit donor, while hardly working and enjoying the cushy job. Is it because I could be?

"I've met her before; she's pretty laid back, so I doubt it," Chris says. "You might get along with her, though I think she is older than me by some years. I just don't think it's a good idea to bring it up because the wrong people might hear us talking. Sure, Elizabeth seems to spend a lot of time with Gogol and he even visits her at the office fairly often, but it's not a sign of an official 'affair' and it's not our business anyway. She's not my wife, not my girlfriend, so what she does isn't really my problem. Besides, Din, you might piss off all of the girls at the office by implying that it's a problem. You could be walking through land mines."

Implication. To imply something is true, to say something that would make someone else think of an idea that is unpleasant in their minds, can sometimes be even worse than speaking our minds outright. I'm starting to get a clearer picture as to why Chris is so frustrated lately, and though it severely pains me to say it, it's not really all because of Miriam Gaw. There are always exceptions, but Chris, like far too many of us, are all but terrified of "authority." I don't know what in his mind that is. If Miriam heard that word was getting around that her friend Elizabeth was having an affair (which is so damn obvious it's ridiculous), she would not want such perception to get around; especially given that it's true. If we can question Elizabeth on anything, we can question Miriam as well. Not sure why any questions at all are off limits but here we are living this modern world.

Hell, even Cathy has told me she's seen Elizabeth come back from long lunch breaks with reddish skin and mussed hair, and it's not as if she's hitting the gym in her business suit, though she is into other exercise it seems. I've even heard Nicole and Cathy far too audibly whisper about Elizabeth's afternoon romps and still, Nicole would treat her with more respect than me.

I suppose extramarital sex is of more repute than no sex at all, presently speaking in my case. I really can't wait to work this event; at least I'll be able to sharpen my skills in the art of what not to say; and careful not to ask why Chris left work in tears after a conversation with Miriam the other day. I'm sure the general emasculation is explanation enough in this case. Chris has his limits, no different than anyone else, just so hard to talk about this when one's very livelihood is on the line. It just should not be.

None of this was ever unfamiliar. I remember I was the center of attention for a bully a long time ago. I was a child but this was no immunity from any abuse. I was beat up a lot for asking why they intimidate and gave me such a hard time, and sent to the fat alcoholic principal's office more than once for the crime of fighting on my own behalf.

I remember being told it was wrong to fight with anyone just as much as it was wrong for being smacked in the face myself. It was never the physical pain, that's was a dodge on their part, to avoid the real problems no one wanted to talk about for some reason. It was never about getting beat up by the bully. It was about them taking away my dignity. No one, young or old, ever used that word once.

"It's not 1663, Chris," I say, attempting to get the subject somewhat back on track here. "It would be great if we could all get together with rapiers and storm Miriam's office because she is a terrible captain and take over this ship ourselves. Sadly, that option is no longer open to us. It would be great if any of the employees could have a say in the direction our day-to-day lives have. After all, we spend more time at work during the day than anywhere else, generally speaking. Why should our fates be left to a handful of disconnected superiors or in this case, one bottomless pit of despair of a boss? So, you have to do something. Spell it out for me, Chris. How is your job search going?"

The Chris looking for a job cat was already out of the bag anyway, and I needed to know if he was having any more success than I was. Maybe I am doing something wrong. Turns out I'm doing slightly better.

"I've had a few calls, and have some feelers out there, just no interviews yet," he says. I don't know if I have too much experience or if I'm asking for too much money.

I hope something comes along but I have to be careful; interviewing can be a full-time job on its own, and it's not like I can ask Miriam for a day or even half a day off just so I can spend time and effort to get the hell away from her. But then again, if she will just up and fire me one day because she feels like it, I would have to find a new job sooner rather than later."

Nice to not be crazy in this instance as well. I suspect Chris will be faking a sick day soon. He has to be careful about that too, as I do. If he is successful with a job interview, then he may be called back for another. That's a good thing. Yet it means more time away, more suspicion; and if Miriam ever gets wind that he wants to leave, she may be crazy but she is plenty clever enough to know that he's leaving because of her. That might expedite his imminent firing if that is indeed forthcoming. No proof, sure, but sadly not at all outside the realm of possibility. What happened to Brooke could happen to Chris, maybe worse; he's just docile enough to keep his mouth shut in front of the boss, which itself is likely what is keeping him afloat, however temporarily.

"Whatever happens," I tell him with my mouth half full of food, "I can provide a reference if you need one. Sometimes we just do what we have to do. I think I told you once I spent a couple of college years working at a video store. I never missed one day there, even when I was sick. The only day I called out was my very last day. I got a more fascinating job at a liquor store and it was on the last day that my new boss called me and said they needed me to help with shipments of wine and asked if I could start earlier. I was left with a choice: make my new boss happy and have the old one pissed off at me; or disappoint the new boss even before the job starts by not going in as requested. Guess which one I chose."

"Thanks, Din. Feel free to have anyone call me too if you ever need me."

I'm tempted to tell him everything. I still feel wrong somehow over the quitting thing. Not sure if I'm more embarrassed that I quit without having another job or that I chickened out of the whole operation. If I had actually left, I seriously doubt Chris and I would even still be friends. He would likely be upset with me just leaving and it's obvious that it would leave him or anyone else with greater exposure to Miriam's wrath agenda. I don't like losing friends. How could I? At least by aborting my quitting mission, I get to be here now with a friend, and not wishing I could still talk to one. We talk as if these are the end times; and for all we know, they may very well be upon us. At least we are still here, for better or worse; and it often does always get worse.

"What are you guys doing here?" an audibly startling, feminine voice interrupts us in the middle of biting into our sandwiches. She almost screamed that at us, at the top of her lungs, at least in our minds.

Time stands still. Both Chris and I literally freeze over our lunch in mid bite. The world has actually frozen in place with this question put before us. She had me going for at least a few seconds. I felt bad about it for a moment. What was I doing here? I'm sorry I did wrong, didn't mean to do that. What was I thinking? I have offended somehow and felt bad about it while stuck in time. It is almost fear.

Elizabeth Tavel is pissed off at us, no doubt about it. What the hell does it look like we are doing here? It's called lunch, try it some time. Isn't that why she is here? Why is she annoyed with us? Not to mention the café is right across from the damn office to begin with; is it that unreasonable to think you might run into your coworkers at lunch?

"We're just having some lunch" Chris says. Elizabeth's reaction is one of confusion and again, annoyance, until it morphs into a fake contentment, trying to be friendly with two guys she absolutely doesn't want to be here. She is dressed up, business like, not the post rich man romp she often looks like, at least not yet. She frowns at us.

"I'm meeting a friend for lunch here," she says, then waves to a generic fat man sitting at a table in the back who of course is Michael Gogol. I don't actually look at him and she doesn't introduce us. She simply says, "Well, enjoy and see you guys later," and walks back to her "date." She doesn't hug or kiss him or anything, but she doesn't have to. She's taking a long lunch today.

"That was awkward," I say to Chris. Elizabeth can't hear us from where she's at and at frankly by now, I don't care; my friend and I can't even get lunch without these ridiculous people and their behaviors encroaching on it.

"The hubris," I say. Chris is quiet, having almost seemed to have lost his appetite by now. "She's cheating on her husband, and doesn't want anyone to know it's obvious and gets pissed off if anyone is around it yet she hangs around that guy at every event. Gogol visits her sometimes at the office and now she's meeting him for lunch right across the damn street. Somehow, we are the bad guys for being in her direct vicinity. What does she expect us to do about it? It's as if us knowing about her activities is wrong on our part and she doesn't want anyone to be around it while she brings it around everyone else."

"It doesn't mean she's having an affair," Chris says quietly. "We should be getting back."

It matters not to me if Elizabeth is having an affair, just don't ask me to fall in line with pretending it's not there; as if we should feel guilty for grabbing lunch across the street from the freaking office. I wonder what vested interest Chris or anyone else has in keeping it all a secret. But then I remember she is the boss' best friend. I am thus obligated to console my own best pal again.

"I get it, Chris. Her dealings are not our business but she's making it really hard not to be part of all of it. I never really had a direct problem with her exactly. Her marriage is not my concern in and of itself but you have to ask questions here. Despite being miserable in her own marriage, she hangs out with and always hires the same type of person.

"It's always the glamour girls. Every single employee that comes down the pike here seems to always have a boyfriend, always engaged or about to be engaged, planning a wedding, and so forth; or they are in the process of buying their first home. All of the things she had herself in the past. Is she trying to live vicariously thorough Cathy and Nicole and whoever else? Granted, her only friend her own age is far more miserable than her so maybe underneath all the fake friends bullshit, she just wants some happy variety, despite probably hating them for the crime of being younger."

Chris just stares at the walls and shakes his head, as if he wished he were somewhere else. Not sure why it makes him so uncomfortable, he hates this place probably more than me at the moment. But that's how our day out went, food and guilt, then back to work; for all the good it's done for us. I suppose we will have to be more careful as to where we eat moving forward.

I hope Chris finds another job though I would miss working with him. I don't want him to be unhappy; he doesn't deserve the treatment he's been getting just for not being able to make a few managers, one in particular happy, for not making her "look good" when it's becoming ever more palpable that she doesn't look good to the people she wants and never will. He keeps trying. I don't know how longer I will be able to. I'm glad Chris and I have each other's backs in a sense; there is still a lot he doesn't know. Maybe I'll tell him next time.

Tomorrow I have another interview. I'll have to pull the doctor's appointment follow up to my last sick day as an excuse, and excuses are becoming ever more in short supply and flimsy themselves for that matter. I have to risk it or there will be no new job. I know I'm lucky to have another interview so soon after the last; which I unsurprisingly never heard from. The work at this other company is similar to one of my old jobs; not exactly the best scenario, but maybe and only just maybe, this one will work. Perhaps it's time for something good to happen for a change. It just seems to be something that's becoming all the more infrequent as time goes on. It's not up to me what happens entirely, but it's nice to know I have some hand in pushing the wheel forward now and again. It's a square wheel, but it can move.

Chapter Eight

Agenda

I'M USUALLY UP PRETTY late. No sleep gives me more time in the day, even if just to think. I don't consider myself that popular of a guy, but I don't mind if anyone calls me late at night if they want to talk about anything. If I'm awake, that's good enough, and if it's a friend, feel free to wake me up with the call. It's about nine at night and my phone goes off. I was really not expecting a call at all, let alone so late at night from a Human Resources coordinator from the company I interviewed with earlier today. Life has been an ongoing calamity lately, but I can't say it hasn't been interesting.

"Hi Din, this is Atousa from Hammerfall, following up on the interview you had with us today."

I barely remember this H.R. person or her name and have no idea why she would call me so late; but again, I'm awake, up for talking to someone, and I usually do not hear from the people I interview with whatsoever so what could I possibly complain about? Then again, I only need to give that idea a small bit of time to take effect.

Hammerfall is some kind of science research company I interviewed with because I applied to it at random as they say they need some writers with business experience. It's similar to what I used to do and with the relative lack of opportunities; I thought it wrong to not apply for the job. I didn't even like the idea of working for a science or tech company and I still am not entirely sure what they do. I interviewed because they called me for an interview and felt like I had to pursue it. I don't get enough calls to say "no" so easily. It's amazing how one cannot actually choose where they work. I could very well end up having to take this job, depending on how all this plays out. So I listen to what she has to say.

"I got the feedback from everyone you interviewed with and I had some notes I wanted to discuss with you. I can say that they are nearly ready to make a decision and are prepared to offer you the position and at the salary you asked for. However, there is a difference among the inter-view team as to if you are the best fit for the position and I was hoping you could clear a few things up for us. Is that okay?"

I just don't know what to say to her. I'm still not even sure I want this job. I feel bad about that but should I just take whatever comes along first just to get away from Miriam Gaw? Not the worst advice but I need time to think on what I am actually going to be doing next. So Atousa here, she kind of has me on the spot, though I appreciate at least the communication.

When I arrived at the Hammerfall office earlier today, I found out I would be interviewing with four people throughout the day, just in different phases: first the hiring manager and my boss to be, then the senior vice president of the department I would be working for, then a couple of girls on the staff whom I would be working with. They had an entire agenda printed for me and everything. It was pretty well organized.

I thought it would be one of those interviews where the main hiring manger makes the decision, then clears it with his boss if it makes him happy, and the staff are just brought in to make it look like they have a say in the matter. It turns out at this place; they actually seem to value the input of the entire team, which is impressive. More companies, if not everyone, should be doing this. Hiring a new employee is more than about just one person, we should all be much more involved with the process; and not just when they are hired, when employees leave too; or is that asking for too much?

Atousa goes through the interviews I had one by one, person by person. She actually says the hiring manager and my would-be boss, Ward, actually liked me. I would have never have guessed by the man yelling at me thorough nearly the entire interview. Atousa never brings up this point but the first man I interviewed with, the boss and official hiring manager actually spent most of the interview time berating me and digging into my resume as to why I left each job and why I'm job hunting now.

It's not so much the usual attitude of a manager wishing he was not there, but more of scolding me for leaving the jobs I have left, as if this was some affront to Ward himself; or perhaps a warning to him that if he hired me, I would in good time leave him as well, and he would have to hire again. He cannot have that.

Ward was the epitome of the "stuffed shirt" office worker; his shirt and tie looked so tight he might have trouble breathing. He was only a little older than me, short but receding black hair and skin as pale as the moon. It was hard to tell but he looked as if he was foreign but not foreign. No sense of humor whatsoever. Though I cannot imagine him comfortable in any other given situation.

Could it be you are overpaid and don't want to do your actual job, Ward? Employees leave, and even "given" this job; I could leave in a few years as well, maybe even less if it doesn't work out well. Indeed, if I end up getting offered this job, it will not be for life. Employees' lives change; they move, they want to try something else, the commute is too rough, or (far more often) they leave for a better salary. We like to ignore it but why would an employee be beholden to any manager, to work for them indefinitely and never be able to leave by their own volition?

This, sadly, is another example of the hubris surrounding the modern manger and job market. They can fire or lay off a subordinate (an inferior), yet it's not acceptable for the inferior to make the choice to end the relationship? Is it an ego thing? Are managers like Ward and Miriam simply offended one of "theirs" left them? Even if the relationship is cordial, rare as that seems, there has to be something wrong after all; and if the employee leaves first, they have the edge on their boss, so to speak. This is but one reason why Miriam did what she did to Brooke. There is no reason to believe a new manger would not do the same, which is only making me more apprehensive of this opportunity, such as it is.

"Why did you leave there?" Ward asked me in a noticeably raised voice while harshly jabbing his forefinger onto my resume. He wanted to know about what happened at IT Corporation, and almost seemed to be turning red in anger, near breaking a sweat and not looking me in the eye; almost shaking. I was admittedly getting a little nervous but was not going to show him. If he could not play it cool, I will have to, or this would be all for nothing.

"The company put itself up for sale and they eventually closed my office entirely" I said. This is, of course, a downplay. Ward was too aggressive of an interviewer, it's like he was out for blood. It wouldn't matter if he was the sweetest guy in the business; I wasn't going to tell him the whole truth because no one is into that. To be fair, the company did close its doors, and I was laid off along with many other employees in different departments.

IT Corporation declared bankruptcy based on some bad business deals at the board level. I'm often made to feel responsible for this by implication. Ward was not making this much easier today. I wasn't sure what to tell him, if a company goes bankrupt and puts itself up for sale, there is little an employee of said company can do other than hope they keep their job amidst the inevitable layoffs or, and certainly more wisely so, start looking for another job. I suppose it's difficult for a manager to, well, manage anyone as the need for loyalty to such a company can easily be superseded under those circumstances.

During this time, when that company was on the fall, I remember my boss, a divorced (though oddly immediately remarried) introvert with an unusual affinity to listening to old Madonna CD's in her office. She was by no means the best boss but then again not half as vindictive as Miriam Gaw by comparison. She often just kept to herself, unless she was working with someone whom she deemed important; usually some upper management director or VIP of some kind.

What I remember most during that harsh time of corporate bankruptcy is that my department's supervisor was in a good position herself as it turned out. Every executive above her was either scrambling to try to keep the company together, or just resigning outright when they realized there was no hope. Everyone below my boss, including me eventually, was being laid off. I suppose the company needed someone in between to actually execute the firings. She was able to keep her job after the new parent company took over as well. Talk about job security. Unfair advantages in any given economic climate. Is this not evidence enough to at least reevaluate middle management? Is it enough to question it, and openly? Do we really need them? Consequences indeed. Maybe I think too much but this more than just a happenstance problem.

Through all this, Ward seemingly accepted what had happened with that company closing and moved on to more current events.

"Why are you leaving your job now?" he asked with the same volume and aggressive tone; while also not looking me directly for some reason. He never explained all the venom. I knew I couldn't question why.

His question was far more difficult to answer as, again, I could not tell Ward the truth. I cannot tell him I have issues with the boss (or that I think she's flat out crazy). I can't tell him I need more money coming in as that, of course, is a far more taboo subject; and he apparently is even more sensitive to the subject of employees leaving their jobs. Charming fellow, really. It's a good thing he could never find out I nearly quit the way I did. I'm sure Ward would love to hear that particular story.

Ultimately, I tried to sell him on the idea that I was simply seeking new opportunities, and that getting a new job would also be an opportunity to reboot myself and start again within a new role. That was a cop out, obviously, but there is some truth to it. It was all I had with this man. Atousa tells me that Ward actually liked me, and that this portion of the interview went well. She did not mention once Ward's obvious concerns that I was a flight risk. For some reason, the man actually wanted me for the job. That or he didn't want to tell the Human Resources rep that he had these types of concerns. He's clearly more than a bit sensitive, maybe he said I was a good fit for the job because he did not want himself to appear as a troublemaker to other departments. I imagine I will never know.

Though it could be the fact that the second person I interviewed with, the Senior Vice President, and commander of the whole marketing and proposals department, Al Russo, who was one of the nicest men that I have ever met; and the mere fifteen minutes we actually spoke were just that awesome. For the first time in as long as I can remember, someone came into a room to interview me and did so with a smile. Al was older than me, probably in his sixties, bald with a small tinge of gray hair on the side of his head, and quite heavy. Al was the jolly fat man. Dressed casually, jacket with no necktie, just very relaxed. His massive size was quite simply part of his overall charm.

It's remarkable how that works sometimes. I am generally thin I like to keep in shape and would take it very seriously if my gut started creeping over my belt, and would probably hit the gym twice a day if that happened. However, men like Al, balding and heavyset, can actually be appealing characters, even downright handsome to the eye of the beholder. Good for him, then. I may be or very well may not be getting this job, but the interview with the Senior Vice President was a lot of fun. For a higher up the totem pole man, he really understood a lot happening on the ground than most do; an honestly refreshing exception to the current trends.

Al asked about my past work, yet not in any negative way. He was simply attempting to follow the story of my resume, and get an idea of my past work and experiences. Never had I before met someone, let alone an upper management man, who had actually made me feel entirely comfortable with my own work history on paper.

"Welcome to the interview day, Din. I know these seem to drag along, especially when you are at a new company you may not feel entirely comfortable with. But trust me, you will survive here. I did somehow, and I started in this business over twenty-five years ago. Just remember when I did come aboard here, I actually had a full head of hair!"

I could not help myself but to smile and nearly laugh out loud. This was all working somehow.

"It's a good thing my wife likes bald guys! I see you worked for an environmental remediation company" he says while casually reading my resume. "That must have been fun, how can anyone be happy working for a company whose primary workload is getting contracts to clean up overused landfills and power plants? I guess we all have worked jobs that we worked at to that pay the bills. I doubt it was your own first choice of work but that is okay, we all start somewhere and work places in which we would rather not. What happened, how did that job end?"

I explained to him that the company went bankrupt, put itself up for sale and subsequently laid off a large number of employees. It was the same old story, yet this time I found myself more confident in what happened telling this story to Senior VP Al; when every other time I was choking on guilt over something I had no control over.

"That's how it often goes," Al responds, "Half the time it seems like they don't give a shit about you, and far too many of them don't, but when it comes to their own company collapsing, they really don't have the time or inclination to care about the employees. Don't let it bother you. It happens to far more people than you know in their lives, they just don't often admit it. Seriously, what's the problem? Companies close their doors all the time, and you have to keep working, so the job ended and you eventually got another one. Simple." This guy is too awesome. I was waiting for a catch that never came.

"I like writers, Din. Especially writers that have business experience. I was a business major in school, and I was always jealous of English majors. They read more than me and were smarter and could certainly write better. I can't write well to save my ass to this day."

Even that felt good, honestly. I occasionally tended to regret or look down on myself for having an English degree; mostly because of everyone else who is not Al Russo had no qualms in doing so. It's nice to be at least somewhat appreciated for what skills I may have. It's nice to celebrate it once in a while instead of being made to regret it; to feel inferior because such studies typically do not lead to positions garnering a lot of money. Though we work just as hard as anyone.

That's how the rest of that interview session went. Meeting and speaking with Al was a ridiculously rare explosion of positivity in the workplace along with hope for the immediate future ahead. I'm somewhat shocked about this even tonight on the phone with Atousa. I was still not completely sure I wanted the job but this Al was making it hard to not want to try. Atousa confirmed with me on all these points; telling me that Al really liked me and thought I would be an excellent addition to the team; and furthermore, he hoped that I would sign on with the company.

I liked where this was all going, almost afraid that I may have to make a decision soon since they were going to make me an offer. Well, that's a nice problem to have. Nothing turned out to be so simple though, and Atousa's tone with me changed rather rapidly. Maybe I should not have been waiting for the catch.

"The problem we have, Din, is that the two editors you met with, Heather and Maureen, thought you were a bit too quiet and don't feel like you would be a good fit for the job. I spoke to Ward and he said the entire interview team cannot come to any real agreement on this, and that's what is holding this up. Can you maybe explain this to me, please?"

This was surprising. But then again, meeting these two girls was one of the, if not the, strangest parts of the day. I reflected on meeting the direct supervisor first, he was basically a dick and grilled me incessantly over why I left my past jobs and my imminent departure from the job I barely have now. He apparently liked me, according to Atousa, though I will probably never know why and honestly thought the whole interview day was shot after just meeting Ward alone.

Then I meet Al and my entire attitude towards working at this place began to shift into a much more positive light. I know I will not be working directly for Al but it was encouraging meeting, and furthermore when that portion of the interview was done, I thought I had an excellent chance of being offered the job. However, the last portion of the interview was to meet with two staff editors who already work under Ward. I was fine with meeting staff, even encouraged by the idea. The problem is these girls had absolutely nothing to say to me.

I thought this was going to be the easiest part of the day; after all, I was merely speaking to staff like myself, and not to management. How wrong I was. They entered the conference room, both young girls, certainly younger than me. They did not shake hands and scarcely made eye contact. I don't know what the issue was but they didn't seem to like the idea of even speaking to me. One girl, I don't remember which one, did not speak at all.

The other editor, who if I remember right was Heather, asked me why I thought this type of company was a good fit, given that I have spent the past few years in a nonprofit organization; all asked with a look that said "No answer you give me will be good enough." What the hell was happening?

I gave her the normal spiel about new opportunities and the need to start again in life. She didn't take that too well and only stared awkwardly at me and then to her friend. What is it that they knew but I didn't? Did they just not like the look of me and didn't want to work with me from day to day? This was all far too awkward, even more than usual lately. I was beginning to wonder if I even wanted to know why.

Then of course Heather asked the compulsory "do you have any questions for us," to which I said I did not. More staring. I could have cut the tension with a knife; I just never knew why. The clock on the wall was running backwards.

They were wasting all of our time, and I just had no idea what they wanted me to say. That was the shortest interview session of the day, easily less than ten minutes time. They left the room as awkwardly as they entered it, and now I am here on the phone, being granted the responsibility of explaining this to the human resources officer.

"Heather and Maureen really felt that you were far too quiet and that you didn't ask them any questions, and it seemed to them that you did not want the job or even be on the interview, this is what they mentioned to Ward and he brought this to my attention. Ward is confused himself," Atousa tells me.

Even she now has this annoyed voice that is disappointed in me for bringing about this problem. Those girls didn't even ask me any questions! I could tell Atousa, this but it would be to no avail. I simply said that I was not sure what they wanted me to ask them and that they seemed unprepared for the interview, and that perhaps we should focus on what the rest of the team wanted to do. This is a criticism, plainly. It is about all over, I am afraid. Atousa herself pauses on the phone. Damn me for making her uncomfortable.

"Well, Din, the thing is, we make decisions on hiring as a team here, and if you cannot give us an explanation to assuage all of the concerns we talked about, we may not be able to offer you the job. Can you do that for us?"

It's come to this. They want me to solve this problem. I have no idea what I am supposed to tell them and it's for a job that at first, I was not entirely certain I wanted and now starting to want it all the less. It's all on me to explain it to them and though Atousa clearly thinks she's helping she is actually obstructing the process to a point it could never work for any party involved.

What are my real options here? Quite simply, I don't have any. I used to complain, and still do, that it was disinterested or (and sometimes and) abrasive managers who were deciding my fate in this world regardless of whatever skills and experience I brought to the table. Now it's two aloof and likely agenda-driven girls who have this same power somehow. I could not make them happy, they didn't even give me the chance to actually try, and now the responsibility falls on me, for some reason at nine o'clock in the evening, to decide what happens next and I don't even have an answer.

This is my life, the next few years or more of my very life rests on the heads of two disinterested editors and subsequently a confused hiring team who want me to solve this problem which is theirs entirely. What a time to be alive.

"I think my resume is representative of my skills and experience," I say to Atousa. "I felt that the interviews today went well, though I cannot explain why the two editors thought I was too quiet. Perhaps you can talk to Ward and Al as we had more to say to each other. Ultimately, I cannot make the decision as to if I am to be offered the job or not. That is all I can tell you."

Atousa immediately gets defensive, "We are not asking you to make the decision," she says. "We are asking you to explain their concerns so they can bring this hiring process to a close. If we can settle this, we should be able to make you the offer that we discussed before." So the carrot is dangled before me, for all the good it does now.

"I've said all I can, I simply do not understand what the concerns were and if they still have them, they will have to make a decision. I wish I had more to say to you, this is somewhat of an awkward situation, I am sorry," I say, clearly implying that what they are asking is ridiculous and it's odd that I am being called so late in the evening to begin with.

Atousa sighs to herself, indirectly thanks me for my time and says that she will be in touch if there are any other developments. Well, so much for that. It all went nowhere. That was a substantial amount of effort, people-managing, stress management, and time for such a flop of a result; and somehow, they have me feeling like I am at fault for it not working out. I don't know what those girls were apprehensive about, nor do I have any idea what they discussed with their boss. Sadly, I am not privileged to such information even though that is exactly what I would have needed. I am quite unaware of what would ever make them happy. Such assessments are out of my skillset evidently.

I have been too naïve of late. I've thought about the "level playing field" or lack thereof a lot since deciding to quit my job. It's one of the reasons I chickened out of that operation, and still somehow have a job. Again, it's presumptuous to expect that I deserve a job; but we all need to work. All of this is moot if a couple of staff editors have enough influence to cast doubt on an applicant for whatever their motives.

I would have enjoyed working under Al at Hammerfall but who knows if it would have worked out. It matters little as I will not be working there. It's just noteworthy and all around sad that this had nothing to do with my skills or even my past experience, despite Ward's intrusions, and it all came down to me not being able to make the right people happy and my options; and indirectly, my immediate life's future were harmed as a consequence of it. Yet this is all with no consequences for anyone at all, besides myself of course.

This job seeking process is becoming all too familiar and all too egregious. It's never on them, not even those editor girls. They got what they wanted, whatever that was, and I did not get the job. What is considered conventional wisdom for some reason states that I didn't "work hard enough for it." I did not make the proper level of effort to make my potentially new employers impressed enough for them to grant me employment. "They" tell me I should have tried harder. I should have prepared more.

The latter may have been true to at least some degree but what's getting to me is that it's someone else's decision where life's employment goes, yet the burden of responsibility is all on me. I make that decision, yet I don't. Everyone still asks me why I work where I do now or have worked in the past. Why did I "choose" to work at these places; and why did I leave? Their answer lies within the mirror. I just can't point that out.

I am not sure when I will have another interview, and less certain of how long I can keep this up. Not everything should be expected to work out, sure, but does everything have to be so preposterous? Chris is more than halfway to being fired and there is no reason to believe that this could not happen to me either. Time is more of an issue than we are giving it credit for. I can't do this forever. One cannot live on edge, in limbo, like this for too long without it taking its toll.

I know it happens. Plans go awry, ideas get skewered to death; and making sense quite easily begins to become less and less of a priority to the point where sense is entirely optional for those who can undoubtedly be called the haves. We are all human, yet tend to forget we share that in solidarity. I just happen to actually notice the road behind me is crumbling away; and the road ahead is flat out opaque. I am starting to wonder if I even want to see what lies ahead, or if it even wants to see me.

Chapter Nine

Tears

"Money," is all she says when the meeting begins. She didn't scream it out or even raise her voice much; but it felt like she was jabbing us with a hot poker with that word. I felt like a hooker who had been slapped in the face by her pimp. The boss will not accept any explanation or dissent; just show her the money and then get more. It's authority time again, not that it ever really isn't. It's ego time. More so it's time to be reminded how much we, the team, do not matter. I can hear her but I don't look at that aging, hubris filled pile of crap of a director in the eye during this entire meeting. Not even once. She likely notices that, and it only makes her rage all the more prevailing. Just not over me specifically. Not yet.

Miriam called this meeting more or less out of nowhere. It's odd because while a year or so ago these get-togethers were usually on a weekly basis, but as time went on and the boss began spending more and more time brown-nosing the Senior Leadership team, it was almost as if she forgot about the general staff as a whole. Not that I am complaining, the less time around her the better. Yet, now that she has us back directly in her clutches, we are all the worse off for it. Well, a specific number of us are anyway. Miriam usually remains in the shadows when it comes to personally dealing with us. She is too important. I don't even like being in the same room with her. She probably knows that too.

"We are a nonprofit organization," she continues with her reading glasses resting way down on the end of her nose, "but this is a business. If we do not meet certain criteria and more specifically, revenue goals, then there will have to be consequences for it. We cannot make one dollar less than we did the day before. That's it. Ultimately, you are all responsible for the financial well-being of this organization and you need to be conscious of what you are here for: generating those dollars. Pursuant to this, you need to be more money-minded and be more aware of your day-to-day practices and what is ultimately good for us or what is going to hurt us in the pocketbook. Whatever it is you disagree with in terms of what is happening with management isn't going to help that either. I don't see why you would; there is no reason to do so."

She goes on and on like this. We are all just sitting around this conference room table, everyone besides me looking at that cesspool of pride with attentive eyes. Well, it's not only just me. I'm more or less faking it, literally hoping she does not notice me not looking at her when I know she can see that because she is damn well looking for it. Still, because she can get away with it, Elizabeth, lest we forget whom is Miriam's buddy (how that evil wannabe executive can have any friends is beyond me), is not looking up much. She's playing with her phone, no doubt texting her rich boyfriend who will likely be at this event we are having tomorrow. She's literally getting all of her affairs in order for this. That said, I know what friends are, and Miriam and Elizabeth are not that; although they think that they are.

Joey LeMari is paying attention but working off a clipboard while he listens. He loves to look busy. I can't think of one single meeting where Joey isn't showing off how busy he is and that he never stops working; at least when someone may be looking. He's a pal so I never once personally called him out for this game but we all know that's what he does. Miriam buys it from them both.

The older types tend to get away with more; superior for the happenstance of being older. They have been around a long time, and they are not going anywhere either. I wish I will live so long but doubt I'll reap the benefits when I get there. Today's boomers have us in a situation where a huge group of what is now older prosper; and they do so at the expense of the younger employees. I am not going to get into how much they make in salary. I could cry, I swear. There are better digressions at hand.

Speaking of which, Cathy is here with us too today, sitting next to Nicole and Elizabeth. She looks ridiculously beautiful; long flowing curly hair that she moves from her gorgeous eyes from time to time with a tantalizing flip of her hand; wearing a tight reddish dress that wraps around her form, accentuating every near perfect feature, and her black stockings running down to her cute flat shoes; legs crossed and I'm not close enough, but probably smelling irresistible to. I try my best to keep my eyes off of her. Even while being berated by the boss, Cathy is still a nice distraction.

"Something else I need to remind you of," continues Miriam, "is that our consultant Jodi Molano is going to be helping us at the front desk at the Alumni and Friends event tomorrow night. I am not a big on hiring out work to external consultants, but she has a good track record on her resume of getting results. Regardless, I want you to represent us in front of her. The last thing we need is for someone outside our own organization to think we are not running our ship correctly and it's not happening with her, is that understood?"

No answers, just subtle nods from everyone, including Chris. I just look at the wall behind us. How did we get here?

Is this really our "careers," and is this what we all went to college for? To have to listen to an authoritarian try to justify her self-centered agenda under the guise of rampant capitalism in a nonprofit organization? Hold up a dollar bill, pray before a revenue chart, or even make the infamous thumb and forefingers rubbing motion, and everything stops. There is no challenge. Chris is dying inside right about now, and it's getting worse.

It's not as if Miriam really wants an answer anyway. Saying anything might show an ounce of dignity and that's something else she doesn't need from us. No questions were asked as if any questions were allowed. It's like these managers are trained to be abrasive, or they somehow inherit these "skills." The end result is not being challenged. It's clear what happened the last time someone tried that. Her name was Brooke.

Brooke was let go. Brooke was let go after she had given notice. That's real, and it's a real problem here. True to form, Miriam does not mention her by name. She knows how to speak without speaking; she knows it all too well.

"I want you all to realize," Miriam continues, the gnarly mop on her head flows along with her low hanging glasses, all employed to their full effect. "What I do here I do for this organization and its mission. I know what is best for everyone, I have been in this business for a very long time, many of you were in diapers when I was working your jobs, and doing better than most of you to boot. Don't resist me, work with me. I am here to help you. For those of you who want to look forward to a good career in nonprofit services, and even those of you who chose to no longer be with us; I remain a sought-after resource and mentor for young development staff and you should take advantage of the resource that I offer."

More staring at her from the staff, notably no smiles, least of all from me. I know she can read my body language, and I know she doesn't like it. Not one bit. She is in her zone and that's for her alone; there is no "we" here.

"I have to say to everyone, I know we are busy with a lot of events coming up and a lot of goals to meet, again, remember the pocketbook; we have to make some tough decisions and we will soon likely experience some layoffs of staff as a result."

Dead silence. Elizabeth is still reading her phone. I want to look at Chris. I need to make sure he's okay, and at least try to give him a reassuring acknowledgement with a glance at him. For some reason, I can't; and I actually hate myself for it. I do not look at him. Miriam does not elaborate on her last point; it just sort of lingers as an afterthought. She offers no specifics of time and certainly not people.

This meeting essentially goes on like this for a little while longer, more money mongering from Miriam, and making sure we put on the best game face for working with Jodi Molano, trying to keep us on the ball even after that bombshell. Those who care enough are in a denial phase right about now. I try to stay engaged somehow. That event I have to work (though I don't know why I bother) is coming up tomorrow.

I have never met Jodi Molano but she was an on-and-off consultant who had done some work with us, mostly regarding big nonprofit events, which are glorified dinners and drinking sessions with rich people. But this event coming up was a big deal, which is why all hands were on deck, not just fundraisers like Chris and Nicole, and the others.

Cathy and Elizabeth, the event coordinators, are more part of the meeting now that Miriam has stopped haranguing us over money and perception. Elizabeth is apparently done texting as they go over the next few events in the pipeline. I tune out again as often do in these meetings whenever they come around. Something else catches my eye. It's Cathy, and this time it's not her tantalizing features.

Miriam and Elizabeth are going over the upcoming events, discussing approved budgets and time frames and the like. An upcoming donor appreciation event; that only Elizabeth's event staff is working, is apparently having its actual date changed. This happens from time to time; Miriam is not even close to angry with this as she is with everything else but she asks anyway.

"Why is that event time being changed? Haven't the 'save the date' emails already go out?" she asks.

"We decided to change it, from a meeting Cathy and I had before today," Elizabeth explains, with only the faintest sense of resistance in her voice. While nothing to get into a twist over, there are some raised eyebrows, even from Miriam herself. Cathy shakes her head, practically sneering in assured confidence. This new meeting has a new date and that's it. Miriam asks why we could not have it on the originally planned date. Cathy slightly rolls her eyes and almost smirks.

"It's Ryan's birthday," she says while shaking her head. "We made our own dinner plans. It's what we always do on his birthday, so I had the event date changed."

"Ok, fine, let's move on to what else we have to deal with today," is all Miriam says to her in return. Elizabeth pulls out her cell phone again. What the hell am I doing even sitting here? It never ends. I can't even attend a nearly irrelevant meeting without her bringing her goddamn boyfriend into the mix somehow. I don't expect too much out of Miriam under the circumstances but why is this happening? A real nonprofit organization, or greedy business as our so-called superior would have it; a professional organization, has just changed an event date on the basis that one pretty girl's boyfriend just happens to have a birthday the same day.

It seems I answered my own question. The pretty girl in the room wants something and it's her relationship after all, so I have to surrender. It must be good enough for Elizabeth, Cathy's boss, who approved this crap and apparently good enough for Miriam as well. If we have less, she has more, so why would she not put her fake iron fist down with Cathy as well? The entire organization just submitted to Cathy. All for her boyfriend's birthday. How business like. No explanation. That's how it went. We eventually leave the conference room, back to our desks. I'm thinking of jumping straight through the glass window, welcoming the multiple cuts as if I could even feel that pain.

I just sit at my desk for most of the day, staring into the abyss. Why am I still here? I was afraid of being out of work, plain and simple. This is exactly the type of thing I wanted to get away from; not just from the maniacal boss, but from the constant reminder of how inferior I seem to be from everyone. I quit my job, chickened out, I keep my job, and it's all the same: Miriam evil, Cathy yearning; while she never stops talking about her boyfriend. Can she even breathe without doing so?

A knock on my cubicle wall and Cathy is there. She has tears in her eyes and for reasons I will never know, she wants to talk to me. Despite all the hell we sat thorough earlier, despite the fact I should be talking to Chris right now, who is probably having a heart attack in his office; yet I want to help Cathy. I can't help but to try and comfort her.

"What's wrong?" I ask simply.

"I'm still having a lot of problems with Ryan. We can't settle the 'home invasion' incident with his dad."

I can't believe we are still talking about this. She goes on with more details I don't want to hear.

"I keep threatening to move out of the house. He's down-playing how frightened I was. I even packed a bag; I don't want Ryan to think I am not taking this seriously."

"I thought you had birthday plans coming up with him. You said so in the meeting." I know her boyfriend's name is Ryan but I hate bringing up that name so I never actually say it. Cathy's tears subside a bit when I asked that question.

"I'm not breaking up with him. I just don't want to live in that house if I'm going to be terrified near to death on any given night. Who else besides Ryan's dad has keys to that house? I just feel like this is something that has to be done."

"But you haven't yet, have you?"

"No. I just can't do that," the tears are all but gone now.

"Why not?" is my only obligatory retort I have at the moment.

"Because this would be a step back. You don't move out of your boyfriend's house together and expect to stay together. It will hurt our relationship. You don't step back."

Damn her and damn Hal Sutts now that I remember it. Always wearing my heart on my sleeve. I have got to stop talking about this girl with my friends. I wouldn't hold my breath on that one. Yet apparently there is more to the story. I don't know if I should be happy or sad that Cathy confides in me this way. Why confide in me specifically? What am I to her? It seems listening is all I can do at this point.

"There are more problems, Din. Ryan and I share a laptop. I was playing around on it and found out he had downloaded some pornography to the hard drive. I hate that stuff, makes me sick, but not only that, some of it was child pornography. So not only is my boyfriend giving out keys to people without my knowledge, now he is a pedophile too. I honestly just don't know what the hell to do. What do you think?"

Well this is turning out to be one of the most fucked up days I have had in a long run of them. Why continue accommodating this girl and not saying what needs to be said? No, I'm not telling her that I love her; still too much of a coward for that and today is not the day, for certain. I tell Cathy something else she needs to hear.

"Move on," I say. She looks at me in shock, if not total disbelief. She's stunned, as if I said the one thing I should never have. "If things are this bad, then it's probably better you move out and move on in life. You will be okay; I promise you that. Move on, that's all I can say you."

Cathy doesn't say anything. She seemingly nods to me and mutters that she has to go back to Elizabeth's office for more events drama, or whatever they do now, and she walks away, and I am alone again. Am I biased? Yes. But nonetheless I can still care for this girl's well-being. I can still advise her to not be in a relationship with a man who downloads child pornography to his laptop, one that he shares with her, no less. Should I call the cops? I damn well should. All the same, I don't think that would make Cathy too happy. Not with me or anything. Am I complicit in this?

If I do nothing, maybe so. Should I even get involved? Why did she tell me that? Can't help shaking the idea that it's all true. I still want to make her happy, and can't help myself; disgusting as all this really is. She has to leave him.

I can't sit here any longer; and can't think about this. I walk down to see Chris and find Joey standing outside his office, talking in. Not sure if they are talking about the imminent layoffs that appear to be on their way but I highly doubt it. Joey smiles at me as I approach.

"Din! How's it going? That's not great news we heard in that meeting but the good news is they are letting me hire a part time writer to help out with all the articles that need to be completed. I get to post the new job soon; hopefully I'll be able to find a good freelance writer to help out. I would love to have a full-time writer working with me but what can you do? Maybe I'll even find a cute writer girl for you, how's that?" he says with a laugh.

Joey is a piece of work. He's much older, gray haired, and it's hard to look at him directly as he just never seems to want to trim the wild nose hairs growing out of his nostrils. They tend to wave in the air as he breathes. It's always on the tip of my tongue to ask him if he will ever cut those things down but he's a friend for what he is, and the last thing I need is more enemies right now. All the same, does anyone else notice? I wonder if he really cares.

I remember when I first met Joey. It was on my first interview with this place and they were walking me from room to room to meet with different managers. Miriam was stopping periodically to berate different people while we walked. That was a little awkward and was a clear sign of things to come. Yet it was Joey who stood as his office door and smiled at me as we walked past him. He wasn't part of the interview process at all but later he told me he was happy that they might actually be hiring a man for a change, as he was feeling a bit marginalized by the gender imbalance with less and less men here.

If he only knew. Joey is happy to have a new writer approved in his budget, especially in the wake of the evident financial constraints that we seem to be having here at the office. Part time work is becoming the new full time, at least in regards to the level we are supposed to appreciate it. Welcome to tomorrow. The idea is that employees and job-seekers should be happy to at least have something, rather than nothing at all. Therefore, getting half the meal with nearly or absolutely none of the benefits has become the new normal. End result: money is saved and the "superiors" consolidate their power even more. It's an absolutely brilliant apparatus, however unsustainable; and they should know it.

"You do that, Joey," I say, "I'll look at a couple of resumes if you want. I am still around to do some editorial work for you on the side if you need it. I just need to talk to Chris for a while; he's working with me on that alumni event tomorrow while you are covering the story."

Lies, obviously. But I need to intervene here. Joey is a guy who generally just talks about sports and about girls which makes him somewhat of a creepy old man. There is no way Chris can keep up a show for Joey and not talk about what we just found out in that meeting today. I'll keep the Cathy stuff to myself. Chris needs a friend. I know Miriam's layoff comment could have been referring to anyone, even me. Maybe me. But to be real, she was saying that in front of everyone to scare the hell out of Chris, to torture him; and she will follow through, soon, and Chris knows it. Joey is a buddy but dismissing him was a rescue.

Joey leaves us. I walk into Chris' office and close the door. I hate closed doors; honestly, I don't like to show off that I have something to hide. I do not care as to whatever Chris was talking about with Joey. Chris begins sobbing and tears swell in his eyes. He doesn't look at me directly. It's okay. I'm here for him. That's what friends do. I'm not going to give him a hug but he knows that I'm at least will-ing to acknowledge what's really going on here. He's losing his job, and his boss is relishing in it. What do I do? What can I do? I still don't know but I'm not going to be that guy who ignores what is happening for the sake of my own job, to save my own ass. Friends don't do that. Friends matter.

"Any interviews lately?" is all I ask to begin. There has to be a way out for him, as well as me. He's mostly quiet, but he talks a bit.

"I've actually had some interviews, one on the phone. Nothing has come of it, not sure it will. She really has the nerve to say shit like that in front of everyone yet cover her fat ass in the process. That was meant for me, wasn't it?" He sobs again, deliberately keeping the volume down.

"Chris, I hate it when people say 'I don't know what to tell you,' so that's not what I'm going to say. It's easy to call this wrong because it is flat out wrong but there is something more to it. Remember how you are always complaining about music and movies today? You know how you get into it; there are no more Sinatras, no more Fred Astaires and we are just waiting for the next generation of greatness that never comes? Well that is real. It may be all in the past, but that's the whole point: it shouldn't be like this here or now. Not with the lack of Fred Astaires but with too many Miriam Gaws."

I go on like this, alike Chris, keeping it quiet. We should be able to have these discussions out in the open yet that was wishful thinking long before now.

"The past does matter," I continue. "People don't think about how things used to be enough at all. The past unfortunately tells us what we don't want to hear. We are both college graduates, we 'work hard,' whatever the hell that is these days, but there is no regard for anyone's livelihood, their well-being. The boss sits up their flaunting the fact that she can just fire or hire anyone she wants at any time. No one challenges her, because they know what happens then. It doesn't change what is really happening. It's so brazen it's like a joke to her at this point.

"She's taking bread off another man's table. Worse yet, she seems to like that. She's never getting promoted, which is not doing any good for her ego; and we have to suffer that. Miriam is on the younger side, I think, but she is a boomer. That makes me even more sick. She and her ilk have lived the 'American Dream' that was promised to them as children. They have benefited, they have been rewarded for the work, which is no more than ours, so why the hell shouldn't they be optimistic? Not to mention she's not retiring any time soon. Apparently, they earned theirs and we didn't. Convenient for them, if nothing else."

Chris says nothing. He's not crying any longer, just sort of spacing out. He's collected some bad scars lately. It's not from working out in the lumber yards but mental scars; it's damage to his very spirit that comes from this entire profound existence. Chris is damaged through his very soul; actually, his dignity. He's not even that old. None of us ever talk about it.

Generational inequality. I started in the 'real world" at around twenty-two years old. Did I really think it would go terribly well with the age fifty-two crowd? Generation and time are a problem, it's true. It's like a generational civil war is waging under all the crap; or maybe no civil war, simply because we are worried about keeping the jobs we have regardless. It is still there.

Chris' dignity has all but flown out of the window by now. That's something else they take away. Because they are within the power to do so does not make it right to take it away. It's not really a financial motive, it's pride, and it's sick. On top of this, we have to live with the notion, if not fact, that at any given time our employment could come to a close, far too often at a "superior's" whim. As such, how can I even speak of dignity in a working environment where one privately feels, or is made to feel, that their jobs are irrelevant, and may not or should not exist? How can this not create a profound sense of resentment, if not rage? It's completely untenable.

Chris is still quiet, but I keep going.

"We have, or damn well should have, the freedom to at least question the boss. I know your job is to raise money, Chris. But how can Miriam expect you to do that well if she gives you such a horrible time with it at every turn? You have a right to question her on the very basis that you are a human being, and trying to take care of yourself and maybe a family soon. Perhaps that's what she's taking advantage of. She knows you have to work, and you depend on her for an income. Does it turn her on to screw with you like this? She's old, a workaholic, likely not getting any sex, not that I want to think about any of that. This is her pleasure. Yet she still let's Cathy dictate when we can and cannot have an event based on the happenstance of her fucking boyfriend's birthday."

Chris just looks at me with his eyebrows slightly raised at me.

"Sorry," I say with a half-smile. "I digress."

"It's okay, that was a little ridiculous now that you mention it," Chris says. "I'm not on the boss' good side, lord knows I have tried. I'll be at the event tomorrow; I still have a job as it is. I just hope that these interviews play out well. I just really don't know what I could have done to make Miriam feel better about all this. She does not make it easy."

"It's nothing for her or anyone like that to brag about, my friend," I say. "Managers do not deserve more dignity or any more respect than you or I, or anyone. Our so-called superiors are like anyone else in that they can't seem to ever admit they are wrong, or tolerate an implication they are wrong. It's just worse because they are actually responsible for others; it's a community whether they like it or not. Yet still it persists. It's a wonderful argument for the advent of cooperative workforces. Why do we need Miriam? Why be at her mercy? This is how bad manager hubris has become and there is little anyone can do about it. Hiring or firing, they hold our lives or at least fates in their hands; and it's wrong."

Chris is not necessarily disagreeing with my little sermon here, perhaps he's said what little he is going to say. I am just about to leave when he grabs the sides of his head with both hands and digs his fingers into his skull, wincing in pain and holding back a cry only for a moment until he breaks down in tears again. I'm glad the door is shut.

He goes on for another minute, like a man contemplating suicide, or near something that desperate. Chris is not a little kid. I don't hug him exactly, only go up to him with my hands on his shoulders, he stifles another cry and holds onto my wrists with his hands; as if I am the only person to save him from falling. I won't do this to him. I don't have to say "It's okay." He knows. He knows better than most.

I tell him I'll step out and shut the door quickly, and to let me know if he wants to talk some more. His head back in his hands, he nods and I leave. I really hope he is okay, the guy can be a little off-kilter; a bit manic, like all of us, but he does not need all this nonsense. He needs some time; and some space. I give it to him. But that's how my post meeting "meeting" goes with Chris, and in short time I am back at my desk; hoping for no more incidents, I think there's been enough. No such luck.

"I really need to talk to you." It's Cathy, standing over me where I sit, and this time not the sweet girl I've known her to be. I want to ask "what," but I can't. I cannot breathe right under the tension. Her eyes are boring into me, she is near red in the face and it's not tears this time, its rage. She's still drop dead gorgeous when she is mad, but this is definitely not good. I've always been a bit uneasy around her, it's true. Maybe it's the old school boy crush approach to the pretty girl. It's not just that though. One of the reasons I wanted to quit this job is because I was always afraid I would come in one day to find her bragging to everyone she had a rock on her finger. Everyone here would throw a ticker-tape parade over that. I wanted out before that ever happened. I may very well want out right now.

"Are you okay?" I ask. I try to think of something, to say anything to make her feel better. I don't want her to be unhappy, let alone enraged; and please not with me.

"I don't need any more of your mansplaining, Din. What you said earlier was ignorant and I don't appreciate it. Don't you realize that it's rude to suggest to me that I 'move on' from Ryan? What the hell is wrong with you? I'm so furious right now. You really upset me, and I don't need that. I can't believe you would say that."

This day can't get any worse. Why did I just think that?

"I don't want you to be upset," I say. At least this time she doesn't talk over me. "Cathy, you told me what you told me. I'm not sure why you decided to share with me all the information that you did, but then you asked me what you should do. I gave you my answer."

I was quite careful not to bring up the word 'pedophilia' as she was in no clear mood to be reminded. It's still an issue if I talk about it or not. She shared that information with me, I have no idea why. Is it because I never accommodate or celebrate her relationship the way literally everyone else here does? So she then speaks to me more so to get me to accommodate?

Maybe I really should have resigned that day. I don't know how I'm going to get through this event tomorrow, not with this happening. Cathy runs these events for Elizabeth, so in effect I'm working for her. I don't even know how I'll make it through today with all this now.

"I'm just overwhelmed," Cathy says. Her rage level somewhat decreased for the moment. "I've been living with Ryan for a while. It's not working out lately, and I can't just move in with a new boyfriend. It means a lot to me so I can't just move on. I can't believe you, Din."

She glares at me again, not crying but pissed off, clearly. The only reason she's not raising her voice is because we are in the office, keeping her entire tone to just above a whisper. Maybe I'm not good at communication with the opposite sex. Most guys are not in all honesty. Nothing I can say to her will help, so I say it anyway.

"You don't have to move in or even be with another boyfriend, Cathy. Life will continue to exist without a relationship. It is more than possible. Do you think you could ever just be single?"

That was some question. She doesn't look me directly. She glances awkwardly at the wall, near smirking and shaking her head as she did in the meeting. Before she walks away, she gives me her answer; as if I should have known it all along and am just plain daft for asking. She only has one word to say and then she's gone.

"No."

Chapter Ten

Tell Me a Story

I'VE SPENT THE LAST hour literally drinking this girl under the table. Well, she's drinking me under the table too. I've been working the front desk for the alumni event, helping Jodi Molano with her boxes of brochures for Learning Tools; something that her own business publishes often, along with other flare; and we are more or less allowed to drink at these events as long as we are not doing that in front of guests while we are helping them. The obvious solution to this problem is to keep our wine glasses hidden under the entrance table, taking swigs of wine whenever there is a lull in guest traffic. There is no love for this job, it's true, but it has its moments.

Jodi turns out to be very laid back and fun. She's noticeably older than me, about ten years or so. She was probably one of the cool girls in high school when I was only in first or second grade, now we are working together as "peers". I have to say she looks great for her age, very beautiful, brunette, pretty smile, such a bright expression with everything, thin; just older. There is a noticeable hint of pain about her. She is sadder but wiser. Not a bad thing at all, one gets the sense that whatever she has gone through in life up to this point has only made her high on life despite it all. That's a rare and damn good thing.

Time flies when you are having fun or not. I doubt anyone would notice our drinking anyway. Elizabeth is off with her boyfriend of course; I haven't seen Miriam all night but she's around. Chris managed to pull himself together and is off talking to different donors, doing his job for however long it lasts. Cathy and I are avoiding each other. I don't intend to speak to Jodi about this, nor bring that name up to anyone anytime soon, if ever again. Not sure that it matters, that's another thing about Jodi Molano. She may be even more cynical than me. Who imagined it possible?

I notice this around the time the odd couple of Joey and Nicole Ramos come by the entrance table. Joey is probably between interviews and complaining about the food; it's what he does for some reason. Nicole and Jodi have worked together before, and I am pretty sure Nicole had a hand in Learning Tools hiring Jodi's services. That said, I don't think they actually like each other too much. I'm not sure if it's the wine, but Jodi just keeps sipping, and almost glaring at

Nicole through her wine glass. I've never claimed to understand what happens in the female mind, but I enjoy trying to figure it out all the same.

Joey introduces himself to Jodi and she smiles. I can't imagine she can miss those nose hairs but consistently, no one says a word.

"Jodi, I understand you used to be a journalist before you started your consulting business," Joey says while she grips her glass. Joey actually used to be this drinking and crystal meth smoking hippie way back in the 60's. You would never guess it now. Jodi probably notices.

"It's tough being in journalism these days," Joey continues. "I was actually laid off years ago from a print magazine I used to write and edit for. It sort of came out of nowhere and I was out of work for a while which was scary for a guy my age. Eventually I met some people here, and I was lucky to land this job. Most of that ends up online these days, but we still mail out a quarterly journal, at least most of the older donors actually read that. I'm old school that way."

"I understand that," says Jodi. "I'm forty-four years old so I fall on the older side of Gen X, whatever that is. I used to cover a county court room for a newspaper, but when that started to fade away, I eventually realized that the work was just going to be less and less, so I got into the consulting business with my ex-husband, and now it's just me. It was interesting living in an age where the medium I studied for and loved started to become extinct."

I could enjoy this open mind all night. I did not see a ring on her finger, but I did not think she was single just based on how pretty she was. It's awful she got a divorce, but I guess that happens more often than we know. Yet that isn't going to fly well in an office environment where it's always about someone's relationship, and one of those in particular.

Nicole jumps into the conversation. I never really got her either. I know she lives with her boyfriend and even bought a small townhouse together. I still don't know why I had to know this but as usual, it was the talk of the town at the office. I remember her taking the whole week off but "working from home" while she had her kitchen ripped out and new cabinets installed. The bosses let that fly to. I can't tell her I don't care to know.

Why do I remember everything? Was that all really as simple as letting her work from home for a few days, or is it because she does in fact live with her boyfriend? Is that what matters? Would it fly as well if she were single? I feel apprehensive asking for being single myself on its own, and that's what she gives me so much grief for in the first place. I wonder more than most, clearly. Still, Nicole is the type who is always tagging along with someone, even Joey in this case. I think he was interviewing one of the rich people Nicole draws donations from. She doesn't like to be alone, literally.

"Well Jodi," Nicole says, "At least we don't have you working alone tonight. You have Din here to help with the muscle. He's a sweet guy, but don't worry about him working his magic too much. He has his type."

I say nothing. I should say a lot. It would fall on deaf ears, I know, but I am beyond tired of the gay implication thing with her. I'm too preoccupied trying to avoid the girl I should stop loving. Still, getting really sick of Nicole and her bullshit. She probably does not really think I'm gay, or maybe she does. She sure as hell feels superior for being in a relationship when others are not. That's how you define your self-worth, Nicole. Maybe you can enjoy a divorce one day. Here I stand hoping, and can't tell which of us is crueler.

Joey and Nicole wander off, and it's just the entrance table again, with significantly more wine. Most guests are inside now anyway. Jodi puts down her glass, shaking her head slightly but not at me. For the first time in I don't know how long, I actually get the impression that someone is on "my side" for a change; have to admit it at least slightly feels good.

"She's a pain in the ass!" Jodi says. "I know Nicole hooked me up with this gig but she's disgusted me since I've known her, trying to feel superior to others because her relationship is ever so perfect. Give it time Nicole, if anyone needs a life lesson, it's you." Jodi turns to me and offers her glass to be filled again with some more chardonnay.

"She's only giving you shit and implying you are gay because she can't understand what it's like to be single, Din. Sorry to assume you are single, but I can tell. Nicole and the other girls here know you are cute, which just confuses them more because how can a cute guy be single? Such a travesty," she says with the best cynical smile I have seen in a long while. "Not that I'm flirting with you, Din. You're too young for me."

I say nothing for a little while. Jodi seems a bit on the bitter side this evening. I don't want her to be unhappy though I have to admit it's a nice change of pace from the usual here. Not all of life is happy go lucky. Sorry, Jodi, you've done absolutely nothing to me but misery does love company. There's always more.

"Sorry if I seem to be in a mood, Din," she says, still enjoying her wine and not much else. "I don't smoke anymore but could go for one. Do you smoke? Or did you ever have one of those nights?"

What she does not know, I swear. "I don't smoke," I say. "Once in a while if I am tempted, I will smoke but it's an extremely rare thing. Crazy thing is, if we were working this event say twenty-five or thirty years ago and more, we would all be smoking; workers, guests and all."

"It's unhealthy but some days I have the urge," she says. "Sorry again, your friend Nicole gets under my skin sometimes, and Joey is a nice guy but he reminds me of what I've lost in life through no fault of his own. I used to be a journalist like him, sure. But that went away before I could really call it a career. Joey was lucky to find the job he has here but good journalists, good writers, or what have you, should not have to be 'lucky' to have a job; no one should. Yet that is what has become of it. It gets harder as we get into our thirties and forties and beyond. It's not like we can retire around fifty something, also like in the old days. It sucks, really."

"I know what you are getting at more than I let on. We want to work, move up the ladder so to speak, but the ladder itself is going away but the expectations seem to be the same," I say, working up another sermon, maybe, yet noticing for the first time that someone might actually be listening.

"I've been there too. This notion that we should stop complaining and start working harder is making itself more of a myth every year, hell, every month. It's like it's a damn religion of some kind, we can't just say it doesn't work. Older generations like to point out we have better technology today, more 'choices' yet we don't actually have the choices they had at all. So weird being in this consulting gig, especially now after being divorced. I could go back to get a master's degree in this or that, but that would take years; and even then, I don't know if I would be able to get a job I wanted. Though I would have more debt for sure along with it. How's that for choices?"

If only Chris was here right now. But he's inside at the actual party. We may hang out with the guys after if his girlfriend is otherwise indisposed. He would certainly get a kick out of Jodi. Somehow, I doubt her cynicism would win over the likes of Dave and Hal but for whatever reason, I would like to find out.

"That's probably the real difference between you and Joey, Din. It's the real difference between you and all the girls here, certainly. Me too. Why not look at these issues in an honest way? We are willing to at least admit they are here, even if it is uncomfortable to point it all out."

Jodi mentioned she's divorced, so that's out there. Can't imagine what that is like and, I don't want to. It's not something I would ever want. Still, at the very least it proves nothing is set in stone and life changes. I will have to remember that if Cathy ever comes into the office with a ring on her finger.

"Maybe it's the wine, but I'm just letting it all pour out tonight. Sorry if that makes you uncomfortable." I tell her it's okay. "It's not the job; truth is the girls at your workplace are getting under my skin a bit more than I thought they could. There they are and here I am. I had one of the worst dates last night. Who would have thought I'd be at a point in life where this was an issue again."

I have to admit this is intriguing. I'm used to the guys telling me they went on bad dates, and used to Chris telling me how seemingly wonderful things are with Tina. I'm not getting into the doggie visitation rights with Jodi tonight, I promise myself. Still, it's another scenario of misery loving company. I still don't wish any of it on Jodi, but it's helping a lot more than I thought it could; this comparing of notes.

"What happened?" I ask of her date. Jodi has no problem at all getting into it, as if appreciating my concern, at least somewhat.

"Last night I went out with this guy I met through some friends," Jodi begins. "He was cute, I guess, just sort of on the disorganized side. That turned out to be an understatement."

"That doesn't sound like it went to well. Want to tell me?" I asked her this not simply because I'm beginning to not care what offends people, yet out of legitimate concern and curiosity. Bad dates are in fact bad; I've had a number of my own.

"Well, we met for drinks at this place I knew," Jodi continues. "He was a half hour late which was annoying but hardly the worst of it. We talked for a little bit, and he mentioned he's divorced and has two young daughters. I don't mind that so much, though I don't have any kids of my own. He complained for a while that his daughters wanted to go somewhere, Busch Gardens in Virginia I think he said, or maybe it was Disney. He said it was too expensive but he still went with his friends to Tampa and Clearwater, Florida recently anyway, in lieu of taking his kids somewhere, so that was kind of cheap of him.

"The real problem with this guy was that he just would not shut up, he kept talking and talking, mostly over me. I was lucky enough to get two words in, most of those words trying to indicate that I wanted to leave. Then it all got worse, he was complaining again, this time about being pulled over for a D.U.I., his exact words were 'these asshole cops with their trademark mustaches got me when I was coming home from a bar not two miles from my place.' I thought that was funny in context but who tells their date they recently got busted for a D.U.I.?"

"Sounds like a charming fellow," I said. Feeling slightly guilty for all the wine I was enjoying on the nonprofit's dime, though at this point it was clear Jodi had a lot more and needed it.

"The date eventually came to a close and we walked out. He said he rides a bike in a tone to make me believe he owned a motorcycle but his bike turned out to be a mountain bike he had chained up outside. I guess that was a result of the D.U.I. incident. On top of that he said he had fun but it was weird dating again as he was actually still married. I had enough of the whole night by that point. I don't regret that this guy didn't work out, clearly that was for the best. I guess I'm just in a mood because I am still 'out there' so to speak, and this date not working out was just a new setback, and a solid reminder. Life gets so crazy after divorce, no wonder no one talks about the subject much."

There was a brief silence but I won't let it get the better of me or her. The more I talked to Jodi now, the less I had to go back into that room for the party, and deal with Cathy, Miriam, or any of those girls. They do not want me around anyway.

"If it makes you feel better, Jodi," I say, "I've had some bad dates myself. Guys go through it as well, even somewhat recently in my case."

Jodi's face lit up and she smiled. "Tell me one," she says, "Bad date stories are so much fun!"

I delve into the whole thing, not caring enough to hold back. Jodi does not seem the type one needs to protect, rare as that is. I'm retrospective by nature, I could run off any single incident I've had in the past, particularly with dating.

"I've never been married," I say. "I've had some serious relationships and even lived with a girl some years back for a while. My bad date stories do not actually have anything to do with her, but you are right, usually the worst dates are the first dates."

Jodi raises her glass at me and tilts her head in agreement. She wants to hear this.

"I was out with my friend Dave once, and we ran into a bunch of girls he used to know all the way back to high school, actually. We hung out with them for a while, in their group was a girl I talked to and we hit it off pretty well. I asked her to hang out again and we met up for dinner the following weekend.

"We met up at a restaurant; the waiter had just seated us, gave us menus and went to get water. As soon as we were seated, her cell phone rang. It turned out to be her brother whom she hadn't seen in a while. I just sat there. She kept talking and talking, on and on while I just sat there. The waiter came back to see what we wanted and I kind of 'shooed' him away, as she was still on the phone. She kept talking; it went on for about twenty minutes. The waiter came back again, she was not done talking, and I simply shrugged at him and raised my palms up, not sure what the hell to tell him.

"My date was actually mad at me for this, irritated with me, as if I was wrong for my reaction. She finally hung up and said she had to talk to her brother for a while as they never get a chance to talk and this was their only time. The rest of the night went fine but the damage had been done. She knew I was annoyed with her and thus she was more annoyed with me. Needless to say, we never talked to each other again."

"Well she was rude," Jodi says. "It's common sense not to take a long call like that, let alone on the first date."

"Well she apparently didn't think so," I said, wanting to keep this game going. "Your turn. Tell me another bad date story."

Jodi thought for a moment. It was amazing to me because it occurs to me Jodi was the kind of girl whom I dreamed of meeting way back when I was in school. She was one of the older 'cool kids,' who could go out when they wanted. Jodi might have been that 80's metal girl I saw on TV and out at the clubs for the next Poison or Def Leppard show. She was probably in high school at that point it time. Awesome time for her.

"I tried online dating a few times," she says. "I ended up meeting this church type guy, I don't know why I agreed to it, but he wanted to go to a four-hour long hymn marathon at his church on a Saturday night. I sat through an hour of it and then I urged him to leave as I was a diabetic and I needed to get something to eat soon. This was, of course, a complete lie. We eventually left and got some food at small place close by. He still asked me if I wanted to go back to church with him again sometime. I didn't answer him, things just fell silent. He actually called his mom while we were sitting there, just to say hello apparently. That was odd to me.

"He did mention that he was a little uneasy that we didn't pray before we ate. I was beyond uncomfortable at that point; not that it matters when an atheist is uncomfortable, ever. He still seemed to like me anyway for some reason. He even dared to say to me that I could have a homemaker life if we ever married as he sees that as the ideal marriage situation and that I would not have to work. Too bad there is not a hell, buddy, because you can go there. This guy even said he voluntarily stayed a virgin all his life until he is ever married. That was it for me. It was a terrible date altogether. It was less of a religious problem exactly; I just knew he was going to be bad at sex. I don't need that in my life, especially not now. Good sex is essential in any relationship, anyone who says otherwise, and girls do that a lot, is full of shit. Your turn."

That was something else. I see no reason why the subject of sex should not be talked about. We are often far too uptight about sex. Not sure why. Probably a power thing. I don't want to be rude and go into detail, but we all enjoy it; and Jodi's right, anyone who says otherwise is selling something. I'm not going to tell Jodi a bad or good sex story, but the one I had in mind next doesn't lack any of the accompanying tension, it just came and went from way out of left field.

"I was set up with a girl by some old coworkers; I find that setups do not often work. Anyway, for whatever reason, we ended up eating dinner together right at the bar and not at a table, which I was fine with. Things were going well, then she had to go in the back to the restroom. She was gone for a while, like a long while."

"Oh, no," says Jodi. "Did she ditch you?

"That's what I thought, but she left her coat and her purse right there on the bar stool next to me so she could not have left."

"Maybe she was doing drugs in there or something?"

"I was concerned with that possibility as well but it wasn't the case. Here is what happened. She went back to the restroom but passed a table with a guy she knew. He was there with his friends, but he wanted to talk to her. I don't think they were dating but there was something there. She eventually came back to sit next to me again but an arm comes between us, flagging down the bartender to get us both drinks on him. Then the not-boyfriend disappeared for a bit. It was awkward to say the least. I just didn't want to look at my competitor, or whatever he was.

"Later, I walked her out to her car, all the while the goon who she knew that bought us drinks actually followed us out into the parking lot. He didn't do anything but watch. What he really did was make things very uncomfortable but I guess that was his whole game. She gave me a light hug and got in her car and left. I got in my own and did the same, our stalker glaring at me the whole time while standing outside the door. The next day she texted me saying that I am a nice guy but we were not a 'home run' match. So much for that."

"That guy cock-blocked you. I hope she didn't start dating him after your date but she probably did. It's this kind of behavior that makes men hate us; nobody seems to care about the effects. Screw her, it was her loss."

Jodi and I could have talked like this all night. Before we could get to any other story, Chris comes by the table, Cathy with him. She sort of smiles at me, I don't smile back.

"Din, great news," Chris says. "Cathy said we can close up shop and let everyone party here. I texted Dave and he's not far from here with Lisa and Hal. They're probably up to no good, but I told them we could meet up with them."

Cathy just nods, not really acknowledging me and thanks Jodi for all the help and that she will check with Elizabeth and Miriam if the need her to work the next big event. Jodi is not as cold on Cathy as she was to Nicole, but the exchange seemed a bit fake. Maybe I'm seeing things. Though I have sufficient reason to at least doubt it. Cathy is gone fairly quickly. She has to work these events until the last person leaves.

She still looks damn good though in the red evening dress that shines in the light and shows a lot of leg. She's wearing a choker necklace I want to get closer to, despite the fact I know better than to even talk to her now. I just hope I can talk to her again soon. I still think her relationship is goofy, even with my obvious bias.

Chris snatches me away from this hell. "Jodi, when we talked earlier, I mentioned you could join us later. It's always fun to have these after work parties with the guys. My girlfriend is out of town to get her dogs so I'm all in for it. You won't be the only gal there."

Chris actually invited her out with us. Was not expecting that; but I suppose I was having fun with her so that works. Jodi's cynicism is enjoyable, and we could use some more of it. Chris then leaves us and says he has a few donors to butter up before he leaves. I admire the guy's professionalism despite the fact that he's two inches away from losing his job. Could be a Hail Mary shot or something; sadly, it's probably just denial but I respect the man for trying nonetheless. It's honestly more than I could do.

"I'll meet up with you guys in a little bit," says Jodi. "Chris is a sweet guy. I'm glad he works here and he told me you are friends. Not enough people are close friends these days; we all take it way too much for granted. We got released from the lame ass party. Want to celebrate?"

I tell her absolutely. Jodi mentions she has to pack up some her stuff and get Elizabeth to sign some consulting receipt or the like but before I leave, she takes me by the arm.

"Hey. You can do a lot better than Cathy, Din. I saw how you looked at her. She's a sweet girl, don't get me wrong but she is way too enamored into her boyfriend to pursue. That, and even if she breaks up with him, she seems the type to just torture you by finding someone else, and finding them quick, if she doesn't already have someone next in line."

That hurts, but I'm too wound up and "wined" up to argue the point. I'm done arguing, at least for tonight.

"It is what it is here, and that's how it is," I say. "Thanks for looking out for Chris, he needs cheering up more than you think."

Jodi smiles at me, almost laughing. She slyly of flicks her tongue in her mouth, as if she can taste something she likes. I don't know what it is.

"It's good you are looking out for your friends, Din. That's why you are great. But don't take that the wrong way," she says again with the tasting motion; almost too close for comfort. "You're too young for me."

Chapter Eleven

Generation Why

MANY OF MY FRIENDS, near all of them, tend to be stuck in the past; much like myself. We are "old souls" with near everything. That night after I quit my job (kind of), I deliberately did not wander into the Skylark Bar down the street from my apartment for fear of actually running into Dave or Hal or whomever might know me. Sometimes the guys call it the Lark for short. The bar hasn't actually been called the Skylark in well over ten years. It's gone through a number of name changes actually. Hangouts are born, not made, and the name of a bar matters. The other guys insist on calling it the Lark.

It has a lot more history going back to the time before any of us were born. We were not there, or we were in diapers at the time, but the guys think of the Lark as all the people going there in the 1970's or even before; there was no internet, no cell phones, yet there was live music, an old jukebox going at least, and the world as it was in greater times not relatively long before the now. It's different today, to be sure, maybe too many TV screens and less dart boards, but good enough for us. We just never wanted it to change, as if we could freeze it in time.

It turns out it's not entirely coincidental I smoked that cigar the night I quit, or that Jodi had asked me if I smoked earlier tonight at the event table. The guys and I had been going to the Lark for a long time, and I distinctly remember walking out of that place on any given night with my jacket reeking of the cigarette smoke residue it collected, which would last well into the next day, and none of us even smoke. Hal himself would have no misgivings of letting us know how much he hated smoke and smokers in general, but he would tough it out with the rest of us, despite all his vitriol on the matter.

This actually led me to believe Hal would have been happier than a pig in shit that the state banned smoking in all public places a few years back. It actually turns out it pissed him off even more. Apparently, the government, local or otherwise, should not make such changes, even when policies were in his own favor. I asked him why he was so angered, as he said many times, he could not stand the cigarette smoke every time we went out to such places.

"My preference is that I hate it," Hal said referring to the smoke-filled bars. "But I think the permission of smoking or not smoking in any bar or restaurant should be left up to the owners of the establishment. If people who like to smoke do not want to go to a bar where they can't smoke, then the owners will have to take the hit of the loss of patronage or change their smoking rules back to what they were beforehand. Let capitalism decide what happens."

I remember not responding at all to Hal's comment. I just changed the subject and asked him to just enjoy himself as we are all still here together and none of us were smokers anyway. Hal gave me a glare I won't forget for that particular comment. It was the type of glare that says I need to either run away or get with the program, his program, really quick. Part of me knows we never got over the tension I evidently caused between us. For two reasons actually, one is not confirming him in his capitalism comment, and the other for brushing him aside with his anger over it. Hal needed to be accommodated, yet I did not even come close to it. It's clear I've never been too good at that.

Everyone is here now. Jodi waited for me outside and we walked in together to find Chris had already beaten us here. He was sitting with Hal, along with Dave and his not-exactly girlfriend Lisa, and a couple of her friends. The fact that the girls are here is why Dave was not late this time. I think I have seen them before, I'm not sure. Lisa would never get along with the girls at the office as she is unique in never committing to one relationship at a time, sometimes going home with Dave, sometimes they are "just friends," there is no way to explain it as it just does not make sense which is probably their idea entirely.

Dave always liked the company and feels better with the opposite sex to have around to interact with, yet he himself has complained on more than one occasion that he was unhappy that the friends that Lisa brought out with her were never attractive, in actuality anything but; and that Lisa was deliberate with her choice of friends. It's as if hanging out with less attractive friends than herself would elevate her own appearance accordingly. She can therefore manage the threat level. Lisa is a cute girl, in manner of speaking. Cute with the foul mouth and faux beer gut, considering her beverage of choice. She does not have to wear makeup but she gives a new definition to a dirty blonde. Dave would know.

Beyond all this, Lisa had a tendency to flirt with other men she met, even while out with Dave. Sometimes, she would not even just flirt but make out with guys she met, losing interest in Dave quickly, forcing him to retreat back to his friends. So glad we are here for you, Dave. It was never as simple as a consensual "friends with benefits" relationship. Dave would often get noticeably annoyed whenever Lisa would meet another guy, often remarking "why would any guy be into her chubby ass?"

I once pointed out the fact that Dave himself would often enjoy that "chubby ass" himself all too often; and if this bothered him, why keep going out with her? He does need her around, though I think we can have just as much fun without her. That will never matter. It all goes Lisa's way. I've come to know that Dave accepts this as immutable, never changing. She is the boss after all, and challenging her could yield drastic consequences. I have implied to question why more than once. There was one distinct answer he provided, even recently.

"These are the times," Dave said to me, near furious at even the implication. "Male chauvinism is out, Din. Female chauvinism is in." Dave didn't skip a beat in his voice or words with that one, as if enjoying educating me on the subject, however sensitive. Epic.

They all see me walk into the Lark with Jodi. The wine under the table sufficient enough, we each nurse one more drink for the night. Chris obviously had other ideas. He has two empty shot glasses in front of him, now drinking a tall beer. I've never seen him indulge much but something tells me he kept up the good employee farce up for long enough tonight and I haven't seen anything yet.

Lisa doesn't say much to me. That's normal, we never really did get on too well, but I wonder if there is another problem here. Is Jodi not fitting Lisa's preferred narrative? That may be happening right now. I'll keep my eye on Chris tonight, for sure, but speaking of eyes, I just can't seem to keep my own off of Jodi Molano.

I've had my mind set on her since we left the event. It's not just because she is beautiful, yet for the first time in probably forever, I met someone who is insightful; enough to be something different, maybe even different like me. Jodi is the only girl in the room as far as I'm concerned. If Lisa is upset with this new "competition," Jodi knocks her out of the park without even trying.

She smiles at me every time I look at her, which is often. I keep telling myself it's not really there. Why does she keep telling me I am too young for her? You would think just saying that once would be enough. This is impossible. How could she be interested in me? I guess I just can't stop thinking of her as the cool pretty girl in her senior year, and I was just starting elementary school at the time. She's not interested. Yet I am, I have to admit. The age difference is no turn off for me. It's quite the opposite in fact. Time has played too many tricks on me.

Dave doesn't make any of this easier for me. Jodi and the others are listening to Chris ramble on about pop culture calamities and Disney movies. I'm not sure if it is Lisa's characterizations of "fucking Dumbo" and "dick nosed Pinocchio in the Disney conversation, but Jodi soon heads to the back to the restroom. How can anyone not notice that Chris is getting slowly but surely hammered? He deserves the benefit of the doubt but that's being stretched thin here.

Dave of course takes this opportunity to goad me about what I can't get out of my mind. Nothing like me walking into a bar with any girl would ever pass Dave's notice or escape his commentary. I'm surprised he does not ask me if Jodi has any friends or sisters. That's usually his first question.

"I always told you that you were the man," he says with that evil grin of his. "Looks like Din has found himself a cougar!"

I wanted to strangle him right there though the embarrassment far outweighed the anger. I usually do not turn red but he's not helping things.

"She's cute, Din," Dave continues. "I'm watching every girl in this place, and seeing who is watching them; and I see all the guys have taken a notice of Jodi just as much as any girl here. These guys are always staring at them wherever they go. They can't walk anywhere without it. I feel sorry for them."

More classic Dave. He's the kind of guy who would feel sorry for a rich man because the taxes on his Aston Martin are too high. Incidentally, Dave really does believe that.

"There's nothing there," is all I say to him. "Chris invited her out with us."

"That's the whole thing, Dinster. Chris told me he wanted to hook you up with her and that was the whole point of inviting her out. It's a plan that's obviously working, you should run with it."

I doubt all this too; I'm too young for her. Chris is still talking on; lord knows how much he's had tonight. I know what is happening. I wish there was something I could do for him to stop it, but Chris' time as an employed man is growing shorter by the second, and he knows it. Elephant in the room for far too long. We can't talk about it here. Why talk about it anywhere? This is where we are all going wrong.

I also can't get myself to talk about Jodi; who's walking back to our group now; again, smiling directly at me. I am the only guy in the room, the only one for her. That's what she is saying to me. I imagine this anyway. It could be that I just want her to be looking at me this way. I don't want to drink much any longer, certainly not as much as Chris is still enjoying. I'm a bit too intoxicated by a girl who is clearly out of my league, and has been all of my life. Jodi is too cool for me and that is it. What I want be damned.

I try to take the pressure off of myself in the worst way possible. Enlisting the quite tipsy Chris, I ask him to tell us his theory of the lack of Sinatra and Astaires destroying or already having destroyed American culture. I'm too good at knowing what not to say. Chris only seems amused enough to get into this so he puts his glass down to make his address. Jodi is enjoying him, laughing; and leaning very close to me.

"There is not much culture left period," Chris begins. "Movies are not what they were. Where is the next *Gone with the Wind*, or *Godfather*? When was the last time you saw a film, particularly in theatres, like those? Music is no different. When was the last time you saw a voice talent like Frank Sinatra? There are great singers today, yet while they can have a great voice, they will never have the persona that Sinatra had on stage or even on camera. Why is this? What changed that we can't have someone that unbelievably cool and collected as a performer? It's just not there any longer. Today it's mostly rap which isn't even music, just catering to the simple-minded bliss with bad poetry set to a beat; yet it sells somehow. Just more indication that as a society, we just get dumber as we go along; and we have lost our way.

"A better example is the long-gone Fred Astaire. He was one of the greatest performers ever to have lived, if not the. He didn't have the internet and expanded cable networks to reach a wider modern audience but this could not stop him. The man could dance better than no other, he could sing, and was even a competent musician whenever he had the need to be one. There is no actor or actress who can even come close to that today. You may be able to find some modern Broadway performer who could maybe reach his level but again, that does not seem to be what people want any longer. Hell, most of us, even those of us in our thirties and forties don't even like black and white classic films. It's old, sure, by why leave it all by the wayside? Things were better in those bygone days than they are now. We are all the worse off for it. Yet we passively accept this as just the times. We are willfully blind. It's so wrong."

Chris takes another drink from his glass. I think I have made him feel worse by asking him to get into this. No one else, well, maybe Jodi, understands or even wants to understand the underlying issue that Chris is getting into when he brings up the Astaire thing. Dave and Hal are old souls, yes, but they conspicuously will never complain about the fallen state of pop culture in front of Lisa and her friends. Indeed, they will hardly ever complain in front of them at all.

Maybe I wanted Jodi to see this part of me, of us. It doesn't make the conversation any less important. It's America on decline, I've never gotten the sense as much as I have recently that we are living in a civilization's fall as opposed to its rise. What a privilege to live in such an era. Culture and even pop culture has a lot to do with it. All the while, we are still losing our jobs. Most of us will never stop to look and think.

"This is it for me," he says, raising his glass as if to toast the end of an era. "Thank god Tina is out of town. I could be saying goodbye to her."

No one says a word to that. If anything, Dave, Hal, and their girlfriends for the evening have lost interest in Chris by now as they often do if the conversation ever turns this way. Jodi, like myself, just nurses her one glass of red wine and gazes upon my best friend with a sympathetic feel; I see in her eyes that she is sincere. All the more reason to keep looking at them.

Chris toasts again, "To the new lost generation!" Oddly Jodi and I toast back. Chris drops the flamboyant act for a moment and almost seems to hold back tears, but nothing is there.

"Sorry guys," he says, somehow almost sober again but certainly not. "I lost a game I never wanted to play in the first place, I know what's coming. Din, you get all of this. You see, Jodi, Din and I talk about this all the time. It's part of Din's charm more than I, trust me. It's important not to ignore it. Plainly, we've become something of a lost group somehow, lost in time perhaps. I am terrified to even think what the world for us will be like when we are well into our sixties, if we even make it that far. The Baby Boomers, many comfortable now even in their seventies, were given everything and barely left any scraps for us. Whatever we could have accomplished has largely passed us by, though they like to tell us it's otherwise. That's a ruse. We just can't point that out, according to their rules. They're not just the 'me generation,' they're the 'me and the hell with you generation.' They are exceptionally well at what they do, I'll give them that."

Jodi moves closer to me, now literally leaning on me, holding her wine, and taking in everything Chris has to say. She cares enough to care. I can all but taste her right now. She smells wonderful. She is wonderful.

"I hate getting older in some ways, but honestly wish I was born earlier in time, had I the choice," Chris continues.

"Din and I would be working in the steel factories, or out on the farm; not this sales, clerical, or any service worker crap. Those jobs have virtually disappeared. You would think as we moved forward into the amazing technological fueled future, we would be granted more time and opportunity for artistic pursuits, there would be more painters, dancers, writers, singers, and musicians. Yet what we really get are all new work sectors like administrative, telemarketing, and heaven forbid, financial services. Technically, I'm on the finance end of my job, in that I am directly responsible for raising money for a nonprofit. It's still not good enough and they are greedy fucks anyway. It's all about the managers and their whims of the day, defended by grade-A capitalism which we can never contest. Indeed, how could we?

"We are working in jobs where we literally have to defend ourselves for our very being. 'Why do we need that' or 'what money can you make' are questions I get from my family, some friends sitting here tonight, and even from my own boss who is paying me to do the very job she is questioning me about, and forcing me to defend. I am responsible for being useless, apparently. I'm also evidently responsible for the absurd cost of buying a house with my girlfriend. Take a look at where housing prices were thirty years ago relative to now. Screw the eight-year olds of the time. My father paid for our house by the time I was out of kindergarten and he raised a family of four on one salary; with no college degree either. I will ask what I should not: 'why did it all change?' That's all on us, conveniently. It's says a lot about the decline of American existence in general. What does it say about our culture that it seems to generate almost no demand for new artists and musicians but has an unlimited need for specialists in real estate finance and corporate law? What is a real profession in the face of the management class? We can't all work those jobs, and even then, we would still have to defend ourselves while our salaries remain disposable in addition to questionable. Theirs are not disposable. That's important."

Chris is damn near out of breath but could probably still keep going. Dave and the rest are practically on the other side of the room by now. They are not here for their friend, quite simply they don't care for what he has to say, or any pain it takes to say it. To that I say fuck them. I'm getting tired of expecting any more. Chris is not complete just yet.

"When I graduated college, I found myself almost superior, sometimes knocking blue collar jobs as inferior to what I had but I know it's not so. I was wrong. It's all wrong. We should not be content with what little we are granted. What would happen to the New York City transit workers were to vanish out of nowhere? That would bring that city or any area to its knees. It therefore shouldn't be run by out of touch managers who do not give a shit about them and would pay them even less if they could, and are still finding ways to do that. I ask what would happen in all the stock brokers and financial analysts, and even corporate CEO's or middle managers, if they disappeared one day. Somehow I think such an incident would be far less catastrophic."

Chris then stops himself. He probably sees Hal glaring at him, who would feel almost betrayed if he had a heart. It's rare for Chris to go on a rant such as this. The guys usually like his problems with pop culture, to the extent they can be a bunch of old men when it comes to art and music, but this would actually be a first for Chris to publicly, or at least not just in front of me, decry his superiors or imply that the very system he lives in is killing him somehow. For all his bravado, Chris knows he's not fitting into the narrative.

I watch him walk away from us towards the back, but he stops and mutters something to Dave and Hal. Chris points at them with his forefinger and thumb, as if to say goodbye before heading to the bathroom in some haste.

Dave, comfortable enough now that Chris has relaxed his address, comes back to Jodi and myself; tells me he and Hal are leaving with the girls to where and what I no longer care. I tell him we will wait for Chris, maybe meet up some other night. Dave gives me his signature weak handshake and he says good bye to Jodi, predictably brazen enough to offer her a hug to which Jodi barely reciprocates. This only makes me want her more. I didn't know that this was possible, but it keeps going. I won't leave Chris, but nevertheless it would be nice if it were only Jodi and I here now. Painfully pleasant yearning.

"Is Chris afraid he's going to lose his job?" Jodi asks me. "I do not get the impression he was too happy with where you guys work, but he seems like he's in a bad way."

I'm not going to lie to Jodi, I couldn't if I even tried but Chris has belabored himself enough as it is tonight.

"He's got it bad," I say. "Miriam and her cabal at work have it out for him. It's mostly Miriam. There was never any real problem to speak of, she just spit back any effort he ever put in and honestly seems to revel in torturing the guy by simply never being happy with his work or his responses to her criticism; and she just enjoys haranguing him to the point of almost publicly declaring he's going to be fired, and soon. They just don't communicate what they want and get pissed off at him for not 'getting it.' He's not the type to challenge the boss too hard, but they probably read something in his body language, figured out he doesn't like their ways, and that's bad enough to bring it all to this point. There is nothing he can do about it; and it's hurting him even more than he lets on, even tonight."

"You care about him," Jodi says while rubbing my shoulder. "You are a good friend and that's important." I am just melting right now. Skin on fire, but in that good way.

"He ranted a lot tonight, it's probably why the other guys took the opportunity to leave, most likely," I say. "Chris is not wrong. It's not often easy on the ears but too many people have fallen on the wrong side of the divide, if you will; and the 'haves' have somehow successfully managed to create widespread resentment of the employees they oversee, at least the ones who don't play the game exactly the way they want it; all the while enjoying their cushy jobs with bloated wages, not to mention benefits; and not to mention the general favor of being in the position of middle management. The higher ups just don't care, certainly not where we are at. There is a reason for it all."

"That is true, I should know," Jodi replies while still giving me the indirect shoulder rub. I hope she does not stop that. Please, don't stop. I don't know how I can keep my composure right now. I touch her back. She does not recoil at all. I still don't believe it.

"It hurt me more than a little to see my journalism career fade away so easily," she says. "It's what I always wanted to do, but the truth is it got phased out by upper crust greed more than anything else, no matter how much we try to deny that. Yes, print is dying, though it really shouldn't; and technology is killing us without reprisal. It's sad." Her hand is resting over my heart now, how could she not know what she is doing?

"You guys are so introspective with the world. That's good, nobody thinks enough anymore. You and Chris are not entirely alike but you watch over each other. I wish I had friends like that but such things are rare and could be far behind me. Still, you run a risk with all the examination and consideration. You can easily turn people off. Not me though. No, hardly me at all, quite the opposite. A lot of people are just protective of their bullshit and you and even Chris when he's drunk seem to attempt to take that away; at least that's how they see it. It's honest, and that's why it's so attractive."

"I'm not good at denial," I say. "Why deny as much as we do? We only end up living a lie. Yes, that's what too many of us seem to prefer but it's not for me. It's gotten me into trouble as well, even recently. But it's not all bad. I'm having the best time tonight with the best company I could ask for."

Jodi turns her head up to me, again with a smile, her teeth stained red from the wine. Everything about her still glowing all the same. I want to kiss her but I don't. I'm an idiot, but I'm just not convinced. It does not stop me from losing control of my right hand, which somehow on its own volition is giving this beautiful girl a back rub with my nails. Her blouse is soft to the touch and she doesn't stop me whatsoever, an expression on her face that says not only does she enjoy this, but this was expected of me all the while.

"I'm having a good time too," she eventually says. "And don't stop with the back scratch." She laughs out loud at herself. "Sorry. I like this. You are too young for me."

My hand does not leave her. That's not happening. "Why have you been repeating that to me all night?" I ask her.

Jodi doesn't hesitate at all. "Because I keep telling myself that, and you are too dumb to realize that I'm just saying it in vain." I don't hesitate either.

"I'm not that dumb," I say. "It took me a while to realize it. I could say something smart but I can't stop looking at you; I can't and don't want to keep my hands off you."

Jodi shudders; in that good way. I don't kiss her yet, I want to. I will. We actually stand together in silence for a while. Jodi is still leaning on me as I continue her back scratch; no one around us takes any notice. I can't let her go away. I know I want to be with her, but what I don't know is how to ask her to stay. This turns out to be more agonizing than any of the work and friend tribulations I have been suffering of late. Part of me wishes I was only complaining about the modern-day workforce culture with Chris. That's almost easier.

I can see Chris coming back toward us, his head bobbling around and both of his hands raised as if in apology, or almost as if he's being arrested. This turns out to be at least somewhat true, he's being led towards us by a bouncer; a huge, bald man wearing a hoodie; and with hands that look like he could snap your neck with just one of them. He has seen us here before, never like this. This man does not look angry exactly, just determined to get Chris out the front door.

"These are my friends," Chris says to the bouncer, who is still steadily walking him past us. Jodi and I follow them to the door.

I found out later that the bouncer heard Chris puking in the bathroom. Chris kept going until the bouncer banged on the stall door, which put an end to it fairly easily. "I wasn't looking for trouble," is all Chris told me later.

Well so much for that. Chris has never drank this much in as long as I've known him and the bouncer is not going to go for the whole losing his job and being humiliated on a daily basis spiel; he wants us out. I've seen this bouncer before, just never had to interact with him for any reason other than him checking our IDs from time to time. He's a professional. No ego, just time to leave. I can respect him for that much.

The three of us make it outside, Chris mutters that he is sorry about having to leave, I tell him it's okay. Chris puts his hands up almost to hug me, yet thankfully doesn't; motioning with his forefinger that he will be right back. He walks himself around the corner into the alley on the adjacent side of the bar. The bouncer remains inside but still keeps an eye on us.

"Is he going to be okay?" Jodi asks, no longer holding me, which is a shame, especially out here in the cold.

"He should be alright, I'll check on him," I tell her, half thinking the moron went into the alley to pee, which I do not need right now. Jodi is perceptibly cool with a lot of things but there are lines; and Chris is jumping clear over them.

I round the corner to find Chris sitting against the wall of the building, taking a drink from a flask I didn't even know he owned.

"What the hell are you doing?" I demand of him. "We have to get you home."

Chris mutters something incoherent, his breath reeking of what smells like some potent brand of vodka. I think of calling him a cab but that may be another disaster; before I can decipher what to do, Chris turns around and starts puking heavily, loud moans and other disgusting noises, I try my best to keep him from falling over. The bouncer comes around the corner; making me stand to attention involuntarily. I can see Jodi behind the huge man with a face of concern. She hasn't left us.

"I don't want him just out of the bar, I want him off the block entirely," the bouncer says, again commendable for not losing his temper but clearly getting pretty close. Chris' head is slack, what little is left of his dignity hanging from a thread. He's not a bad guy, I tell myself. We have all been here at one point or another, maybe even drunker, though I just honestly can't remember when, least of all with him; and less so with Jodi here.

"I'll take him home," I say to the bouncer. "My place is down the street. Sorry we became a nuisance. This does not happen that often."

"It's all good, brother," he says.

I guide Chris down the street. Jodi follows along with me. We make it far enough to be away from the bar and more importantly, that vigilant bouncer. Chris mutters that he needs some air and wants to walk ahead of us with some space. He's heading into the direction of my apartment so at least he gets the right idea where he has to go. I let him walk ahead. Jodi is still beside me.

"I'm sorry about this," I say to her. "Like I mentioned, he's just been in a bad way, it's not like him to drink so much."

Jodi takes my arm with both hands. "It's alright," she says. "You are looking out for him and that's gentlemanly of you. It's damn sexy, really." Jodi then puts her arms around my neck and pulls me closer to her. We kiss, all too briefly; there is the other matter at hand. Chris is on his knees again, puking his guts up into the street, the flask still in his right hand. How much can this guy drink? That and damn him for the worst timing ever. Jodi lets go of me and walks towards him. I just stare in their direction blankly.

Jodi, small as she is, starts to pick up Chris, draping his one arm over her shoulder, grabbing and tossing aside his flask with her free hand. I can hear her laughing. "We'll take care of you," she says. Jodi looks back and me, beckoning me with a nod that says more than come hither.

"I need your help," she says to me with an anxious smile. "And I don't know where you live, exactly."

I don't argue the point. I take Chris' other arm and we walk him to my apartment, Chris apparently done being sick and both Jodi and I smiling and even laughing at all this.

"Hey," Jodi says to me. These will be the real memories."

We continue to my apartment. Chris is not a burden at all. I really love my friends.

Chapter Twelve

Chronos

Ilook across my apartment living room from the kitchen to see Jodi pulling Chris' shirt off. He decided to cough up or dry heave, (I was too afraid to turn the kitchen lights on), into my kitchen sink of all places so I clean that up while Jodi takes care of Chris like a mother caring for a sick child, helping him lie down on my couch, stripping him down to his undershirt and untying his shoes for him, then pulling a blanket over him and petting his head.

"I'm sorry," Chris mutters to her. "It's just hot in here."

Jodi takes the man's shoes off and places them neatly beside the couch while he gradually doses off into a drunken sleep. I can hear him moaning somewhat. I just hope he's actually done with the getting sick part of this ordeal, and doesn't choke on his own puke during the night.

I can give him a ride home tomorrow. He's crashed here before, just never like this, and certainly never with someone like Jodi taking care of him.

"It's okay," she says to him. "You will be fine because you are with friends who love you and will take care of you."

Chris comfortably rolls on his side; snuggled up in one of my throw blankets. I continue washing out the sink and then my hands; taking a good drink of water from my cold pitcher in the fridge; my mouth still parched just from hanging around Jodi all night. I look over towards Chris again, yet she's gone. It's as if the apartment is empty; no lights and no sound; with enough moonlight coming though my windows to see; and I do not hear Jodi shut the door to leave. My apartment is small enough, I could never really afford more. I never really needed more, though that would be nice. That's no matter at the moment. Jodi is still here.

I quietly walk past the sleeping Chris to find her in my own bedroom; sitting on the edge of the bed patiently; almost beaming in the dim light that makes her skin glow a beautiful ivory tone. She's not looking directly at me, as if nervous somewhat. She's never been here before. I don't want her to be uncomfortable. Still, I sit on the bedside next to her. She keeps her head down, glancing at the floor as if she's scared to look at me. She can't leave; all the weight I've been under for I don't know how long lifts with her being in this room, as if it was never there to begin with. Jodi is unreal even to the touch.

"I know it's getting late. I can walk you back to your car, it should be fine parked where it is," I say to her not at all realizing how absolutely dumb that was.

"That sounds like a dismissal," she says, this time looking at me.

"It's not," I say, nearly in vain.

"If you don't want me here, I can go, and you don't have to walk me back," Jodi says in a nearly rushed tone, sitting up from the bed only slightly as if indicating a desire to leave. I gently touch her on the shoulder; she knows. Jodi stops moving yet is seemingly disappointed at my "suggestion" of her leaving. She cannot be more wrong.

"Listen," I tell her, looking directly at her, somehow commanding this situation, if only for a brief moment. "I don't want you to leave. Believe me, that is the last thing I would want right now. There is a brief pause as she looks away from me again, her beautiful skin still glowing even as I edge closer to her. "I don't want you to leave," I repeat. I didn't have to say so again.

She lifts her face up to mine, half smiling, but almost smirking at me. She knows she has me now.

"Then convince me to stay,"

I don't think any longer. I lean in towards her, I don't kiss her mouth, but her neck, first gently then forcefully; she lets out a noticeable sigh. As I kiss her, I look up, and I see her grinning from ear to ear; like a happy Cheshire cat, content beyond any form of reasonable expression, no words needed with it all written across her face. I love her smile. It glows more in the moonlit room. Her teeth, still red stained from the wine she had earlier seemed almost predatory now; she's only getting started. No more thinking, no more needed.

We kiss again; Jodi immediately pulls off my shirt to which I return with her in kind. Still kissing every chance we get in between these motions, she removes her sensual, black bra, and then unbuckles her own pants. Time remains still. It is yesterday or tomorrow for all I care. We continue to undress as I kiss and massage her breasts, her body bathing in the light coming in through the shades. This moment a living work of art to which I cannot have enough of. Neither can she.

Naked, Jodi is breathtaking. Her entire body glows in the dim of the night. I want to taste every inch of her and in time I do just that. She's older than me, yes, but more sensual and confident than any girl I have ever been with. It's not just that her skin is somewhat older. This makes her no less alluring. Jodi's body is somehow made of beautifully scented lotion for me to bathe with her in. I want to touch her even more. She is that beautiful girl I saw as a child, the hot all-night girl down the street; completely out of the question because she was older than me, yet I learned at even that young age what beauty was, and now she is here with me, naked in my own bed.

Jodi wraps her arms and legs completely around me, squeezing me even closer to her while working complete magic with her lips and tongue; she is just that damn good at kissing. I don't enter her just yet; still taking every chance to touch every single part of her body, she then grabs my right wrist and forces my hand further down to where she wants it to be. I do not deny her.

We go at this for a while. I feel her becoming increasingly moist as we go on. She does not want me to stop this at all, why should we? I want more of her, still kissing her neck and mouth, all but owning each other yet never having enough. We are fundamentally strangling each other, sweating in the dark, breathing not a priority. She eventually comes up for air herself. Her mouth perhaps as slightly worn as mine, if it's pain; that's perfectly fine with us. She nibbles and whispers in my ear.

"Make love to me, Din." I only pause for half a second until the next demand she provides, less than a whisper this time. "Fuck me."

All sense of immediate time and space seems to melt away at this point. Jodi and I are somewhere else, and I do not want to ever leave where that is. She invites every single desire, both welcoming and initiating all variables of positions, accepting me into all of her body and being, riding when she pleases to, and wrapping her legs around me when I take her beneath me; looking back directly at me with starving eyes when I place myself behind her; demanding I grab her hips and thrusting against her ever harder. She wants even more of me, and I am hers for the taking as much as she is mine.

This goes on for what seems forever, and forever is not enough. I don't want to finish, enjoying giving her multiple orgasms too much to want to tell her she can't have even more. She throws me down on my back, straddling her body out on top of me, climaxing once more with a muffled scream, her head and hair flailing wildly, near passing out yet straddling just a little more, then indulging me with a finish in her own fashion.

We collapse, out of breath and dripping with each other's sweat; and contentment. Jodi relaxes her head on my chest, wrapping two legs around one of mine like a knot, gripping tightly, as if she is afraid I would leave the room. She won't allow that.

"You taste sweet," she tells me. She feels me catching my breath, and continues kissing my chest and stomach, caressing me with the tip of her tongue, as if enjoying the last remainder of a delicious dessert. I can't help but to watch her. She knows, as if inviting me to do so.

We lay there in bed for a while. It's a good thing I closed the door. I nearly forgot Chris is sleeping just outside, I really hope he didn't hear any of that. I look around the room, my contact lenses are somewhat faded from all of the heat and activity, I look over at the clock and I think it is two-thirty or such. I ask Jodi if she wants some water, she shakes her head and kisses me again, reaching down to touch me, yet hesitating for a moment.

"You are not sore or anything? I can have you again?"

I answer by kissing her; she continues to feel me until I am hard again and takes no time to initiate all of this over again; clearly forgetting this time that we have a guest in the apartment. Jodi screams over and over now, begging me to thrust into her more, no other care or concern in the world for either of us. I almost try to tell her to be quiet on account of Chris in the next room. I don't. This is where she and I belong. We continue through the night.

The next time I look around, Jodi is asleep, and the sun seems to be coming up through the shades on the windows. Jodi eventually wakes, clearly tired but like me, not wanting to waste such an evening asleep, even as the dawn comes in. I kiss the top of her head and she smiles, while not as aggressive as before; she still enjoys tying a knot around me with her legs. I could lay here all day with her, and would if I could have my way of it.

"Tonight was incredible," Jodi says with her head on my chest again. "Or rather last night was fun, is it morning already? Your friends are good people. Not so much Hal, but they are fun; and your friend Dave is oddly obsessed with his not-girlfriend, she clearly dictates everything he does and where he goes. It's amazing that he tries so hard to pretend it's otherwise with that her."

I don't answer. She's not wrong. "It kind of hurts though," Jodi continues. "It's ridiculous, but I'm jealous."

"Why?"

"I don't have many friends," she replies. "You have a lot, and that's near impossible these days."

"I don't have that many friends, hardly Mr. Popularity," I say, still amazed that Jodi is lying here naked with me.

"I barely have any at all. I grew up with a lot of friends, my sister is still married and has kids so I don't see her that often, and half the time any female friends I end up hanging out with only end up hating each other soon enough. I honestly can't say the last time I hung out with a bunch of friends like we did last night. So, I am a bit jealous. Having friends to pal around with and discuss your life issues with is more valuable than anyone will admit for some reason. It's rare and I'm envious. I want what you have."

"In a lot of ways, I'd say you actually had what I have," is all I can say, trying to get off my one-track mind somehow. Jodi giggles and kisses my chest again. Despite going on about my friends, she doesn't seem to remember Chris is sleeping just outside the bedroom. Still, Jodi has got me going in other ways besides the purely (and I have to say again, unforgettable), sexual. She's dead on with my friends, it's true.

"I've always been closer to my friends," I tell her. "It has always been hard if I ever lost any. I've always been on my own for the most part. No family really and serious girlfriends are few and far between, so I spend a lot of time either alone or better so with the guys. Chris clearly wants to get married to his girlfriend soon so that will be a thing when it comes; and it will. I should feel happy for him, but I more often feel sad for myself. Is that cruel?"

"It's okay," she says. "I completely understand that, believe me. You are selfish for your friend. You saw him first, after all. It's cute. Chris is the 'girlfriend guy' in your life; someone whose relationship drowns out anything else by the sheer volume of it. It's good that his girlfriend is a nurse or you would probably never see him. That itself can be cruel.

"Let's be cruel then," she continues. "Why don't you have a family? Not judging you there, my real father is dead and I don't talk to my mom or stepfather at all, so I get it."

"Not too much there," I tell her. "Like I said, I've been on my own since I was in my teens. I think I just developed a different background then the one my parents brought me up in and they took it personally. They took my very opposite personality personally, as if being that different was a slap in the face. Let's say they were a bit too old school. They were just happier with the world of the 50's or 60's. We did have better music then but I digress. People just so often need to be accommodated. I just would not do that for them; it drove them crazy, and drove me away."

"You are a runaway, then?" she asks with noticeably curious eyes.

"Not exactly. It's just a scenario that's all too familiar. Oftentimes, the ego wins, maybe even all the time. We'd rather cut off each other from our lives rather than to have to even indirectly admit we are wrong, or worse yet imply accountability. I was the insubordinate employee who just left after a while. They were like the abrasive and sensitive bosses who got pissed off at the very challenge, even the implication. The fact that we don't talk is proof that there are still personality issues, among others. Some people are more concerned with how they are perceived than how we can exist alongside one another. I know that's human behavior, that's who we are unfortunately. It's just somehow gotten worse over time."

Jodi does not delve (to my great appreciation) on the issue. I don't ask about her family. Still, Jodi continues with her naked interview.

"Tell me about your ex-girlfriends. You were never married, right? No kids?"

"None of the above," I tell her. "I have done the cohabitation thing with girls before and I have dated single mothers, but no, never married, or any kids of my own."

Whenever I am asked such questions, I feel like I'm on an actual interview. Is she reviewing my "resume," so to speak? We all have a past, a background, though I don't see how mine could be any more or less evaluated than her own divorce. It's not really who we are, as much as the past does matter more than we appreciate. Jodi and I are something else now, something more. I hope.

"Tell me about one of them, one of the serious ones. What happened?"

I can't believe I am even explaining this, and I remind myself I am a bad liar. This is so very often not good for me.

"I dated this one girl for a good while," I tell with some hesitation. "When we met, she was already in a serious relationship though that didn't stop us from spending time together and essentially actually dating. Sex, spending time with friends, everything. I should not have got involved with such a girl; I know. However, most gals I meet already have boyfriends, and have little qualms about telling me so. I really liked this girl, she liked me; I can't just wait around forever to find someone without a boyfriend, or one who has been single for whatever the acceptable time frame is, so I ran with it. She eventually broke up with the guy so she could be with me full time."

"Ah, the never being single girl," Jodi says with a deliciously cynical smile. "Perpetually in a relationship. I know a few of those. What happened?"

"I lost her to airport security."

"What?" Jodi is in complete confusion. I'm not at all a fan of speaking to people about past relationships; let alone to a beautiful girl I just spent the night having sex with, but here I am. Yet when I do mention it, I always tell the same joke.

"It's a figure of speech," I tell her. "The girl I was dating was a criminology major in college. She graduated but never really found a job related to her degree, she was always working general administrative office jobs, glorified secretary, things like that; and that frustrated her. I always sympathized with her, which is maybe a big reason she liked me for a while.

Eventually, she got a job working for Homeland Security at an airport. Still administrative and working computers but she saw this as more reflective of her studies and justified her major; airport security was criminology in a way after all. The problem is, the airports never close, are busier on weekends so we saw less and less of each other. That got me asking questions, implying or outright telling her I was not happy with the new scenario. This in turn got her unsettled with me; for being frustrated with it. She took it all personally to say the least."

"So, she just left at that was it?"

"Hardly," I say. I try to make light of this memory and many others, or at least try, though I just always seem to fail in the end. Somehow, I am not nearly upset as I normally am, not here and certainly not now.

"She kept her ex in the picture to fall back on. Literally. She went back to him, explaining to me that she was still 'deeply' in love with him. He then gave her a ring about a week or two later, probably to make sure she did not leave him again. I can't hear the word 'deep' to this day without wincing a little every time. I guess I should have seen that all coming. Hard not to look over my shoulder more often than not. I've met and dated other girls just like that since. She had her options; and here we are."

"You sound a little bitter about that. Not saying I blame you."

"It's okay. Maybe I am, but I have my reasons. I'm not sure what hurt the most, losing her or the fact that she just went back to the old boyfriend so easily. It's not a good position to be in life. It's probably why I get into the economy and workforce issue so much with Chris and everyone else. This is never well received but I don't like being involved in relationships where I am disposable. If things go bad or even a little sour, then they can just throw me away or fire me like a boss who doesn't want to deal with me any longer, and any challenge or question to the contrary would only invite more vitriol; and replacement. Therefore, one must never ask questions, do not criticize, and so forth. It's not tenable. None of it. It can't be. We can live better than this, but we don't."

Jodi remains cool with her silence on all that. What is there to say? All I can think of is that I want to have her again. Jodi brings the interview back into play.

"If it makes you feel better, it probably never lasted with her going back to the ex-boyfriend. It never does."

"I know. It never did. Eventually I found out she broke up with that guy, never married him. She was always in a relationship, even engaged a couple more times from what I could tell. She's married now, no kids. Lives on a chicken farm, and yes, I'm not kidding, she lives on a chicken farm with her now husband who inherited it from his father. Life has its ways. Don't ask me how that all happened."

Jodi just blinks at the chicken farm thing. Who wouldn't?

"How the hell you would know all that, Din."

"The internet is an amazing invention of modern times. More so amazing when you know how to use it."

"Cyber-stalking? Never took you for the type." Jodi is still grinning at me and massaging me with her fingertips.

"Call it what you will. Information is something that is accessible. More so when that information is laid out for everyone to see. Perhaps she wants me to know. Perhaps that's the whole point. To me, it's admittedly hard to keep things in the past. I have a memory, after all. I'd say there is a fine line between forgetting things and pure denial. I am bad at denial, very bad in fact. People usually do not like that. Maybe denial is what keeps all together and keeps us going. To call it out or even mention it, hell, even imply it; has disastrous consequences. Deny it or not, it hurts when someone you know becomes someone you knew; and it always leaves a scar."

"Can't deny that,"

"What happened with you?" I ask her. "I hate to say it, but I always found divorce rather interesting. I don't wish it upon you or anyone else, and I would never want to be divorced myself, yet I find it fascinating."

"Why fascination?" Jodi does not seem offended at all.

"Marriages can end for any kind of reason. I don't know why yours ended, but clearly it did. I'm sorry it did. There are a lot of reasons the subject of divorce fascinates me. I guess it's because when someone gets married. It seems so finite, as if this is the end of the story. Happily ever after. It's written in stone and if there is a marriage; then that life is untouchable, unchangeable, forevermore. We throw a ticker tape parade at the mention of it. This is how we react when anyone gets married, or plans to. Why? It's hardly the end. It's still a relationship, and marriages seem to end far easier these days. We ignore that until it happens, I guess."

"You are telling me," Jodi says, now ready to get into what really happened, or so I presume. She still looks amazing laying there next to me. I hope Chris doesn't wake up any time soon.

"My husband and I were married for years," she says to me. "We both wanted to get away from our crazy families, we actually moved to the Netherlands for his job for a good few years. Eventually we came back to the states and things just fell apart between us. You can always see this coming. The sex we were having was perfunctory at best, half the time we didn't even want to be around each other. It all just kind of stalled, and we didn't talk about it, probably because neither of us wanted to be held responsible for all the problems. As if the less said, the better. The silence and the staring was the real cancer. It was as if not talking at all was a way to cover his ass, the less said, the less to be held accountable for. It works, immature as it is.

"Then he started disappearing on most weekends and sometimes during the week. I got sick of that and finally confronted him on it. He started crying and admitted he had a new girlfriend. She was a hooker, some Russian girl, that he picked up one night probably out on the street and that's why he was crying. He was so ashamed that he cheated on me with a hooker. He kept dating her for a bit but it didn't last. We've since been comfortable just living our lives pretty much separately. That was all well over a year ago. Time flies.

"I'm sorry I haven't told you, but we are actually still married," she continues. "The lawyer my friend Kim found for me was an arrogant feminazi who just got off on the idea of me torturing him and making superiority comments in her separation documents to hurt him and thus make herself happy. The lawyer said it would help. I was never into that. It's not me. That and she was only a part time lawyer, mostly a wannabe TV talk show host on local channels. Emasculating men was apparently just a hobby for her and she liked the opportunity I brought. She was a piece of shit who will only try to get ahead by bringing other people down. Sick that she has kids. There is bad and then there is worse. I needed to get another lawyer, but haven't had the courage to get around to it. Besides all that, I get to stay on my husband's health insurance which is admittedly pretty good. I would not have it otherwise."

Unbelievable. I had to ask her. "I don't understand," I say. "By 'dating' a hooker, you mean he was continuously paying this girl he met with for regular sex?"

"No, he apparently only paid for it once. They just hit it off and started dating for a while. He did identify her as a girlfriend and I even saw the two of them together once. She cashed in with him, regardless that it didn't last. So no, I won't go into denial and pretend that never happened. It sticks with you."

I don't believe her. I really just don't buy that story whatsoever. Her husband buys a Russian hooker and they just hit it off? The story has too many holes in it, and that's an understatement. She's not telling the truth. Should I humor this? I told her the truth about myself but after last night, I just don't care about anything but Jodi. The fact that she is still married be damned. I want her again. This has to be the start of something new.

She leans up as if to get out of bed, the last thing I want now is for her to leave. She stops herself from getting out.

"I don't want to leave, but I wanted to say how much fun I had last night, all night, it was incredible. And talking to you now, it's so nice. But Din, I can tell things are not going to well for you. Sorry, but you are brooding way too much and I'm concerned. I don't want you to be unhappy. What's going on at work?"

"For me?" I ask.

"Is there anyone else here?" Jodi has clearly forgotten Chris is in the next room, probably still passed out on the couch.

"I'm having too good of a time to get into it," I say. "We are all having problems with the boss, you know that. It's gotten out of hand lately, who knows what the hell I can do about it. Even what I have tried has not changed anything. All the interviewing, dodging, and futile head ducking has got me nowhere. Just something else I'm not good at denying. Seems to be becoming a theme now."

She looks right at me with dead serious eyes, not condescending but of genuine concern. "Well, what would you want? Do you have a dream? What kind of job would be best for you?"

She has me there. I wish I knew. Not the job I have, clearly. I could never ask for a promotion or raise; the boss thinks we are all paid too much as it is; and should be kissing her ass for the privilege of even working under her. The times allow her to get away with that and more. My only dream is to not have to feel lucky for having a job that makes someone else happy. At least not so blatantly. I want to belong, to really be needed, not to mention respected. What happened to mutual benefit? I can really be part of a team. I am admit I am rambling as I say all of this. She doesn't mind.

Jodi kisses my cheek and says she'll be right back. Both my pleasure and horror, she's not putting her clothes back on, and is about to walk back outside the bedroom where

Chris is. Both he and I do not need that. I choke up. I can't say a word to stop her and she goes, still completely naked. The bedroom door is now wide open. I don't hear anything from the living room area. Now I'm happy the guy drank so damn much last night. Please, Chris, stay asleep.

I still can't believe any of this has happened. I can't remember when I've been this content, dare I say the word "happy." All this for having sex with a beautiful, yet significantly older than me, divorcee? That's quite a cure if it really is one. I sure want it to be. Who would have thought it would come to this? I remember being the nerdy kid, never once as cool as the "big kids," never possible to be with the cute high school girl down the street for not only was she out of my league, she was out of my age. I was in first or second grade when Jodi was a senior in high school. That alone is incredible. We just had incredibly amazing sex; and she is here in my home.

I've always been that kid, bad at sports, head in the clouds, always reading, never competitive enough to make anyone happy, let alone the prettiest girl in the high school. Where are they all now? If only they could know where I am, what I have done. I have spent the night having sex with the 80's rock concert girl, the girl who could go to rated R horror movies when I wasn't even close to old enough, and those jackass older kids, the bullies, and the idiots who thought they were my superior for simply being older now have no idea at all. What else didn't they know?

I am beyond them. I have conquered the god of time, if there ever was such a thing. There is not, but it's good enough. I always mattered, however young or naïve. Time has come back my way. Jodi is with me, my friends, and my life. This is too good.

Jodi comes back into the bedroom, again not noticing the still sleeping Chris but at least shutting the door behind her. He is just dead, and I hate to tell him that is a wonderful thing right now. Jodi stands there, naked in the morning light now, no less beautiful than before; and smirking at me in her playful way. She almost poses for me, there at the door, her one hand leaning on the wall, her other on her hip, as if she's wondering what to do with me next. I am in her hands yet again. I reach out to her, not saying a word though beckoning her to join me in bed; to crawl under the covers and let me have her yet again.

Jodi almost slithers into bed with me, under the covers, making out as fervidly as we did hours before. She grinds on top of me, not shy of her desires; clearly noticing how hard I have become now that she's here with me again. The god of time. She smiles and whispers in my ear while handling me again where she wants.

"I was hoping for this," she tells me and licks her teeth and lips like a vampire demanding her next meal. She leans down towards me and whispers "Again."

No response necessary. It's not a request. I do not disappoint her.

Chapter Thirteen

Another Road

WE WILL NEVER STOP the clock from turning. If I could put a name to the fire in which we are burning, I expect that name would be time. Too much has changed since that night with Jodi Molano and then again, nothing has changed at all. It's been weeks since she left that apartment; kissing me goodbye while a hungover Chris drank coffee on my couch and awkwardly said farewell to her. Brave new day.

It's all changing even as it changes. I have barely spoken to Jodi since that night; she's been "busy" with things yet I'm still holding out that there is something still there. She did light up at the prospect of hanging out with everyone again; though I'm having trouble getting my hopes up for any repeat of that last evening's activities. Two days ago, Chris texted me to tell me he actually found a new job. That's great for him, it's just we haven't spoken of it much at all beyond him letting me know. I suppose I'll find out more in time; would have been nice if he told me more right away. That said, I had another interview myself which actually went well; no hiring drama, other than the increasing stretch of time without any word. I don't know what to do next. Have I ever?

When Jodi and I finally emerged from my bedroom (clothed this time), we found Chris sitting up on the couch drinking from a soda can he found in my refrigerator. He looked absolutely hungover, probably because he was; his rim of brown hair mussed from the heavy sleeping, not wearing his glasses and exposing his red, bloodshot eyes while he looked at Jodi in slight confusion. I can't imagine he remembered much from the night before and he certainly did not expect to see her the next morning.

I made coffee for everyone, Jodi had some, yet told us she had to leave and could not hang out too much longer. She doesn't ask how Chris was feeling, to be fair neither did I. He'll be okay, at least with the hangover. I excused myself for a moment to place eye drops onto my contacts, everything was still a bit blurry after wearing them all night. I sometimes wear glasses, and I was too distracted (really glowing) to bother taking out my contacts. I just did not want Jodi to leave.

I explained to Jodi and Chris that I actually can't see well at all without contacts or glasses. It's been an issue since I was fourteen. I remember my mother being angry with me that she had to spend money on glasses, as if it was my fault my vison worsened at such a young age. Someone had to be the blame, and I was an easy target in retrospect. I made the conversation with Chris and Jodi interesting by explaining that without my glasses, I could see the black soda can that Chris was holding, but cannot read the text on the can, not without squinting very hard. I don't know why that was interesting but somehow it was.

Jodi finished her coffee rather quickly. I asked Chris to stay while I walked her outside. She doesn't need to be escorted back to her car; it was difficult to let her go. I really tried not to act like a swoon teenager but the fact was she did not make that easy for me. We kissed again.

"No brooding today, okay?" she told me. "Enjoy yourself, you might have some reason to."

"It's what I do. Talk to you soon?"

"Uh-huh," is all she said with another smile and kiss on my cheek. "Last night was incredible," she whispered. Then I watched her walk away.

After going back upstairs Chris asked the inevitable question.

"Well, what the hell was that?" he said, not sounding so sick any longer.

"You didn't hear us?" I was still really hoping not.

"No, I was out pretty hard last night. I don't remember much about even coming here. I didn't realize Jodi was here all night. You had an interesting sleepover."

"There was not a whole lot of sleeping, actually."

Chris just looks at me for a moment. "No, I don't suppose there was much of that," he says.

There was some more awkward silence, not sure why. I remembered being told that Jodi coming out with all of us was actually Chris' idea. "Dave told me you set the whole thing up; that you wanted us to hit it off. Is that true?"

"Yeah, it is, I thought you guys might get along but was not expecting this on the first night," he says, almost sounding disappointed.

Dave and Hal would have completely different receptions to talking about a girl I just spent the night with but that's something else Chris does not get into much; as if talking about sex is somehow cheating on his girlfriend. It's not that bad but Chris is sensitive to relationships almost as much as to his employment situation.

"Well, we like each other. To each their own," I tell him.

"No kidding. Do you think this will go anywhere?"

"I would like to think so. It wasn't just the sex. Jodi is really amazing and she's sweet. She also likes you, she felt bad you were so upset last night. It wasn't me who took your shoes off so you could be comfortable. She's good people. I want to see her again, absolutely."

"I just find it odd you two would hook up on that level so soon. Tina and I were not physical until months after we met. I think that was for the better in the long run for us."

I can't believe half of what I am hearing. "Not all of us are you and Tina, my friend. Everyone goes about things differently."

Chris raises his eyebrow and frowns at me. It is almost as if he is disappointed in me for having sex with Jodi. Is it simply the change in routine? New can be hard to accept, especially for those enjoying the status quo. I can only speculate as to why for any of this but it's not implausible.

"You going to call her?" he asks. "I would not do so too quickly."

"I was planning on it. I want to see her again. We don't have to have the same activities we had last night, though I'm not exactly against that idea. I'm fine with just getting some food or hanging out somewhere. At least I know she's interested."

"I don't know," Chris says without looking at me. "I would not call or text her anytime soon. You might end up offending or annoying her. Just take it slow."

"Ah, the old unwritten rules," I say to him, half joking, half annoyed. "It's a three-day thing, right? Or is it more? Or less? I'm not sure; and I'm also very good at breaking unwritten rules. I suppose they are not written down for a reason. Yet we are expected to follow them, and the reprimand for breaking a rule we have not been informed of much if at all is rather hasty. Where do we find the time?"

"I'm just saying," is all Chris had to say at that particular point.

"You are also just breathing, or just drinking coffee, or just hung over from drinking your ass off last night. I'm here for you, Chris, it doesn't bother me that you puked in my sink, among other places out there, or that you don't remember ant of that. I didn't think Jodi was going to spend the night here but she did, and it was damn fantastic for lack of a more explicit description. I haven't dated a girl in any serious way for a while, haven't been in this good of a mood for even longer. It's a good thing, whatever it is Jodi and I have going."

"Just take it a day at a time, I guess," he says. "I'm sorry I got so drunk last night."

"No apologies needed. No judgement given. We've all been there from time to time," I said, knowing last night was not just about me. Chris, despite the uncomfortable morning watching Jodi come out of my bedroom, was still no better off than he was before.

"I guess it's coming," he said. "Miriam is flat out evil for announcing those layoffs like she did but she's not going to back out on her word. She would lose too much face and frankly, it's just wishful thinking that my job could last much longer. I haven't really told Tina anything, to be honest. She doesn't know what is going on."

"Why layoffs plural?" I asked. "Who else could be on the cutting block?" It's not like I feel particularly secure there either. Miriam has her radar, sure. But don't think it's just you alone she's after because she enjoys keeping you in the center of it. It's not power anyone should have; sitting on a throne and observing who is and who is not falling in line to whatever her preferences are alone. It's not a measure of success for a department of employees; it's a measure of success for her. We don't need her; we don't need that."

Chris gathers his shoes and the rest of his clothes. Time to run. It's always time to run lately.

"Chris, if you get fired, do you really think I plan on staying? She will probably come after me next just by association. I try to keep quiet but Miriam reads body language, I can tell. Don't think I've forgotten what she did to Brooke. I know we are not supposed to say that name but it's real, and it happened. We should not allow for things to get that bad. There is no reason to suffer the whims or vices of a bitter, aging director with a god complex. What the hell makes her special anyway? Why even remotely revere her?"

Chris was looking down when I mentioned Brooke's name, sadly. To his credit, he did look up when I told him about the Jodi 'envy' story.

"I didn't tell you that Jodi actually mentioned that she's jealous of us," I said. "She thinks we are cool, apparently. We are nothing special but if you get fired, we will still be friends. I don't want it to happen to you or me but if it happens, Miriam can't take our friendships away. Do you think that pile of crap we call a boss has friends? Elizabeth maybe. She gets away with a lot but she's afraid of Miriam. I can't be friends with someone I fear. Friendship doesn't work that way. Maybe they hate us. We have something they don't. Fuck them."

Chris was just not buying what I was selling. I don't care for the lack of support for Jodi and I, but he's been through a lot. He is still a friend. I remember what he said just as he left.

"I respect you, Din. You're not afraid to speak your mind, or what you think is the truth, even if it will cost you your neck. Just understand it's not always what you say, it's also how you say it. I advise you to be careful, and do the right thing if or when it comes."

That was the end of that morning, eventful as it was. It was also the last conversation Chris and I had before he just sent me that text saying he found a new job; another nonprofit, this time a university. That's very good for him. I want to talk to him again. Isn't this important? I would have liked to have received more than just a text, which is all I got from him. With all the pain and tears that he had been suffering, one would think he would want to talk to me more directly about this; particularly how he's going to handle Miriam when she finds out. There's a lot going on with Chris and it's finally good. Though I feel like I am missing out.

I admit that even after Chris and I had that conversation, I can't take my mind off of Jodi, off of her beauty, off of the sex, and above all off of her personality. She is just that great. Should I be ashamed of thinking that now? I don't see why, though there is an implication somehow, and I hate admitting it, it's kind of gotten worse.

I've only talked to Jodi for the past few weeks over text, and short ones at that. She didn't pick up my one phone call. I won't push this too much more despite really wanting to. Apparently, she had more consulting gigs and some travel up to New York. I asked her once or twice to hang out again but those ideas were more or less ignored. Maybe Chris was right. Perhaps he's looking out for me, perhaps he has his own motive for this to fail. I don't want to believe that.

I never know what to do about these things. Again, so many unwritten rules. Usually it starts with don't call or text a girl the day after you get her number but Jodi and I went far beyond that with the whole all-night naked thing. That has to amount to something. It still all comes back to the main question I have been having since forever: what is a relationship?

We act like there are all kinds of set rules but there really are none. Jodi is older than me, yes. We had sex after hanging out for one night; I have no idea if she's interested in a relationship, that's true, but what would be wrong with that? I haven't smothered her with texts or calls but I want to keep the relationship going, and not just for sex again.

Everything else is acceptable in this brave new world, why not a cynical thirties guy dating a girl some ten or more years older than him? Even if they just met. Is it always wrong when I do anything; or is that just me?

Another reason this all troubles me is that everything for so many years has seemed to be quite established. We all have ours, just not me. Can we imagine Cathy without a boyfriend? Could we ever expect to meet her one day and for her to tell us she is single? Or Nicole for that matter, or even Chris? They have theirs, well, good for them. Can it be my turn, or is that too much to ask? It would be a change of pace, a change of establishment, and that could upset things. Was Chris right? Is this why it may not work out with Jodi? Because we are used to it? Is it true that in order for one person (or two) to be happy, another must be unhappy?

I don't need to be in a relationship. I've been in several, but I've always "admired" my own ability to live alone in this world while at the same time absolutely hating it. I don't want to be alone, either. We are all human. Jodi has clearly been through some shit in life. For this reason and more, Jodi is more real than the Cathy's or Sara's, or anyone else I can think of in my recent life. I could be another road for Jodi, another way. She deserves such a path as much as I do.

Maybe I am asking for too much. Call me criminal, but I actually took it that Jodi would reciprocate more than she has. I presumed that her being older was perhaps something different, not that it's simply a sexual turn on, but that she should be mature enough to see a good thing when it comes along. What is a good thing? Why not run with it? What can I do about any of it? Perhaps it all needs a little more time. As far as I'm concerned, any amount of time is worth it for her. It does not have to just go away.

I didn't spend all my time since the wild Jodi night thinking about her. I actually was on another interview that went pretty darn well, even in retrospect for a change. More waiting though. Applying to any job is like a dice throw, one never really knows what will happen. I can't help but to see what is wrong with that very truth, and I continue to try.

Such was the case at this interview, honestly the most remarkable of all my attempts to find another job and escape a pending fate under a "superior" that seems to almost thrive on the idea of firing employees for the sake of unchecked ego. I interviewed at a company that creates advertising materials for law firms and private practice lawyers across the country. It was something new and what was interesting is that I interviewed with my potential supervisor to be via video conference from his office in California. Not a big deal. I just don't know how much he could have evaluated me from seeing me on a projection screen. That and I found it interesting that my potential boss would be located on the other side of the country. That would at least remove the problem of him firing me over body language. Food for thought.

The man I interviewed with was Kevin Roberts, very friendly even through the video conference. What amazed me most was that he spent no time at all trying to delve into why I left my previous employment positions. He was the most "aware" manager I have ever spoken to, he really seemed to understand the plight of the job seeker; and his hubris was not nearly as abundant as to challenge me in the way so many other managers have done for reasons only to benefit themselves. I just wish his follow through was as impressive as his interviewing skills. I have not heard a word in almost two weeks, and this needs to move.

"I can see you worked a few places in the past, Din." Kevin says while apparently reading a copy of my resume on camera.

"Your resume tells a story. I like where you have come from. A lot of managers waste time interrogating potential employees why they left this job or that one; most of them don't realize that times have changed. While the expectation is there for no good reason, we still wonder why people only seem to work at jobs for ten, or probably even more likely five years, then move on to something else. There is a reason for it. It's likely those jobs do not exist anymore, or the company in question itself is gone. So I find it better to focus on the substance of a previous position over the time served. We all learn something and add to our skill set regardless, we should focus more on skill and character, as opposed to holding individual workers responsible for the state of the economy. I don't like the tricks and games thing. It's probably why so many other mangers I've met in the past tend to hate me."

He was okay with me laughing out loud at that one. This guy was awesome. It's a welcome change to feel good about my past jobs as opposed to feeling guilty for them. It's rare for a manager to really emulate with a "subordinate." I don't think it's pure arrogance, but ego has a lot to do with it. It's that, and exposure. If one's nose is too high in the air to smell all the shit down here, one can quite easily forget what shit smells like. Good for them but not for the rest of us; it's a cancerous imbalance of perception. This man was different. Unfortunately, this is no guarantee of the job working out. I didn't talk much on this interview, just tried to stay in sync with Kevin. He was slightly youngish for a department head, whatever the proper age is, I don't know; older than me, certainly. It was hard to tell, again, it was a video conference. I listened to him continue his oddly positive rant.

"There is nothing wrong with someone trying to move up or around a bit in their careers," he said. "As I often see it, a major problem is that retirement age people, whatever that age is now, are staying in the work force a lot longer than in times past. It makes it harder for everyone else to find or keep good, satisfying jobs because now it's often just perpetually out of grasp as a result. They are not going anywhere and actually enjoying it in most cases.

"This is probably a moot question, Din, but how receptive are you to learning new software programs and procedures? I ask because we have a lot of changes here in that regard, and will likely have more new software applications come in as we expand and negotiate new deals with all the different vendors and firms."

"I am quite ready and familiar with that," I said. "Even if we are working with something brand new, I can get a handle on it with a little bit of time. Everything is new when it is new, then it becomes second nature."

Somehow, I found using the word "we" gave the impression to Kevin that we are a team and it's not just me searching for a job for myself. I want the working experience to actually work for everyone. I'm glad he was receptive to this type of positivity. "We" can and often does eclipse "I."

He's right. We simply just do not let that happen much. Even through the video camera, I could just tell that Kevin was on the same wavelength as me on that interview. This was something else entirely, and it was good.

"Another thing that's happened," he mentioned, "is that companies today are far less inclined to train new workers. They don't think about how that hurts morale and widens the divide between staff and management; and it keeps them prone to find that perfect candidate who has exactly the training they need before hiring, which is damn near impossible to find unless maybe hiring internally; or at least they want to find someone who can hit the ground running."

If this guy ever knew. He was dead on, though. Some of the worst situations I have been in after being hired is the far too typical manager being slow or non-existent on the training of a job, yet quick on the reprimand when the new employee still has some things to learn, and questions to ask. Every new job is new, even with experience. Again, it's that hubris factor that allows this ignorant scenario to even exist. That and the whole "don't question the boss" thing. Don't even imply it. Unwritten rules indeed.

Can it really be the modern phenomenon that older and in "power" employees just don't want to work beyond what is acceptable to them? Did they earn this power? Must be nice. What is "earn" to begin with? They are paid well. The very reason I have a job (for however long I do) at Learning Tools is because I could run the damn database better than their established employees. Perhaps I benefited from the lack of interest. What great success. I could have said more but Kevin took the words right out of my mouth that day.

"That and college itself is a problem," he says. "I know you are not a fresh out of college guy, Din, but let's face it, college is not exactly preparing anyone for what happens in the working world, though to be fair, far too many companies and their management are not interested in new blood enough. I don't know why it is so, but it only hurts, if not ruins, the experience of the younger worker as a consequence and it's wrong. We should be happy that we have generations of new employees, even if they are more experienced, coming in an being a part of our lives here. Too much of the opposite is the modern condition, however."

Kevin paused and held whatever else he had to say in, as if laughing at himself. "Thanks for tolerating my digressions. I think you could really work out well here given your experience and attitude. You are a team player."

That was something else. We talked for only a bit longer and that was it. I proved to Kevin, even though video chat, that I actually am something he is looking for; and open to new ideas. He was the only interviewer I had to meet with, so no one to push their agenda on him this time. He didn't ask about salary needs, and I didn't ask him about money. When is the appropriate time to talk about that? Again, it's often an afterthought, yet we never talk about money. Maybe if he ever follows up on this, and I need them to, it can be discussed. Such a taboo subject, I wonder if I had asked Kevin about salary what would have happened. I didn't risk it. All I can do now is wait.

That all happened before now. It's been a couple of weeks and I'm running out of excuses for why I am out of the office lately. The last thing I need is more attention. Miriam is having one of her infamous staff meetings again tomorrow; not sure how that will play out now that Chris is leaving us. I don't even know why I'm so scared. I could lose my job at any second is one reason. Precarious thing to live in fear every day. I actually quit this job if only for an evening; and then I backed out. That was more fear. I could quit again but if Kevin doesn't get back to me and move the hiring process along, I could be doomed to look again; and this time without a paycheck. I know Kevin is not obligated to hire me, but my fate is in his hands.

Am I wrong that I just don't want to suffer any longer? I know this new job won't fix everything. We all suffer, I get it. Never really stops. Suffering is the realization that the world is not what we want it to be. Suffering is what makes us real. The haves are keeping us from being even conscious of it. The world is working for them, yet it all is, in its very essence, a lie.

Chapter Fourteen

Ground Zero

So I NEVER REALLY liked this job. That's not too abnormal but then again with me, it's really getting there. One of the aspects of the entire experience here and pretty much anywhere else I have worked in my life was a noticeable frustration, more a feeling of loneliness, in simply not feeling like I was important at all. I never wanted to be the man in charge. That's the last thing I would want at this place; however, there was always a sickening feeling that I don't matter. This place could and would exist without me. The bosses certainly have no interest in ever promoting the likes of me, raises are practically nonexistent; yet in addition to those unfortunate fundamentals, there has been many a day here at this job where I felt insignificant, regardless of being employed; or being part of the team. It's natural to feel that way sometimes. I just didn't think today would somehow be the absolute worst and then some.

Today was also the first day I walked into Chris' office feeling like I had no right or reason, or even permission to be there. I have no superhuman abilities, yet I could somehow feel it in the air that things have changed here and they have changed for the worse; my worst specifically. I thought I was just kidding myself until I walked through his door and realized that even my worst fears are far from overblown paranoia. I can't think of any other time where I've wanted to be wrong.

Chris looks up at me when I come in, not annoyed at all that I am there, and noticeably less uptight than he normally is. That fear and apprehension that has been a part of him for too long and drove him into at least one drunken stupor was all but eradicated from his persona now. What I see in this office is a man of renewed confidence. That is so great, at least it should be. Though I don't actually think he wants me to be here.

"Hey," Chris says in a friendly way. There are no words I can find to perfectly describe it but he almost seems very formal now, nearly the opposite of the friend I have known. He's the same man, Disney toys everywhere and dog pictures the same. Yet he's not.

"Sorry, I don't have too much time to talk," he says. "I have a meeting with Miriam and Elizabeth coming up." He seemed far less afraid at a prospect of a meeting with them than he has of late. That and there is a full staff meeting scheduled in an hour from now. Can't wait.

"You going to tell me about the new job? Where is it? Are things okay here?" I barrage Chris as he looks at me with half confusion, probably half annoyance. Did he somehow forget that he is leaving the employ of a megalomaniac who sent him home in tears over this job, probably more than once? What immediately lies ahead?

"It's at Andrews University," he says. "I used to work universities after I graduated, it's how I got into nonprofit work in general. It will be good to get back to my roots that way."

I can't help but ask. "Did you speak to Miriam about this? I don't blame you if you haven't yet. I dread how that will go. But I'm happy for you, congratulations, buddy!"

I do mean that. It's great that Chris got a job; he deserves it, we all do. I just can't imagine how well anyone here, Miriam specifically, will take it. She has to know that he is leaving because of the differences (to say the least) they had. I can only imagine the retaliation tactics she will enact to save face for herself. Not that I care about the management's feelings, they deserve such a reprisal and then some. The boss needs to know that behavior has consequences, and her employees are not beholden to her. This is a good thing.

"I talked to her earlier this morning," Chris says while seemingly shaking his head at me; no gravity felt whatsoever as to the state of affairs here. Does he even comprehend what I am asking him? Judging from him looking at me like I am from Mars, I would deduce the answer is no.

"And?" is all I could bring myself to say.

Chris shrugs. "It went fine, I told her that I got a job, and I thanked her for the opportunity here. I told her I learned a lot. It went fine."

I stare at him for a while. I've never been a fan of staring; it's too effective of a defense mechanism for those who want to avoid accountability, which is far too many of us; so I try not to humor the practice. But I don't know what to say to him. Chris is not looking at me now, just fiddling with some paperwork, an important man going into a meeting with the boss; as if this was always the case. Apparently, all of the abuse this man suffered never happened; as if he has magically swept it all away.

"Are you going to talk to anybody?" I ask.

Again, Chris just looks at me, just as annoyed with this question as any other I could ask. "I have an exit interview coming up. I'll still be here for about two more weeks."

"I would hope you would talk to someone about how horrific it's been here. You and I have been discussing this for some time. Miriam treated you like shit, remember?"

He shrugs again, now a brick wall in the form of an overgrown nerd. "I'm sure it will go fine. Now I'm sorry, Din. I have to go. Will see you in the staff meeting."

Chris walks right past me, I don't know if it's my imagination, but I really think I see him roll his eyes at me as he passes, leaving me alone in his own office. I stand there for just a little while. Am I wrong? Clearly, I just imagined the past six months here and none of it happened. The crying, the hiding from his girlfriend, being tossed out of a bar like a drunken lout that he was that night; apparently none of it ever happened. All an afterthought, if that. He's not going to tell anyone the truth, let alone Miriam herself. How impressive of you, Chris. Glad I could be there for you. Perhaps I've outlived my usefulness. I should have quit that day. I know that now.

I don't exactly know why but before I leave Chris' office, I pull out my cell phone and text Jodi.

Who knows when she will respond to that, or even if she will at all. Not when things are going so well. I wander down to Joey's office. I just need to talk to someone. I'm running out of allies fast here. I still haven't really spoken to Cathy since I suggested she break up with her pedophile boyfriend; and with the Jodi adventure I've had little time to think about that, maybe not even care. I don't forget people that easily, I'm afraid.

I've seen Joey taking some interview candidates in and out of his office lately, not really making any good on his claim to find a cute freelance writer but I never took that seriously. I could not care less who he hires, and my mind still drifts back to Jodi. It occurs to me that Joey probably has no idea what went down between her and I, and the less said in the office of that, the better.

"Any luck with the new writer?" I ask him while he fiddles with his paperwork. He knows I don't care if he's working on anything or not, maybe he is really busy but he's admitted to me before he likes to play that game. I just offhandedly find it dishonest. Though I'm in no mood to argue with his nose-haired nonsense, there are more prominent battles ahead.

"No one yet," he says. "I just started, more or less, so hopefully someone soon. The resumes are still coming in. I want to get someone here quickly; I could use the help. We have that meeting coming up soon. Chris mentioned to me that he is leaving. He's clever to take on such a good opportunity."

Now I get to play the part of the disinterested party. Joey does not really know how frustrated and emasculated Chris has been here working under Miriam. In fact, I doubt Joey even notices how vindictive our august leader is half the time; and the other half he is in denial like most of us. Both are equally wrong; yet what is wrong with no consequences? I don't press him on it; Joey may walk out just like Chris did. Even in that likelihood, I won't forget why. I stay in Joey's office for a bit, talking about nothing really. Joey's mouth moves as he goes but I hear nothing because I just don't want to. Why am I here? We head to the meeting.

I'm reminded that last time the boss, in her own cavalier manner decided to tell all of us that not "all of us" will be here any longer after some indeterminate amount of time, presumably soon. Usually at these meetings, I distract myself with ogling at Cathy while hoping no one would notice I was looking. Today, she was just another face in the room. Still gorgeous, for certain, nothing has changed there. Call it progress; call it acceptance, at least Cathy doesn't know my mind is on a far more amazing girl and I will take no course to let her know I have found someone else. I don't need to.

Something else I notice is that Elizabeth is sitting directly next to Miriam, as if she's being allowed to run this particular meeting. I think too much, and I admit I do have a habit on dwelling upon the worst-case scenario in nearly everything. The worst tends to happen though, whether I dwell upon it or not.

What I fear the worst of is here is more talk, if not perhaps real details, on the layoffs that Miriam said were forthcoming. Is that why Elizabeth is kicking off this meeting? Managers do so love to cover for themselves; they want to be the bad guy without actually looking like they are. That's where stooges like Elizabeth can come in; she's the mouthpiece for this purpose. Avoiding responsibility for oneself is also an art form in and of itself.

The rest of the staff eventually trickles into the conference room. I don't think I've regretted backing out of my decision to leave this job without notice like I did more than right then and there. I do not feel like I have a friend in the room, or perhaps worse, anyone who really wants me to be there any longer. I have failed at accommodating anyone. That's another sin to add to my list from that morning. I'm not sure how this can get any worse. Once everyone settles into the room, Elizabeth takes care of that problem for me.

I was expecting something about the layoffs or other such trouble, yet taking another look at Elizabeth, I see she's actually smiling. Not only that, it almost seems as if she is containing some kind of joy, nearly ready to get up and dance on the table, or jump around like a teenaged girl even though she is probably in her late fifties. She puts her hand up as if her mirth is infecting the rest of the room, which with the notable exception of myself, actually seems to be happening.

"Okay, everyone, we have a very special announcement to make," Elizabeth says. "That's why Miriam has let me start off today's meeting. But I'll let the lucky girl of the hour announce it herself. Are you going to tell us?"

She was looking directly at Cathy, sitting there somehow looking a little older than usual. She looked beautiful as always; from the way she was dressed, her makeup, and her general manner; she looked older. It wasn't real though, as if she was playing dress-up as the new look was a costume, as opposed to really an actual change.

It doesn't matter if it was real or not. I watch Cathy hold up her left hand with her palm facing back at her, waving her hand back and forth to show off the new piece of jewelry on her third finger; the light shines off the diamond right into my eye sockets. There is no stopping this.

"I got engaged!" she shrieks, and the entire room erupts in a frenzy. Everyone, including Miriam, standing and clapping, shouting in admiration, and hugging this girl to the point where I can't even hear myself think. I am the only person at the table to remain seated. I just stare with my jaw slightly disengaged from my skull. I can't bring myself to fake anything. At least a few people are bound to notice; I know at least one of them is Cathy herself.

Elizabeth yells over the roars and applause. "We will be having a happy hour party for Cathy tomorrow night, everyone here is invited to attend, I can't see how you can't though. This is so fantastic! Congratulations, Cathy!"

More screaming. Cathy and Nicole stand next to each other almost in tears, Joey actually walks over to her and kisses her on the cheek in congratulations; or at least I presume he says that, I still can't hear anything. Everyone continues to frolic and worship before her for what seems forever. I'm still sitting here; at this point wondering when the ticker-tape parade will come through.

I wonder why I should even care. I won't accommodate this but I'm just about to give up resisting it. I haven't really talked to Cathy since she chewed me out for suggesting she break up with her boyfriend. I can't hear myself think. If they only knew. I dare say that if any of these clapping seals knew about the pedophilia boyfriend, they would still have reacted in exactly the same way. There would be no questioning it. Why should they? No need to make sense. For whatever reason, Cathy only told me. Maybe that I am the only person seated is why she wanted me to know; so as to somehow validate what was coming, which is exactly what just happened. I won't indulge.

I think I can hear her telling everyone that she got engaged just last night. I try not to pay attention but everyone is making that effort damn near impossible. Are there any other single people in this room? Would it matter if there were? Regardless of the fact that I haven't thought about Cathy much these past few weeks, am I even allowed to believe this is wrong based what she shared with me? Why do I feel like the bad guy? Miriam of all people cuts off my thoughts with another announcement.

"Well, we have some bad news, but good news for him," she says to a finally quiet room. "Chris, how about you tell everyone what is happening with you?"

Chris actually stands up. "Well, first, I very much want to say congratulations to Cathy, I think that it is awesome that you are getting married and your boyfriend, or should I say fiancée, is very lucky to have you. I really wish you all the best."

I am more than half tempted to get up and leave at this point. This new version of Chris is terrifying. Maybe this isn't really about me but he knows how I've always felt about Cathy. He can see me sitting right here, and yet he coddles her all the same. To what end?

"To dovetail on that piece of great news," he continues. "I have to share some bad news; I will be leaving this organization in about two weeks. I was offered a job elsewhere, back in my old university realm, and it's been wonderful working with everyone, I'd like to thank you all for the help you have given me; and to you, Miriam, for all the guidance, I have learned a lot from you, and I'm sorry to go."

The sounds coming from the staff. I can akin them to nails on a chalkboard. What happened to Chris? Who is this man standing in front of me? He's like a total stranger; a kiss ass diplomat, completely disinterested in the truth which he himself has suffered. It's good that he got a job, he needed that, but why is he acting like this? That abrasive mound of pubic hair he called a boss made his life miserable for months, sent him home more than once in tears, all in the name of humiliating him for her own satisfaction, while nearly costing the man his very livelihood and enjoying it all the while.

Speaking of contentment, that is the look on Miriam's face right about now. I had feared that Chris would be fired similar to how Brooke was. After all, despite all the showmanship, it's still damn obvious that Chris is leaving because he doesn't like working here, not just disliking, but loathing. Miriam is far too clever and more so sensitive, to not be aware of that; and that's no compliment. What will she do? Is this why he is lying? I'm not the only person here thinking this, but very likely the only person admitting it to themselves, which should count for something, yet it doesn't.

The meeting goes back to par soon enough, Miriam takes the time to humor herself with a goofy idea she had several months ago that fell apart. The mood in the room is slightly dampened when she begins complaining about the work logs, which was something she invented to keep us on our toes.

In addition to coming into work every day, Miriam wanted us to catalog each and every one of our tasks or projects going on at any given time with the progress that had been made on each; and then uploaded to an intranet application she could then review. Nobody liked this, obviously. It was just another way to make Miriam's occasional helicopter management style more effective and perhaps a way to show off to the Senior Leadership team, so as to curry favor and indirectly beg to be among their ranks; which they will never allow because they know she's crazy. They are not concerned with those "beneath" her. How could they be expected to be so?

We all entertained this new process for a little while but it did not last. Everyone, myself included, trusted each other enough that while there may be some quieter days, we are all working and do not need to log every project or task we do, and that this "work log" as Miriam called it, was only hurting our daily morale and we just gradually turned away from it. Half the time Miriam was too busy kissing upper echelon ass, and Elizabeth was probably exempt from it entirely. Even Chris, despite evidently being a changed man today, complained about this often. He and the other direct fundraisers already maintained a database of all donations coming in and events going on; so what need for the work log other than to give Miriam more power over everyone, as if she needed more.

"The logs are not being entered," Miriam emasculates to no one in particular. The conspicuous Cathy engagement vibe having clearly not affected her much, hardly a surprise. "I introduced this process to help you, not for you to ignore them. If there is a good reason for these not being completed, I invite you now to explain to me why that is, or why you seem to think this is not a good idea. As I see it, it's only for your own benefit to remain organized and enjoy your work."

True to form, no one provides Miriam with any answer. No one is going to say that they just don't like being monitored as such. Chris doesn't offer an answer either, though considering his newly found brand of confidence; he is hardly bothered by any of it. He already found his get out of jail card, so why need he be concerned? He's got his, after all.

It's not as if anyone is going to offer criticism of any kind, not even pointing out even to themselves why Miriam offers any of us to challenge her when the price of criticism has been well established in all of our minds. This is not your job, it's Miriam's department. Important distinction. I offer my own.

"It was an idea," I say; everyone rather astonished that anything was said out loud, let alone from me. "The problem may be," I continue with everyone gawking at me, "that it's difficult to log each and every item we work on in such a manner. Most people are more comfortable, and even work better, when given some degree of independence, and we still have the main database for the fundraising and events, and so forth. Whatever the intent may have been, it did drop off for after a few months; morale has a way of pushing back on such discomfort. We can take it that this is not the planned result, but it just doesn't work altogether, and that's okay.

Miriam's glasses are hanging down on the bridge of her nose, looking down upon me. She does not waste much time to retort. Chris has his hand over his face at the moment.

I'm not sure if he's afraid for me or just him. Whatever he's thinking, I was asked to speak my mind, so I am. If you don't want your bullshit challenged, then perhaps it's time to cease the bullshit.

"I'm not here to make anyone uncomfortable, Din," Miriam says, her volume noticeably turned up. "I'm here to help. No one is uncomfortable with the work log. No one is uncomfortable with anything. The main database is for generating reports for management and the CEO, the work log is for us, to help us do our jobs better. I don't see any reason that it would not work for everyone, yourself included."

I smile. That's correct, I smile. What she wants is subservience and simply to never be wrong; and not even for that to be implied. Implying is what I do fairly well; though it seems even that's unwelcome.

"Ultimately," I say right back to her, "the work log didn't take. As you pointed out, no one is really using it and we haven't used it for months. We are still getting our work done and the wheel is still turning, so to speak, even without logging in each and every task we do. The idea of it simply doesn't work, and that's okay. We should be introducing new ideas and processes that will help the department over all. This was one such idea and it did not work, so we can now try other ideas that will. That is the nature of ideas after all."

I know I just punched everyone in the gut with that backhanded defense of a bad idea. No one is speaking up;

in fact, most won't even look at me, and keep their heads away, or simply look for Miriam's response because they can translate what I said just as well as anyone else. We are not as dumb as we act. This isn't theatre. We shouldn't have to act to begin with.

I wonder if anyone else can hear Miriam's heavy breathing through her nose, probably gnashing her teeth under her repulsive lips; in a lame attempt to contain the steam that would not be there in the first place if she was at all effective a leader. Admittedly, she has never given me that much direct attention, even though she is in fact my direct supervisor. She was always just so busy brown nosing the higher ups; or if not that, busy making Chris' life a living hell. I never indicated to her my many issues, not the least of which was the dismissal of Brooke Mesa. I wonder if I did, would it be any less awkward than it is right now? Before Miriam can defend herself even more, Chris steps in. I wish I could say it was on my behalf.

"I can't speak for Din," Chris says out loud to no one in particular. "What he fails to point out, I think with all due respect, Din, is that the work log is good. Miriam and the other managers need to know what we are working on, they are busy people and really just don't have the time to watch us and the log helps them when they have the time to follow up on the day to day work going on here. It doesn't have to be dismissed. Let's make their jobs easier on them.

Miriam likes snapshots, short and sweet; we can trust our commanders and that will be the best outcome for all of us."

Some of the others, including Elizabeth and Joey, nod in agreement. Cathy is probably beyond disgusted with me all things considered. I start to tune out even more from this meeting, beginning to wonder why I should even pay attention to what is going on here at this point.

I remember Miriam saying something along the lines of "Thank you, Chris. I'm glad you appreciate and respect the reputation of our own methods here. Not to spoil the great news we had today, but keep in mind I have been in discussions with the Senior Leadership team regarding possible layoffs; we are not the only department here who may experience them but regardless, the team and I agree that both performance and attitude should come in to play when deciding to eliminate positions so please bear that in mind."

I'm getting noticed, if they didn't notice before. The meeting eventually concludes, some stay behind to hold Cathy's hand and analyze her unholy ring; Joey pulls me aside for a moment.

"That was a ballzy thing to say in there, you know."

I only respond that we were asked to speak our minds and I did so; to which Joey raises his old eyebrows to me in seeming disgust. Not to mention the damn nose hairs; and then he leaves. Chris mentions to me that we should talk. I tell him I'll think about that. I'm here, but I am not here. I should be flat out gone. Yet still, I wander back to my desk, which likely won't be mine for long.

I keep telling myself it's good that Chris found a new job and is getting out of here. I don't like being selfish but that seems to be the name of the new game. New to me, at least. I'll have to talk to Chris; I don't want our friendship to end. Maybe I'm overreacting as to the egregious level of his behavior, but something is happening. I need friends. They are all I have. I miss Jodi. Can't imagine how she will react to the Cathy news, though I hardly think it would be jumping up and down for joy in Jodi's case. I'm not texting her again yet though. I am desperate, not for her, but for something. It's a Hail Mary shot, but I text Dave.

Yes, desperate. Really on my last leg if I have to depend on Dave Huston for emotional support. Stop gap solution at best, it's not really what I require. I need a new job. Not soon, now. I suppose I should call Kevin Roberts and see what the deal is. That was a good interview; he still hasn't gotten back to me. Can I at least get an answer one way or the other? He's not responsible for this particular predicament but the timing would be most welcome. That would be nice, a call from Kevin that I have a new job; and a new life, both of which seem more essential as each minute passes by. Wonderful emotional cocktail: fear, yearning, and outright pissed off.

I still want Chris to be happy, and he can't be that here. It still doesn't explain his behavior, but what if it was me leaving? What if I do get that job offer? There's a clock on the wall, it's always been there. Still, I know how I would approach leaving this place if given such an exit. I also know how ill received my resignation would be.

It's quite simple on its premise. I would have to set up a brief meeting with Miriam and tell her I am leaving. I don't need tell her to take this job and shove it. I don't need to be snarky or berate her in the slightest. That's not the way. However, I would simply tell her that I am leaving because I was able to find another job; and I sought another job because I am unhappy with this one. I disagree with the policies and manners of the present management, and this is why I decided to leave. You may continue to manage this department as you see fit after I leave, I do not expect otherwise, no one would. I thank you for the opportunity here, such as it was; and if I am asked why I'm leaving, I will speak the truth to them as I have spoken the truth to you. That is how that meeting with Miriam Gaw should go.

Naturally, I would probably be fired right there on the spot, but that is what I would say. That's the conversation that should happen, and another reason I want this new job and need it. A good part of the reason Miriam behaves the way she does, why she can treat the likes of Chris Allen like shit, is because she can; and the reason she can is because the economy usually sucks and jobs in general are hard to find. The advantage goes to the abrasive director to the point where we are treated like this and evidently like it so. That all said, I don't know what to do now, so little has been improved. I'm not going to tomorrow night's Cathy celebration. Should I be sitting here right now? That front door is not too far away.

A text message from Jodi comes in.

I admit it, I have no control over anything.

Chapter Fifteen

It's Never on Them

Today is the first day since the day after I nearly quit that I woke up feeling like it was all exactly the same day. Well, not entirely. That morning in particular I was afraid that someone would have read that resignation letter on my desk and realize that I had left. I rushed back to the office for fear of officially losing my job; I never hit the send button on the email because I was a coward. Perhaps anyone else would feel the same way; most would just never have put themselves in that position. Today I don't care; I'm not afraid of it and part of me wants to be fired. I just don't want to be out of work for too long. Not at all ideal. So for this I'm afraid, and these two mornings become quite similar. Notwithstanding when I left my apartment for work this morning, my neighbor was nowhere to be found but the milk crates again are on the street, reserving her space. I didn't remove them then I don't remove them now. I can't and won't do anything; apparently for anyone or anything. Paralyzed.

I do occasionally try positive thinking. It can be practical if the circumstances grant the leeway, but I am not a good liar. It would be dishonest to pretend that things are going well at all. I could lose my job, and I am still afraid to quit. I really need to hear from Kevin. I'm ready for a new job, and that's an understatement. I should not place so much of my faith in him but then again, he holds the key to a potential new life Is it wrong to want the rest of your life to get underway as soon as possible? I can't stop thinking about it.

Yet back to work I go. I may be not long for this world, but my job is still mine, for however long or short of time that may be. I don't really try to speak to Chris; his door is closed, probably in another one of his now apparently more important meetings. I can't help but ask if Chris is still a friend. How could he not be? He's been distant if not transformed of late. I don't even know what they are, but are any of these differences reason for a friendship to end? I'm not a popular guy here at the moment. I need my friends. We all do; we just so easily forget.

I pass Nicole and Cathy in the halls, no one seems as uneasy with me as they did in that meeting, but I'm not pushing my luck; and still would just as soon rather not hear any more from them. I'm still tempted to text Jodi; and still want to see her again tonight. Maybe things are not all that negative. We were something positive. I just hope it's something that can last.

I never heard back from Dave, not that I was expecting to, and not hearing back from anyone has somehow become a very disturbing trend. Dave never stops, not responding is him putting it out there he is busy; he is in demand. Why should it stop now or at all? I could lay into him about this, yet considering how things have been going of late; that would probably be it for my friendship with Dave, and indeed he's not even that good of a friend. I'm not left with many choices; other than accommodate, or not have any friends. I would not know what to do without them; though I can't shake the idea that absolutely none of this should persist. All the while it does.

Joey is still here. I don't know why I always wind up in his office, or even just talking to him. Maybe he needs friends. He's older, sure, but we are all getting older. Maybe I'm one of the few who can tolerate his specific lack of grooming, maybe I appeal to the writer in him. Maybe could be anything. At least he's here. I can't survive stranded on this island.

I find him today as I always do, fiddling about with his day-to-day, the morning newspaper strewn about; the paper itself becoming what charm is left here. I would like to think he was taken aback by the Miriam retort because he feels it could have been done more privately, not in front of everyone. Sadly, I know the reason is because of how he generally deals with authority. I get it, he's older. As such, our divine superiors are more respected by the likes of him; and it's not like Joey could easily get a job at his age. He has more to lose. Still can't accept it as an excuse though. It's doing far more harm than good.

I feel like I could tell Joey about the interviews I've had lately. Not sure if I should but I could. Unfortunately thinking about that new job is starting to become an obsession. I want to at least know where things are. I enjoyed speaking with Kevin and genuinely think he's a good man; and I could call him, or email; and ask what the status of my application is. Would I be doing Kevin's job for him? Is the lack of communication an indication that I did not get the job? I almost don't want to know in that case.

Looking at him now, I realize I'm not the only guy here stuck in the past. The only difference is that Joey actually experienced the past. Good for him. As a baby-boomer, it would be just as easy to see Joey as a man out of his time. Quite literally in his case. But he had it different than I did. Was it better? He's doing pretty good for himself and he can retire fairly soon. That is something. Will it be something again?

"Any news on the new hire?" I ask him. Joey doesn't seem too troubled with me or much at all, I'd rather not talk to him about Miriam. I'm tired of feeling like I shouldn't be here.

Joey looks at me with half disinterest. "I think I'm done interviewing, there might be more. Just have to decide where to go from here. It's been busy."

"Busy?" I ask him. "All the more reason to hire someone, as soon as they can get started, the more it will help you. When was the last time you interviewed someone? I try to keep notice of who comes in and out of here but things have been a little off the wall lately, you can call that 'busy' if you want."

"Over two weeks ago," he says, not looking me in the eye with that one. I need to know why. Joey is a manager, not the manager, but someone in authority. He is someone bestowed with the power to hire another human being; he can decide their life's course. He's stated numerous times he needs the help, why drag his feet on hiring?

"What's taking so long?" I ask him.

"I don't know. It takes a while, there were a lot of applicants and the resumes are still coming in. This process takes a while." Joey clearly does not like the direct question, though I don't stop. Just can't at this point.

"There's no doubt you had a lot of applicants, Joey. I don't expect you to talk to each and every person who applies for your writer assistant job, but what about those you have interviewed? How many have you actually talked to?"

"Six," he says. "Though one already contacted me and said thanks but no thanks, she found another job. Full time job for her." Joey almost sounds disappointed at that one for backing out, as if it's a waste of his time that someone found a full-time job over a part time gig. Shouldn't that be a good thing?

"Well, you can talk to the five applicants left that you did interview. I'm sure they are looking forward to their next job, and would want to know one way or another if they will be working with you, working here."

"There's too many applicants," is Joey's only retort. I swear, the fact that his defense is so lame is exactly why he's getting so defensive. He was actually almost gritting his teeth at me when he said that. There is a clear reason for this sensitivity.

"What about the five people you have interviewed? Can't find the right person there? Do you think you owe them an answer, or your time?"

"I haven't decided. They are all qualified, otherwise I would not have interviewed them."

Clearly. Is Kevin Roberts and who knows how many other hiring managers I have spoken to thinking the exact same thing Joey is? That is to say if he's really thinking at all. Why the delay? What need for the resistance? I dare say that if any of Joey's five applicants were to call him right now, he would be annoyed with having to provide an answer, and that in turn would hurt their chances.

Is it that difficult to hire? Neither Joey nor Kevin can ever expect to find the perfect candidate; they should only be expected to hire the best they can find, the best of their given pool of applicants and interviewees. Is it such a burden to hire? What is the issue? If anything, a person in the position of a hiring manager might well be excited to work with someone new. New ideas, new personalities, and yes, new changes.

Maybe that's the issue. Why would someone want "new?" Change is bad. After all, even the smartest and most experienced job candidate is someone you have to work with every single day. You have to interact with them, presumably train them, and answer questions. It's quite the burden, indeed. Furthermore, why hire someone who is the best person for the job? That could potentially ruin our daily lives and routines quite easily; let us not consider why they are so brittle in the first place.

"Joey. I know it's not easy. But it's part of the job. You said yourself you were almost surprised they gave you a budget to hire someone part time. You need the budget to hire someone full time."

"That's right," he says. This time on my side for preaching to the choir. At least we agree on at least that. Though he's not going to challenge the bosses on money. Even with good reason.

"Those applicants are depending on you though," I say to the man looking away from me. "I highly doubt they discussed it with you on their interviews, but they have bills to pay, maybe kids to feed. If they get the job, it's their own next step in life. Even if it's just a part time job, sadly. They can't know or act on any of the above if you do not follow through. You can't drag your feet, easy as it may be to do so."

Joey's face is getting redder by the second; nose hairs flailing.

"That's not my responsibility," is all he says, though I can't help but think he's holding back more than a bit more.

"I didn't say it was your direct responsibility. This does not change what is for them. The burden to hire is the burden of power, my friend. If you don't want to deal with it, how in the hell should they be expected to? It's really sad that they are putting in more effort into getting the job than you did in creating the actual position."

Joey inhales deeply while looking away from me. "I just don't like to hire," he says after a discernable pause. "Most of us don't. Keep that in mind. I will get around to it eventually. But as you pointed out, Din. It's all at my discretion, not theirs."

I appreciate his honesty, if that's what it is. I wonder if there is more to this though. Is Joey just lazy? Is this hiring process taking forever because he is simply disinterested, and is disinterested because he can do so with little to no reprisal? Or is hiring, even approved hiring, the proverbial money going out? It's not money coming in. Employees are seen so much more and more as an expense these days. Employees do have to be paid after all. The paycheck, as essential it is to all of us, does cut into someone else's bottom line. That could be another reason for the blockade here. Joey won't talk about that. I know Kevin and everyone else I've interviewed with would not be receptive to that subject either.

Am I so out of touch, or are they? I know there is nothing so mutually exclusive but there is something to be said for the haves and the have nots. Again, not so simple but Joey is from a particular generation. This game was different when he was younger, when he was the man looking for the new job. It should not have to be a game. He no doubt does not realize how good he had it. He's on the younger end, but he is a boomer. The twenty or thirty something boomer in his time is night and day to the same person that age now. Joey never exemplified "boomer" to me; we always got along too well. But sitting in his office now, Joey may not be of the boomer generation, though he is of the "me generation," which is more or less the same thing. Perchance the "me and the hell with you generation," which is far more befitting here.

I doubt Joey realizes these differences here. I know he doesn't. He lived that different life that was his. I don't know if all of his applicants were younger than him but that's very likely so. They were all probably Gen X, or worse yet, Millennials. Gen X is easily forgotten and I don't know why everyone gives the even younger generation such an amount of shit for simply living in the time that they do, and at the age that they are. Do boomers like this state of affairs? Do they like that the two generations, varied as they may be, have less than they do? Gen X in particular, which I think is where Chris and I fit in to this, is in fact the first generation in modern history not to have it better than their parents had it. Not even the same. This hiring process here that Joey and I are so enjoyable chatting about is no exception.

"Not everyone had it as good as you," I say. "Opportunities are drying up left and right and you know it was not like that when you were in the job hunt way back when. I know it wasn't easy for you either, but in comparison, can't you see any of the differences? If it's all up to you, perhaps you can be more cognizant of it."

Joey raises both of his hands out in disgust. "Don't give me that crap. I worked for everything I ever had, and you are right, it wasn't easy at all. Maybe the newer generations are not as resourceful as mine, or my parents who went through the Great Depression and then the war. If you want something, work hard for it. I see younger people today; they don't even have their own homes. They are renting forever or living in their parent's basement. We never did that. Not even into our twenties and thirties."

"It's sadly true we don't own homes much these days, Joey. I'm a lowly renter myself. I don't know why that makes me less of a person, yet somehow it does. Yet if you look at it, younger generations are not less resourceful; they have fewer of the resources. At age thirty, let's say, adjusted for inflation and time factors, Gen X and Millennials actually possess half the net worth of boomers at that same age. Talk about have nots. How long do you think something like this can last without more people taking notice? Even given that everyone is still scared to death of pissing off the boss."

Joey just stares at me. He did not want this today. He didn't want it any day actually. I always liked Joey and still do; we don't really spend time outside work together but he is a friend. That means something, at least to me. Does he think it's good that the generations to follow him have less? Do others who are older like him, particularly those in power, think that? The present circumstances do increase their own value. Boomers are known to be selfish. Having access to more resources and wealth than any other given time in modern history would do that. It's dangerously plausible.

"Sorry if I'm making you uncomfortable, my friend," I tell him. "I don't want to. It's just frustrating to play these types of games, just to be able to support oneself, and then play all the games more once you even have the job. I know why Chris is leaving, after all."

"Din, Chris is leaving because he found a new opportunity."

I can't believe I have to explain this. "Joey," I say, not caring what offends him at this point, "Chris would not have found that 'new opportunity' if he had not been looking for it in the first place. He always hated it here. Miriam berated and humiliated him almost on a daily basis. He's been looking for a job for months, maybe longer, which should be obvious to anyone. That's why he's leaving."

Joey just shrugs. "Well, that's good for him. He's not frustrated here, and his bosses never had a problem with him. He gets along with them fine, from what I can see. I'm happy for him. Speaking of happy, I can't make it, but are you going to Cathy's party after work tonight? She's a pretty girl, very happy for her."

Incredible. Joey has managed to ignore nearly all of my points and counterpoints, and completely pissed me off with that little reminder while doing it. He particularly became a brick wall when I mentioned Miriam's name. Denial works. I suppose it has to. If he has his, he has to keep his after all. Perhaps these advantages outweigh the shame of being a sycophant. This is who we have become.

Even in the face of this clear indignation, such ire would never be directed towards the bosses, to those above us, to the real haves. We can't find work to support ourselves, there is no follow through even when presented with an opportunity, and it's all because we did not work hard enough. Why not be angry or even disappointed at upper management for allowing this to happen? We can say it's "just business" but this theory is flawed. The hiring phenomena, even the lack thereof, would not be what it is without the key-holders, with those in charge. We can't say this though. No criticism. What's mine is mine; and certainly not yours. It's never on them.

Joey and I, despite whatever generational differences, at least have fear in common. Fear is everything. It shouldn't be. Younger Americans have simply been exposed to such fear at an earlier time in their lives. The fear is losing one's job at any given time, and for any given reason, and at someone else's own discretion. Thus, we have come to be afraid of the times themselves, while increasingly accepting it as the norm.

I want Joey to be working. It's not so easy to retire these days, or find a new job at his age; and that's another reason he may not be so eager to hire someone else. Hiring someone, even after all the interviews, could quite potentially devalue his own standing, his own job, his own livelihood. A particular byproduct of this is that many workers are living long enough to yield a precarious degree of demographic disparity; or simply a scenario in which a large group of people, namely older boomers such as himself, prosper unfairly at the expense of those who just happen to be younger. For the crime of being born too late; they atone by watching their quality of life decline over short time, with no end in sight.

They are hardly saints, though the younger generations have been doing a pretty good job of keeping up appearances. They don't seem as angry as they perhaps should be; and maybe they are. After all, it still comes down to criticizing authority, and the consequences of such. It's completely unsustainable. This will only lead to substantial declines in standards of living, and a growing number of resentful employees, or in this particular case, applicants. Can we keep taking this while the haves have theirs without concession?

"Joey," I continue, nearly exhausted. "You are certainly not responsible for anyone's living situation, debt, financial circumstances in general; none of it really. But think about it. You are only hiring for a part time job. That can give anyone the window of downplaying how important hiring actually is to everyone. What if it was a full-time job? Humor me. You have an open position, you post it, then interview for it, it's all moving along. We don't think about this but if you are going to hire John or Jane Doe, then the direction of their lives is in your hands. You ultimately will decide their fates. It's a responsibility. It should not be shirked."

"I'm not shirking!" he almost jumps up, practically snarling at me by this point. "I will get it done, but the more I'm asked, the less likely I'm going to follow through, my time should be respected too. No one is getting a job by cross examining me." He fidgets about with his papers and tapes now, as if wanting to leave his own office.

Hubris unchained. Maybe it's not just the economy. The economy is hardly ever "good" and even when it is, the haves, the keepers; are still cheap as hell. Somewhere along the line, probably around the late seventies when I was conveniently born; we figured out we could pay less for the same amount of work. We can pay less for more work, actually. We certainly pay less for more suffering. Don't forget you are lucky to have a job. If you had yours, why complain? Joey and his ilk feel happier, psychologically speaking, in their work than those who have come to this game after. Talk about job satisfaction.

At the end of the day, I agree with Joey on this much: we are responsible for ourselves. If you want to get ahead in this world, you have to hoist yourself up, and climb the ladder by your own strengths and abilities. Yet the rungs on that ladder are not being shared much any longer. Wealth, even middle-class wealth, does not come from nowhere. It has to be shared, or released. It was shared with Joey and so many other boomers, not so much with the following generations, and we are forced to accept this as normal somehow.

Joey is a good man, I know this. Working with him has been one of the few good things about working at this goofy and greedy nonprofit organization. That said, he knows he had it better; it's probably why he's getting so pissed off at me right now. The rules were never laid out here, but I can finally say I get it, not that I'm happy about it. These are the unwritten rules. Do not talk about what I'm talking about right now with Joey LeMari. Don't spoil the game for anyone, particularly those above you. Don't even attempt to take away our advantage. After all, why would anyone, the boss or not, want to give up any advantage they have over another? If your playing field is level, then there is clearly something wrong with your approach. I would add one more rule: don't take our bullshit away. Don't even try. Though try I do. Why respect bullshit?

I'm batting zero here. I leave Joey in peace, hoping I didn't hurt any of his applicant's chances of getting a part time job. He is still responsible for what happens to them next, indirectly (perhaps more so) of what happens in their lives. He is not likely to ever see it that way. Why would he?

That leaves me with what to do next. My last interview went well, at least as it happened. What comes after is far more important, and thus far there is nothing to speak of. I'm concerned with my life moving forward; be that by gaining new employment, or losing the current job. Losing that is not outside the realm of possibility; and with Chris soon gone, I wonder if I should even stick around.

Still need that paycheck. I am exploited thus. Why do we behave like this? Why can't I ask why? I feel like I'm in a civilization long in decline. We get by with near threatening each other on a daily basis; mostly with money, but whatever works for oneself. We act like we can get along with being this selfish and isolated, but we really cannot.

I want to call Kevin about the job, maybe I just should. If I'm going to call out the egos and pride of everyone else,

I should be able to check my own. Dignity matters, though there is not much of that left, it seems. My chat with Joey was not hopeless. We should talk more about it, even if it could destroy our friendship. Sad that it could.

I keep comparing haves and have nots. It's not without reason. We want to have, we want to be well off, or even rich. Yet for someone to be rich, it would seem invariably someone else needs to be poor. Someone needs to lose, and we don't want that someone to be ourselves. This doesn't do well for human connection very much.

Connection. I miss that with someone in particular still. I do not want to go to this Cathy party tonight. Yet Jodi is going to be there. She sounded like she wanted me to be there too. Who knows if that will go well at all. I won't give up trying, and not just for her, for me too. I can be selfish, and make others happy at the same time. It's sadly becoming too much to ask. If it's really all on me, I'll do things my way. I just don't want to move forward alone; and it's all getting remarkably quieter here.

Chapter Sixteen

The Times

Digging her hand into mine, she pulled me into a corner; away from everyone at the "Cathy is engaged" party. She asked when she was going to have me again; apparently, I had more notions in that sequel than I thought. Then she threw her left arm around my neck, pulling me closer to her and kissing me, much harder than I would have expected. Her other hand briefly cruised below my belt. This would better wait until we were in more private quarters but she was making it difficult to object.

Jodi got here before everyone else apparently. This was the first time I had been back to the White Dog since my lunch with Chris and visit with Elizabeth and her "friend." There really is no shame, I'm convinced. I was already dreading this party. Why do this? Why have a whole office event for a girl who got engaged on a whim? Of course she must really love him. Most of the staff, if not all of them, do not know this and probably would not care, but I ask again: what is the point? Is it because it's a happy moment, so to speak anyway; or because they want to try to inject some positivity given recent turns of events or impending layoffs; or is it just because Cathy is the prettiest girl in the room? Could be any or all of that, though probably the latter.

Jodi has already had a few, not nearly drunk at all, though she's already started to wear it. It's lightened her up, to say the least. She asked me to come with her as soon as I walked into the place. Fine with me, any less time around those cackling idiots the better, that and it answers my question if Jodi was at all still interested in me. I remember walking in and seeing her there by herself yet and wanting to greet her with a kiss as if I was her boyfriend. It did not play out like that at first, not sure if she was worried about appearances in front of the staff or if it's just more teasing. There was something else there when she saw me; as if she isn't here for business, yet here for me. Or at least that's what I saw, what I really wanted. There is not much left of me, but I can still have my imagination.

"I'm here because I pretty much have to be too," she tells me. "I'm not too keen on these engagement parties thrown at the office. They are questionable, to say the least. I wish her the best; but can't help but feel more than a little cynical. When I announced I was getting married back at the old newspaper I worked for, everyone jumped for joy and they even had a mini-shower for me which was nice. Just so embarrassing in retrospect, and not for just me. So unfair to the single people too. Part of me wishes I could turn back time just to apologize to them. So you, know; 'if I knew then what I knew now,' and all that."

I can't imagine ever finding another girl like Jodi ever again. I just wish I was not so apprehensive to see her. We haven't spoken too much since that night out with Chris; and despite the kissing around the corner from the party, I still have no idea what is really going on between us. I won't ask lest it won't last.

"They invited some other consultants and vendors, bizarrely," she tells me. "That's why I'm here. Have to be sociable if I want to at least keep my business relationships up, particularly with Elizabeth and Cathy for more events. I heard Chris is leaving, what happened?"

I just want to kiss her more, but I don't. We just stand there; close enough for anything despite all the relative nothing. I won't count on anything, not at this point. Doesn't make me want her any less.

"Yes, he's leaving. He's been looking for a job for a long time. I thought it would go off a lot more honestly than it has, but he's making it work. Not sure if he is smart or just clever in this case. I hope his next job works out for him, won't be the same without him here."

Jodi discreetly kisses me on the cheek. Just one more minute here with her would be enough; at least that's what I tell myself. I want her again, I know it. So does she.

"What's wrong? Is it Chris leaving? It sucks to lose a friend, and that will not be easier come each day. It won't be all bad after he's gone. If he can find another job, another path in life, then so can you. It's not an impossibility."

"It's complicated," I say. "I wish things were so simple. Sorry for not explaining. Maybe I just can't get into it. I'm just not feeling so good, if that isn't at all obvious."

Jodi smiles again. Irresistible, even if subtly condescending.

"Well, stick around for the rest of the night with me," she tells me. "Stick around and feel better," she says with an amorous whisper. How could I provide any other response? We rejoin everyone. Amazing that all but my two friends at this job, (if they are that at this point) Joey and Chris, are not here. Chris doesn't actually tell me why, I'm sure it had something to do with his girlfriend; yet maybe he feels the less he's around the better until he's really gone. Maybe he's trying to loosen his association with me. Maybe there is actually a reason for that.

Miriam is here. Strange seeing her mingle with staff in a social situation. She's not one to spend time with 'inferiors,' and this is not her kind of party. Maybe some of the higher ups were invited. It's possible, though I don't see any of the senior staff types here. Who says they can't be sentimental?

I consider that this turn of events; an engagement party, makes Miriam and her staff "look" good. The truth be damned. Like Cathy, she's keeping her distance from me, as if I am not here. Everything is a show. Why should tonight be any less?

Nicole is unfortunately here as well; next to Cathy, doing very well to absorb all of the energy from that source. Cathy still looks incredible. She doesn't seem to mind that I'm here, at least not exactly. There is always something else. Nicole does not look at Jodi and I much; this leads one to wonder if she suspects something is going on, whatever "that" is, even I don't know. Perhaps Nicole notices but refuses to acknowledge it. She probably still thinks I'm gay. If Jodi and I were in a relationship, if she were my girlfriend, even fiancée, I would see no reason to shout it from the rooftops. Like Jodi said, that would not really fair to the single people; even if there are none here.

Elizabeth is enjoying a drink with some of the other staff. I don't see her boyfriend anywhere. Maybe he has no use here. She's not likely to divorce and get engaged again. Having him here might not be in her best interests. Too many people to ask questions, she freaked out badly enough when it was just Chris and I here that day; we cannot even enjoy a meal without all this. It's all music in the background. Time for a new tune.

I never fit the narrative too well here. Being single was always a part of that, though hardly the main problem. If it was Jodi sitting there with a ring on her finger that I gave her, it might very well upset the established order. Same if Cathy was ever just single. She won't be. Nicole thinks I'm gay; it was always her one and only explanation of why I never bring up a girlfriend in any context of conversation. Is it such a stretch to assume my experience with Jodi fucks things up for everyone? Change is cancer, after all.

I wish I had such power. I've always said we accept Cathy's behavior because we expect it. She's the pretty girl with the boyfriend, now something slightly more. That's good enough. We accept Miriam's behavior because she's the boss after all. Sadly, that says enough. Everyone knows that Elizabeth is in the midst of an affair even today, but that's alright, after all we expect it. It's predictable. Expected. A relationship between myself and Jodi, or anyone for that matter is not predictable. Who wants that?

Chris can resign if he wants, but is he not telling anyone why he's really leaving because of the issue of predictability? If I had actually resigned, that's something no one would have seen coming. No one wants that. Is it why I backed out? There's something to be said of routine, something to be said of consistency; we do not take well to any real variation in the process. There's something to be said of its demise.

Give people what they want, even if they don't know what they want; even if it's only what they think they want. It's what's happening right now with Cathy. I never played well in this sandbox. To be fair no one ever told me the rules. What if I was the pretty girl? What if I was the boss? We believe what we want to believe because we wish to believe it. Evidence and truth are trivial matters at this point. Yet this is power. I don't want it. It may very well be time for me to leave. I feel as though I have walked into a party comprised entirely of willful strangers.

I want to be alone with Jodi and tell her all this. To her credit, she is not as cynical as I am tonight. It's good to see her happy, I only wish I could keep her that way. I've hardly had a drink at all tonight but am not discounting my own options to do so just yet. I'm could be turning into Chris; or at least into what he was. I won't turn in to what he is. Why do I have to lose a friend?

Jodi knows this hurts me; even without knowing much of the details. It's real. I'd rather lose a girlfriend than a friend; more so given the circumstances here. I've been alone too much in life, and it's become a sick psychological study I can't let go of; and I'm the only one in that classroom.

Jodi does not spend all her time with me; I can see her talking with Nicole and Cathy; nodding her head because she has to. I can't imagine she's so into the engagement nonsense; not just because she is divorced, because she's smart enough not to humor them for the sake of it. She's also smart enough not to say that in front of them. We are her clients after all. "We," as if that is how I identify myself with this organization while I'm practically at death's door with it. It's all going to give soon.

Cathy is still the girl of the hour. How could I forget? I'll never know how many people involved here knew what a crush I had on her. Cathy herself had to know it. Chris knew it. Joey knew it, I think. Maybe everyone knows, I don't care any longer. With Cathy, it was only a dream at best, and dreams die pretty easily. Memories do not; not for me.

I listen but don't listen to Cathy talking to Nicole. I'm not in the mood to hear wedding plans but that will become part of the background noise soon enough. I don't know what she's thinking, but it appears Jodi listens in along with me. I wish I never stepped through the door tonight but I like looking at her all the same.

"Not everyone knows I'm getting married yet," she says to Nicole though she knows more than one person can hear. "My mom will probably be done telling everyone in my family about it before the night's over. Word gets around. I know a lot of guys will be hurt by this. I still have ex-boyfriends who call or message me sometimes. Other guys have asked me out, even when they knew I was with Ryan. I doubt they will take too well to it; they will be hurt."

The girl is not smiling, not really showing too much pride in her face but it is there. To appear to be something while not being held to account. That's just a fine how-do-you-do moment here. It's not enough to be happily (well, for now), engaged; and have the office throw a party for you right after the announcement dropped. Cathy has to take time out of her busy schedule to make it known she's hurting others. She's hurting me. Or rather, she did. One way or another it's become more past tense when it comes to Cathy. I'm not blind to it. She is cruel for as evidently sweet as she is; and that is what really hurts.

Unfortunately, I really need clowns like Dave and Hal here; if nothing for the entertainment value of it. I should talk to Chris. Maybe he wants to get married soon. There is no maybe about that. I'm happy for him, I am. Am I going to be a part of it; a best man, or even invited at this point? That must have been quite an "opportunity" he picked up. He's leaving, that's happening. What happens to me? I never said it to him, but it seemed obvious even to me he was on Miriam's layoff hit list. He had to be first in line. Am I next?

Time stands all but still until the boss makes her way into the center of the crew and announces she has to leave. She never wanted to be here and the indignity of having to say goodbye is just as bad. She likes at least one thing about tonight. I still can't get comfortable, near hating the fact that I am "hanging out" with Miriam Gaw.

"I can't stay any longer," she says. "Cathy, I want to say congratulations one more time. It's good to see you growing up; we all have to go through it. It only gets harder, believe me. Nevertheless, I admire your conviction. You all need to show much more resolve and less negativity. We often forget that everything is taken into account; and if you can't get over your own personal frustrations in life, well then the consequences should be fairly cut and dry to you by then." The boss rolled her eyes as she left. She doesn't say goodbye, just sort of disappears; yet she's still here and she knows it.

What indignity having to take time out of her evident busy schedule of ass kissing and humiliating to attend a party celebrating someone younger and far more desirable than her. Miriam doesn't hate Cathy, that's clear. Though I doubt I'm too far off point. Per usual, no one says a word in response to her. They don't have to.

Elizabeth and much of the others trickle out the door soon enough. The younger girls, along with myself and Jodi, remain for some reason. I spoke up before, I know what it means. I actually hate myself for not speaking up now; for all the good it will ever do.

I've been promoted, I am Chris; I am what he was only a few short weeks ago at least. Breathe it in. All that exists is screaming in my head at this point, I either can't or won't hear anything else. I think I hear Nicole mention that one of her ex-boyfriends cried when she moved in with her own current beau. Cathy is finished with her particular spiel, and Jodi chimes in. I want to believe she would say something true, at the least indicative of all the bullshit here tonight. What I want is becoming less and less signifi-cant. I'll always appreciate her brazen and straightforward manner, even if it is for the last time.

"It's fun to reach back in the past and slap them, isn't it?" she says directly to Cathy and Nicole. Jodi's face is flushed red from the wine at this point, the girls are all laughing, having a good time; and she will indulge.

"Men think they know what you have going on, but they really don't. We only let them think we know." The laughing continues.

"Ryan did the right thing by snagging me up," says Cathy. "He knows that's what I wanted. He had to know what would happen if he didn't."

"It would be his loss otherwise," says Nicole.

Jodi bursts out laughing, leaning into Cathy even closer. Cathy is enjoying this. They know I'm standing right here.

"That's what we do, isn't it?" Jodi continues. "That's just how things are, why not run with it?"

"I know!" says Cathy. I almost expected her to hive five Jodi.

Jodi laughs some more. "It's great! You don't even have to stay with one man all the time. It depends on whatever your mood. Sometimes you want an alpha male, to tell you what to do because sometimes you just like that; again, all depends on the mood. And sometimes you want a beta male, a guy who will be there at your every beck and call. If they piss you off and question you, then they can enjoy a cup of tears while you find another guy who probably already found you."

The laughing has transformed turned into cackling; all of them screeching, even Jodi, and certainly Cathy; it's her party I suppose, why not behave so shamelessly? There is no accountability, why even look for it? The injustice of it is everywhere, the air sucked out of the room, I can't breathe; part of me doesn't even want to. I'm convinced they don't know I'm here. Options really are power, both in love and war. I've been unceremoniously discarded. They don't even know that, doubtful if any of them care.

My back is turned to them at this point. I don't remember much else. The restaurant was crowded enough at this point that I could slip out without a word, the cold air outside never felt better. One thought was on my mind. It was time to go, and go I did. There isn't one reason to stay. Not any longer. I never heard from Jodi again; and still ask myself as to if I should be surprised. Tempted as I was, I didn't call or text her, no carrier pigeon, nothing. Hard as that was, there was no question to any extent of doubt here; it's better to have never loved than to have loved and lost.

Memories are that treacherous. I did find refuge in the most unlikely of persons, and what is left of my friends. Interestingly enough, it was Dave who texted me while I was out at the hooray for Cathy party. Rarely does he reach out to me, let alone for when he has a problem in life himself. I would say this is a better sign of things to come but I've simply grown beyond the hope of it. I can't rely on Dave; his shoulder is hardly one to cry upon but I am done crying anyway. It makes me sick to my stomach but somehow all the more gratifying to see Jodi Molano shrink within the rear-view mirror. She is gone. No texts, calls; it might as well not have happened at all. Thanks for the memories.

Dave asks me to meet him at his own apartment of all places. He says he's in for the night; apparently after a bad day for him. At least he can't be late this way; though he actually forgot I was coming when I arrived. Dave's apartment is something else; all hand me down furniture, he barely ever cleans or bothers to dust anything or even leave towels in the bathroom, the kitchen; any comfort to be found is long gone. Within the dried and greasy kitchen, his refrigerator is almost always empty. He offers me a beer, which I nurse only to be polite. That's about all there is in the place. That and his guitars lying around. I've never seen him play them. He's still on his one-track mind.

"I was out with Lisa; Hal was there for a while, but he managed to fuck everything up for everyone and she left."

"What happened?" I ask, feigning interest in this tired subject, yet still happy I have someone to talk to. Dave apparently needs a friend to, so here I am. It's good to be there for someone, but it's far too often just a one-way street.

"We met up with Lisa and one of her friends; I think her name was Kyla. This girl was cute; which is rare considering Lisa's track record of girlfriends. Actually, that's probably another reason Lisa didn't stick around with us. Still, we were all just hanging out and Hal gets on the subject of politics like he does and he ended up going on one of his tirades, saying things like the Iraq war was proper revenge for what happened in New York, and going into all the American exceptionalism sermons like he does. Talk radio come to life. He doesn't realize that most girls don't want to hear that.

"I never talk politics around Lisa, and you know she's liberal as all hell. She took the red pill. Kyla was offended big time, saying that other countries have it better and that she spent a lot of time in France after college. The mention of the nation of France alone triggered Hal. I just sat there and watched Hal and her argue over the war, the very existence of the city of Paris; and all kinds of political differences, and he would not stop. There was nothing I could do. Then Kyla fucked off to other friends she had there and Lisa left. Then I called you."

So glad I missed this. What Dave neglects to mention is that he himself is just as conservative leaning as Hal. Dave just never brings that up in front of the girls he is pursuing as he knows that's never going to get him laid. I never get into politics, even with the guys, though I know I don't fit very well into whatever ideology they developed. It's probably why Hal never really liked me which is fine, I'm doing something right. It's just tough whenever Dave and Chris bond over the real estate and stock talk; their indulgence in money tells a lot more than it shows, more so lately. This all hardly matters in this case as Dave will say what he has to say to make sure girls like him. He won't get what he wants by challenging their beliefs, and he knows it. He'd rather talk about girls than politics any day, and he doesn't disappoint.

"You still enjoying that cougar girl or is that all over?" Dave asks, taking a swig of his beer and smiling with that damn shit-eating, unshaven smile of his. I'll never know why that always bothers me but it does; and why shouldn't it now? I'd rather not be asked, but then again, I'm done sidestepping the issue.

"Whatever was there with Jodi is gone, Dave. I hoped it could have been more. I thought it was more, clearly. The more I think about it, I was likely just part of an elaborate plan of hers to get revenge on the world for her divorce, whatever happened there. Divorce fucks everybody up, sometimes we have to play the part of the strong character just to get by. Our little fling helped that effort to some extent for her. I won't be a part of it. I just saw her earlier tonight at Cathy's engagement party. I probably should have known after she all but ignored me that it was never going to work out. But I hoped."

Dave stifles a laugh, almost knowing how much all of that actually hurts me. In my position, he would still pursue Cathy, even if engaged. He would still randomly have sex and pursue at least a physical relationship with Jodi. He would never walk away as I did. The man has no heart. So,

I guess he's doing fine. Old soul like me, however, he does get along better in this brave new world than I. Good for him. I won't be Dave. There's just too much wrong to ignore.

"I heard she was engaged," he says. "Some girls just have to have that. You're right, she's likely just in love with the situation. Nothing you can do about it. You should keep pursuing Jodi, but I get the frustration. She might be bitter from the divorce but there could be light at the end of that tunnel.

"Din, you should stop taking things so seriously. You analyze too much. Don't think I don't get jerked around too, and not just from Lisa. Yes, we have hooked up in that way before, but that's always on her terms, always. I have this theory. Girl's like sex just as much as guys do, if not more so. But that urge, that impulse, that desire to have sex; they can turn that on and off like it's a fucking light switch. On. Off. On. Off. On. Off again. We can never know when the hell they will be on or off, so we just have to be pretty much 'on' all the time."

Dave's use of "we" makes me wonder what exactly he is and what we are. Am I too loyal to goofball friends like this? I enjoy hanging out with him for the most part; yet his one-track mind keeps getting worse over time; and more so whenever challenged. Dave is an unreliable friend, indeed a toxic friend. Friends are getting harder to come by, but the energy it takes to maintain such relationships has become exhausting. I want to leave again, even with nowhere to go.

Is Dave my last resort here? It's really come to this. I have a choice, bad friends or no friends. Dave's relationship with the evidently fairer sex, how he interacts and perceives them, it's not for me. I still don't know how to lie.

"Maybe it's time to stop playing all the games, Dave. It's almost as if you want to have some level of power in this game, whatever the game is. I can kind of see where you are coming from. It's an options game. If one party has more options than the other, that's an imbalance. You don't have to just have your conquests, nothing wrong with a real relationship. It's a game but it shouldn't have to be a game. Playing it constantly will be good for no one in the end."

Dave just stares at me, as if he would need to do anything else. "It's like the boss at the job," I continue. "If you tell them what you really think, and if you disagree with them on one point or many; you are not going to get what you want. Indeed, you will likely be reprimanded or even fired in sadly more than just a few cases. So don't tell them what they don't want to hear. After all, they have other options to go to. I wish I had a job where if I was unhappy, even a little unhappy with it, I could just get up and leave to find another. That's not reality for many. The bosses know that, they know it's almost always a bad economy, and you are beholden to them, lest you want to be so easily replaced.

"It's untenable. But make no mistake, you are not playing them, they are playing you; and our illustrious superiors would not behave this way if we had equal options. They would simply not be able to. But they can. Create whatever stories or justifications in your mind that you will to cope with it; in the end it's all the same.

"The first step in solving any problem is realizing that there is one. It just simply should not be, and if the least we can do in opposition is talk about it, then that's what we should do. But we don't even do that. The fear of consequences is sadly enough. No honesty, none expected."

Dave looks at me for a moment and looks away as if I'm not there at all. The silence only lasts for a moment. Then he does what he always does. He laughs. He will laugh enough to sufficiently downplay every word I just said. He doesn't want to hear any of it, and goddamn it, he won't.

"Come on, nobody's honest," he says with a smirk, still giggling. "Whether it's girls or your damn boss, no one likes criticism. Girls don't like cynical guys. You try to hold them accountable for themselves and they will run for the hills. Or in your case, just say 'nice working with you' and show you to the door. It's not on them even if you want it to be. You shouldn't. You are not going to get anywhere that way. I advise you take the sociology shit elsewhere. Trust me, nobody cares."

There is nothing else to say to him. I didn't stay much longer at Dave's. That turned out to be it. While I'm not surprised in retrospect that it turned out the way it did, I can say it did in fact hurt more to lose a friend. It always meant more. That said; to hell with him. To hell with Jodi.

I may be a smart man; I am not so much a clever one. But I know what friendship is.

The whole world seems to hate me today for not dancing to their tune, and I can't change for them. I don't think "want" has anything to do with it. I would have to lie to myself and that's where I lack any clear ability. I don't want to live a lie. There is one thing I can do.

I don't know where he is or what he's becoming but the friend I have in Chris has got to mean something. I care enough to try, even if it's the last chance to do so; and if I have to find my answers at the bottom of a glass, then that's what I will do. I believe in friends, I always have. I can be a big kid like him. One can't play on the seesaw all by himself. So little has changed since the schoolyard; and we seem so much less than now than we were then. Where is the way we were?

Chapter Seventeen

What Matters the Most

"I'M THINKING OF LEAVING," I say to him. "Or maybe I just want to tell them I'm leaving. They need to know that." Chris just looks at me, wishing I was saying anything but this. I've been out of the office for two days straight; feigning the sick act; not for the sake of any new interviews, which there have been none; yet for the fact that I don't want to be there any longer. They must notice by this point. I know they do; and part of me does not care.

No interviews. No word from Kevin Roberts either. I never contacted him. It's his job to hire an employee, if I'm going to be doing his job for him then I'm likely going from one bad situation to another. After that minor tiff with Joey, I have come to realize if I want that job, I am not to hold the boss accountable for not following through with the hiring process, or I may very likely not be hired for even asking. They have all the power and control and probably don't even realize it; or maybe they do, they simply just don't think on it much. Nothing has changed. It needs to.

When I called Chris and asked him to join me at the Lark, I was half expecting him to just blow me off, pull the whole "I'm busy" routine. That and the fact that the last time he was here he was nearly thrown out by the bouncers, and Jodi and I had to carry him home. None of that seemed to matter to him now. Tina was working the late shift and Chris actually said we needed to catch up and he looked forward to seeing me. This was a welcome change, for whatever time we have left.

"Are you saying you want to resign? You don't have a job lined up yet, do you?" he asks. I still don't tell him everything. Yes, I want to quit, and yes, I want a job. I'm in no position to just put myself out of work, mentally I have been there and back again several times but the hard truth is that financially, I am nowhere close.

"I haven't found anything yet. Some interviews and I am looking. Nothing solid, unfortunately. I've actually been thinking of leaving for a long time, more so now that ever. Miriam is a serious problem; you know she is. I'm wondering if I tell her I am considering leaving, maybe at least the political landscape will shift, even a bit. No one ever really talks about it. I don't want to lose my job but am always failing to see why that can't be discussed."

Chris grits his teeth while breathing a heavy sigh through them, shaking his head at me; his face carrying a hint of sympathy, yet mostly despair. Chris is above me, looking down; in fact, talking down. How dare I say or even imply any of this? I remember picking him up while his head was face down wallowing in his own puke, and with good reason. I feel like he's disappointed in me now for even being a reminder that all that happened.

"That's really not such a good idea, Din. You need to understand that Miriam is rather sensitive about how she is perceived. You are putting yourself in a bad situation. If you let them know that you are willing to leave, then you are basically telling them that you are a flight risk and therefore a liability. That can be used as grounds to fire you."

"Even if it's the truth?" I ask him. No answer, as if I should expect any. Some period of silence goes by; maybe a couple minutes if that; it feels like hours.

Maybe I just can't or won't accept that this is a new Chris I am so enjoyably chatting with. Since he found his new job, he's been different, as if possessed by a long-lost twin brother who has a lot more ego and attitude; not the fairly meek, nerdy, and all-around good man I've known him to be. He looks the same, yet he carries himself about in a manner entirely alien to me. I know I read into everything, and what I find reading into him here is something that makes me far more than afraid. He's not only "leaving" this job. Though somehow, I've gone from reliable friend to grasping at straws in a vain attempt to change what I cannot. Nevertheless, I try.

"Chris, you are leaving. I know that's easy for you at this point, but you have been in my situation before, quite recently I might add. I never knew what all your conversations were about but Miriam did send you home in tears, more than once. Did you tell her you were unhappy, or just unhappy with her? I am willing to bet you told her none of that, and what you could have said or did not say hardly mattered. Only her ego matters. You know it. You've been agonizing over it for months, longer even. That's why you are leaving. I don't blame you for it, I am glad you found something."

"It was a new opportunity," Chris replies, looking away from me, likely clenching his teeth in subtle rage even more. He cannot be wrong here; and I'm pointing that out. People really do hate it when you read into them. They get really cranky when it comes to questions.

"Are you comfortable losing your job?" he asks me. "You have to decide to what degree you are comfortable expressing that and yes, even to them; it's their discretion after all. Miriam hired you; she has every right to let you go, even if you disagree with her reasons; even if she doesn't give you a good reason. If you are willing to show them this side of you that they don't want to see, then farewell promotion, farewell raises, and altogether likely; farewell job. You will have to live with that. Not them."

Hypocrisy tolerates no boundaries. This bastard is clever, I'll give him that. If I criticize this man, even criticism with clear evidence (especially that, actually), I may likely be out of a friend; just as I could be out of a job. Is this what Chris and I are? Are we just two people who expect to be told what we want to hear, have things go the way we want them to go, to be accommodated at every turn without question; otherwise to turn about face and run from a friendship; in what is ostensibly within a change of the wind?

A job is something of value to lose, to be sure. That's why Chris was so morose for the past few months. He was not about to lose his job and income, but was steadily losing his dignity and would lose that even more once Miriam let him go with "justified" motives; within her mind at least. As an honest man, how could Chris have behaved any differently than he did? How could there not have been tears, pain, and the drink; all of it. It was real. Then he got a new job and forgot any of it happened. Was that all part of the plan?

What of losing friends? Are they of value to him? I've had more than my fair share of failures in life. Family, failed relationships, jobs that tanked, everything, yet I've always had friends. It may very well be my one notable accomplishment in life, all I ever had. That's losing something of real value, even if it doesn't pay the bills, purchase a house, or buy the ring. I don't like feeling superior to anyone, I can't be so with money, really. My friends are another story. Is it wrong to be proud of them? I don't think Jodi was lying when she said this all gave her more than a hint of jealousy; my friends, and her lack thereof. These past many months have been a ride, to say the least. I could feel so profound if not for that nagging sense of feeling so useless. This is wrong.

What happened here? Is Chris not the friend I know? Maybe I just can't accept that he's become the person I knew. Can't accept what's in the rear-view mirror. I was the pal he relied upon when he was down. Was my purpose served, and now by arguing these points, I have thus become a liability? Some program. When will I learn that no one is interested in the truth, save if it benefits them? I won't walk away from this, not yet. I have obligations to my friends, even if to lose sight of what they are.

"We are only trying to do better," I say. "To get better. Can we live with what we have and can we do better than the generation that came before us? We don't have to compete with them. They didn't, though they probably think they did. We've talked about all this time and time again, Chris. The American Dream is dead, and it's because we killed it. 'We' being everyone who has just accepted this as it is. Why can't we talk about it beyond closed doors and quiet rooms? Others besides us need to hear it."

Chris looks all but annoyed, exactly that actually, superior and embarrassed to be any part of this, yet hardly for himself.

"Din, people are going to behave the way they want to behave and not many people change, if ever at all. Do you want to keep your job? Do you want to move up, or get a raise? That's not going to happen if you are going in the direction you seem to be implying; and you will find that out, I promise you. Maybe try impressing your betters instead of questioning them and you might find better results."

My friend is clearly less concerned about the complete role reversal here. Could he be here for me as I was for him? I could not solve his problems. I would if I could have; now I'm causing more trouble for him somehow. I don't want to believe Chris is less than he was. My friend is still under there somewhere, it's just a phase. I'm bad at denial.

"Chris, did it ever occur to you that Miriam's narcissistic personality disorder, a malady that you yourself have pointed out over a dozen times in her prior to now, exists largely because we allow it to exist? People don't change much, which is frequently and unfortunately true. Yet we seem to have no trouble feeding it. Feed the monster, or it will eat you. How do we live this way? How can we possibly keep it up? I suppose quite well considering the energy we give up to it; and there's evidently more to spare.

"It's become an almost simple process, at least for those at the top, or those directly above us. If we have less, they have more. It's not just money, though that's the largest part of it; but also, an intolerance for any verbal or emotional high spiritedness. So not only do they deliberately pay less than they could, they also punish those who question them or imply dissent in any way. This is also known as bullying. You do remember Brooke Mesa, don't you?"

Chris holds his beer and smirks. He's not going to run from this subject this time. He doesn't have to. I wonder what Brooke would think of all this? I wonder if she's doing well, and if she could handle all this crap better than I could. She most certainly didn't deserve what she got. The fact that her very name is such a sensitive subject tells us a lot more on its own. Maybe if we talked about it more, "executions" such as hers would not happen.

"Yes, I remember Brooke, Din. She paid a heavy price for speaking to Miriam the way she did. She should have known better. What would you do if she undermined you like that? A boss has to be concerned with her reputation."

"At any cost? Brooke lost her job and was humiliated on a whim, all for the sake of Miriam's worthless ego."

"If Brooke was upset, she could have complained to Human Resources. She didn't. That's on her. Miriam did what she felt was best for the department, that's her job. If you don't like it, you can always move to Cuba." Again, Chris smirks, believing in his heart of hearts that he's right. He does believe that. I know it now.

"As if complaining to H.R. would have done anything," I say. "What would they do? They would never fire Miriam. Brooke was a subordinate to management, if they gave her such a victory, that would undermine all of them, not just Miriam. The boss saw her chance, and she took it. They will not bend if one of us suffers. Why invite chaos if it is not in their interests? Forgive my blatant lack of faith in your wonderful institution of capitalism, Chris; but does it hurt that you may be just lucky?"

"What?" He sounds like he wants to murder me right now, as if I am a stranger he never met who cut him off on the road, on his road. No consequences. None at all, apparently.

"You got lucky. I'm not saying you are not qualified to have the job you are moving to, or the one you had, any of them. It took you just as long to find a job as it would anyone else, none of us are so in demand. Employees are an expense. Is it right that we are 'lucky' to have a job, lucky to find one, and easy come easy go when lost at the hands of another human being with no interest in the livelihoods they are responsible for, no matter which way it's spun? Miriam would have gladly had your head on a platter and fired you, if nothing else than to make an example to everyone else what happens when anyone tries to cross her. Yes, we are so lucky.

"I wonder if your luck, or even mine for that matter will last. I find that doubtful. Where can we go? You conveniently pretend to forget, and don't seem to have an issue with that dishonesty, yet you yourself expressed dismay in the very opportunities that were once abundant, before our time, and have not been around much lately. We don't say it but they are never coming back. That fact doesn't go away because you got yours. There are others. Friends matter, at least they always did to me.

"All the opportunities are going away; the teacher faces underfunded and crumbling schools, even dumber students; the aspiring college professor can only be an adjunct, with no benefits; but lucky to have the job. The artist can go fuck himself. Those who came before us, the Miriams, the Elizabeths, all of these old bastards; they could not have worked harder than us. They think they did. Good enough for them. Why is this the way it is? What happened?"

Chris sips a drink and frowns. "I know it's easier to say we worked for the results when there are results, Din. But you have to make the results. They are not the keepers; and like Brooke, you will suffer the consequences for believing otherwise. I'm imploring you, do not tell Miriam you want to quit. It's not the right thing to do."

How can I not realize that those who have theirs would normally tend to be more conservative, to just about actually celebrate selfishness? Boomers had results. Miriam and company had results, even Chris has results, however questionable. Therefore, why ask questions? I (and Chris) will likely have over five or six, maybe more, full time jobs before we reach retirement age. That's if we are lucky, not to mention lucky enough to retire. Why do we have less? All the more, why even be "loyal" to a job that will only last four or five years, if lucky? All this evident respect for authority has its purpose. Why question it if you have yours?

"I understand it's rude to criticize what one believes, Chris. It's become a bit of a religion rather than a way of work life; believing that if you work hard, and keep your nose to the grind, that in short time you will be rewarded in the forms of raises, promotions, or general favor from management. It actually didn't happen to either of us. We can at least be honest with each other." He is already laying his money out on the table, ready to leave.

"We can't even criticize the awful boss because they 'give' us the money we so depend on. We are beholden to them, no matter how subtly, or even blatantly abusive they may be. We won't get anywhere by questioning them. We know this, because we don't like criticism either; and we want to be them. So play by their rules. There is no 'us.' Maybe we don't really need the boss to lead at their discretion, or at the discretion of rich donors or shareholders. If the team ran things, a cooperative based workforce; there would be, at the very least, a lot less heartache and pain. Maybe jobs would not so easily be shipped overseas, pensions would not dissolve for the sake of it, people like Brooke would never be fired the way she was. The interests, the money, and the decisions, do not have to be in the hands of a few; at the clear expense of the rest."

"That's a pipedream, Din. No one would ever want to give that up. Show your value, not your dissent. How long do you think anyone would last if they went to war with the upper crust? Do you really think you will get ahead with sharing these ideas with everyone? Will you get anywhere in life by pissing everyone off, and making them uncomfortable? It doesn't work like that, Din. I've honestly had enough. I hope you find peace with yourself. I have to meet up with Tina."

I don't want Chris to leave. But if he leaves now, he will not ever come back, not this new man. I get it, Tina makes him happy, that's clear. As such, what need has he of me? No balance, sadly. As if having friends somehow negates the power of one's romantic relationship or marriage. Almost as if having close friends means something is missing, and going outside the relationship is an indication something else is wrong. What happened to balance? What happened to just having pals?

The epidemic is not implausible, least of all with Chris. He would do anything for her, even exchanging an ex-lover's dogs like they are children. Even miles away; hell, he'd cross an ocean for it if he had to. Would we do that for a friend, especially one in need? Can't we walk and chew gum at the same time? Can we not have friends and be with our loves as well? What love I found is gone, almost as quickly as it came. That's probably why I even notice, and why I dare to ask.

It violates every fiber of my being to think I am now talking to my friend for the last time. Our friendship was not a flash in the pan. It can't go away. Chris and I always wanted the same thing: home. Job security, life security, love, the quest for contentment, whatever that may be for me. We are only getting older. This obligates us to create our own home. If those options are failing, if they are disappearing; then so are we. We can't even get to where we want to go if we do not even have the opportunity for any true balance. Without that, what good is home?

"It's not right that one person's ego decides the very fate of our lives, Chris. Ignore or downplay it all you want, but it's wrong. They can destroy lives, set fates, and destroy friendships, all at their whim. Such power should warrant far more responsibility than it apparently does. The workplace is where we actually spend most of our time. We need only think about it, even from time to time; a bully director guiding our daily lives is not a healthy situation. There is no course of action in accepting it. There's nothing for it."

Chris stands up to leave. I stand up with him. He extends his arm out to me, almost as if he's afraid to reach into a yawning alligator's mouth. The motion goes slowly. The handshake that follows was by far the most reluctant I've ever had. Worse than any bad interview, the worst of any goodbye. That is exactly what happens.

"Goodbye," is all he says before he walks across the Lark and out the door. I watched him fade away into and beyond the crowed until he disappeared. Even then, I kept watching. He took our friendship with him and threw it all away before he turned a single corner. Gone.

Chris was someone I knew. Maybe it was all me. I served my purpose, that's who I am, that's why I was needed. Din Swift is the friend you need when you are down. He's quite helpful. Not so much when all is going well though. Is he a downer? A joy-kill? He doesn't want to be, though he is a bad liar, I know it. Maybe right now I am actually making others feel better. It's just for all the wrong reasons.

I never mentioned to Chris, and probably shouldn't have, that I actually received a calendar meeting request from Miriam herself earlier this morning. The meeting was even given a title: "What do you expect from a manager?" It could very well mean that I'm being let go. She has done this to others; and within her good discretion, according to Chris. This meeting is far more likely just to get that process started, work on me, humiliate me as she did Chris, and then fire me after that's done to her pleasure. That's what this meeting is really for. Charming request. Not one that I would ever indulge in. Nor will I. If I was going to speak to any of these stage actors for the last time, it would have to be Chris. I'm glad it was.

I can call out Chris for being less than he was. It's not outrageous to consider. Yet what I know is I myself am less now than whatever I was before today. Maybe (hardly) it was for the best but not without its worst. Far from it. I thought I was disillusioned for not finding a new job, failing with Jodi, with Cathy, failing everything. None of it measures up to this. Friends are all I had; and now there is not. I had a job, even some fleeting prospects of a new one. They are gone as well.

I'm still standing here. Alone in the Lark, where I was never alone. I hate drinking by myself. Yet I remain, for at least a little while, feels like so much longer. My best friend, Chris Allen walked away. He's not here any longer. I watched him leave. I keep looking up for him, as if maybe he stopped to talk to someone, maybe he was not actually so willing to go. I look. I listen. Why? Nothing; and I don't even know what the hell I'm waiting for. He's gone, and that was the last time I ever saw him.

I stand here, by some means having two daydreams at the same time. The first is of myself walking out to find Chris strolling down the street to his car. I call out to him and he turns to my attention. I punch him directly in the face, his glasses flying off his bloodied face and shattering upon the sidewalk. He grunts in pain when I hit him, and I enjoy it, almost hoping he gives me another reason to do that again. He just stares at me, tears in his eyes and red faced, telling me I'm a sick bastard, and he's pressing charges. His breath is heaving, and he picks up his broken glasses, all the while staring at me with nothing but hatred and disgust. I tell him none of it matters, even if he wants it to.

I don't like that dream; though that's by no means the last time I thought of it. The other dream I had which I dream of even more was of Chris coming back into the bar, wanting to talk to me again, to be friends again. I dreamed we would both get over this and we would continue on, and not out of each other's lives. The reality is we didn't; and for the life of me I can't imagine any way to ever really make peace with that. Friends. What we are without the other, I can hardly imagine.

Chapter Eighteen

The Truth

IT'S AMAZING HOW CALM I am now that I've made up my mind. I have been avoiding this for a remarkable amount of time; I fought it off for as long as I could, for whatever that was worth. Once that meeting request came in from Miriam, I knew it was time to leave. I actually half doubt I was going to be fired in said meeting, which itself would have been easier to accept. What I can't accept is what was more likely, that being the beginning of a humiliation campaign that Chris himself underwent for all those months. It's not enough to just fire someone, they have to suffer first, and they need to know who wins in the end. It is not enough that they succeed; everyone else must fail, and do so miserably. This must happen without question, and certainly without any reprisal for them.

That and the so-called superior would have to keep her hands clean by setting me up for failures; damaging in a potential performance evaluation, thus making it all look good on paper. The score can't end with them just winning; my score has to be zero. Not giving them the pleasure, I simply won't stand for it any longer; no reason to stay here at this point anyway. Not even for a paycheck. Capitalism may be unbeatable but it doesn't need another victory dance. I just came to enough being enough. I don't know what comes beyond this line.

I have been out of work before; one never knows how long that will be. Since my conversation with Chris, I have been trying to get used to the idea that I now do not have a job. It brings about that dazed and confused feeling; losing one's employment, losing a source of income, losing a part of life. At least it was my decision, not theirs, and not on their terms. I resigned early on a Monday morning, logging in remotely, having already come into the office on Sunday to remove what little possessions I had. I did leave my office key right on my desk, they won't miss it. I could have just left everything. But if I'm going to be gone, then I will be gone. Without a trace.

When I woke up that morning, with my neighbor aggra-vated at me over her milk crates, I realized I was in fact out of work. Then I intercepted my own folly. Nobody knew I resigned, and I backed out. Not this time. This time I hit "send all," and to the entire department and human resources. They will know when they come into work for their day. All of them: Miriam, Chris, Cathy, Joey, Elizabeth, everyone. Enjoy it.

I didn't change a word of that resignation letter, just the date. One of the better or at least more notable works of my career, such as it is. No concern for reputations any longer. I sent everyone that letter because we are everyone. Who am I to leave anyone out of a farewell?

To whom it may concern,

Good morning, this is Din. You likely may not have been expecting a message from me today, or at all. Nonetheless I hope this letter finds you all well. As you likely have already gathered from the heading of my email, I am officially announcing my resignation from the nonprofit organization known as Learning Tools, effective immediately. Please do not let this cause you much alarm as there is no real need for it. I realize that many of you may not have expected this, let alone from one such as myself. I think a lot more than I have ever let on; this is often to my detriment, but to paraphrase a saying: watch out for the quiet ones, they might be too honest. Somehow, I feel that no explanation is needed for as to why I am leaving. Nonetheless, I will elucidate the circumstances.

Whatever you thought of me, I have come to accept that I am no longer what I was. Maybe that's a good thing, and we've all been lacking good things, despite ideas and events to the contrary. What has not changed as much as I would like is my own certainty that I was simply born too late. I am not a man of my own time, none of us really are is the truth of it. I've been at this "working world" for over a good ten years now, I never imagined it would actually come to this but even as an admittedly slow learner, I have come to accept that this needs to happen, and all of it needs to be said.

I simply will not stand for the methods and procedures, as well as the subtle (and occasionally outright) abusive manners of the present management of this organization. Manners that take obvious pleasure in feeling superior to and humiliating their "inferiors" for the sake of their egos, or world view, or often all of the above. This behavior, common as it sadly may be, does not deserve an ounce of the respect we so easily give them. I will not wait for this to play out with myself as a tragic hero, only to be removed with little to no remorse and then forgotten. All of which enforced by a great number of unwritten rules that we inexplicably follow.

I acknowledge (quite fully, actually) that I'm committing two rather unpardonable sins as they exist in our brave modern world. Firstly, I am resigning my position at this organization without notice, only this letter. As you are reading this, I am gone. The second sin is that I do not have another job lined up for myself at this moment in time. Though I do see time granted to me now to continue to explore opportunities, whatever they may be. I realize that I myself am responsible for these sins, and I accept this. Even if I didn't, the burden of responsibility could never be on this office's management. We cannot and do not accept this in any tangible sense, though this is the reason for our behavior after all.

If I was good at this job, then I thank you for the opportunity, such as it was. I am rather good at surrendering into self-pity, certainly in regards to these two sins. However, in a rare moment of positivity, I find that maybe I will cease such activities in time. If nothing else, a great number of changes have come about, they could and likely will change even more. We do not like change very much, change often violates our plans, and does not often stand well with our perceptions, particularly our own perceptions of ourselves. Still, I am gratified by the recent past that I have lived, which has granted me a faint but clear sound of ambition to make the decisions I have. This is all where we have come to today.

If I seem to have digressed, let me further explain myself. I plainly no longer wish to subject myself to the bullying, verbal abuse, abrasiveness, and "C.Y.A." mentality that now grips the office due to management. I don't think I have to explain to anyone what "C.Y.A." means. All of these transgressions are the features of a totalitarian; and we are allowing this to happen under our very noses, *if not with wide open arms. I choose to no longer be a part of it.*

On the subject of my own crimes, or sins as I have mentioned, I cannot help but to ask if I really have directly offended anyone who is not in any real position of power here. Does the fact that I move on from this organization without another job mean that you in fact work for an organization that is questionable enough for one to leave in this manner? Is the thought of it alone too much of an implication to handle? Are you uncomfortable for the right reasons? Are you offended that I asked?

I know I am breaking more unspoken instructions; yet I feel more than just slightly obligated to mention a name that has not been spoken of once since the day she departed our company. That name is Brooke Mesa. We don't think about it, or speak of her. We should. Maybe you do not remember that our colleague was fired on day thirteen of her own two weeks' notice to leave. Brooke has not done what I am doing now. Perhaps, she was stronger than I, and I commend her for it. She suffered for us all the same; while we said and did nothing.

Brooke suffered the wrath of Miriam Gaw for criticizing the boss. This is unquestionable, and it is shameful. It is also to our shame that we likely saw this coming, perhaps expecting it, perhaps understanding it, perhaps even liking it. Make no mistake now that I have reminded you of something you do not want to be reminded of; the removal of Brooke Mesa from our ranks was not a business-related decision. It was ego; and ego is not business, nor should it be. Though we seem to like it. What have we become?

Are employees allowed to leave, be it in a scathing resignation letter, or by traditional submittal of a two weeks' notice? Consider, if an employee leaves for any reason, it's harmful to the company; and certainly, its management. If an employee leaves for a better salary, that means we don't pay enough and therefore are in the wrong. If they leave for differences with management or even other staff, this implies that the organization's people, or workplace culture, is wrong. We cannot seem to live with this. It's not business, it's all rather quite more personal than we have any courage to admit, as evidenced by our complete lack of courage to even speak of it.

I dare to ask: who is it that decides what level of money we make? Not just here, anywhere. There are only twenty-four hours in a day; exactly who decides what compensation is to be distributed among us? Are they thinking about you? That's quite a power for another human being to have, and for us to have not.

I reprise, Brooke was fired because and only because of one person's ego; and not for the betterment of this organization's business or financial well-being. We offered only a blind eye to her departure. Why was a personal decision such as this unchecked? The answer is painfully simple: we fear to suffer a similar fate.

What kind of a mad house do we work in, where employees who express dissent, or even simple disagreement are fired for the sake of what I can only see as instilling fear into the staff which is allegedly supposed to respect the authority above them? What kind of workplace has employees sent home in tears after meetings with the same "superiors?" Why do I even call this a mad house, or even a workplace? Perhaps a play pen might be a more accurate description given these circumstances we conveniently forget. This is what we work under. This is the manager's play pen, and you are going to play her way. If you are not going to play her way, well, then she is going to show you; as she did Brooke.

How little has changed since we were all children. Do you remember those years with any vital amount of detail? Maybe I remember too much. If I speak of bullies now, I can ask as to what our relationship is with them. Maybe it was you, maybe it was not; but do you remember that one kid (perhaps more than one) that was friends with the school bully? Remember they were chums on the playground? He (and even she) saw something in the bully. No, the bully is not that bad, I see something in them that you don't, and you just have to catch up with the program in order to see what I see.

The bully is my friend. Well, I'm sorry; you were full of shit then, and you are full of shit now. The bully does not care about you. Miriam is not your friend. You just want her to be. There is something about being "in" with the wrong kind of person isn't there? I am not impressed with anyone with such friends.

I emphasize this so profanely, and I also ask: do you care? Do you understand the consequences of turning away? Or the consequences of denial? This behavior is completely untenable. If there is nothing but "me" and no "we," the game is up before it even began. If this is how we all behave, it is not an excuse, it's an indication that there is clearly something dreadfully wrong with all of us, and we will in turn pass that on to those who come next to follow. But then again, if we are this selfish, why do I even speak of others? If the boss does not care about any of us, how can we care about each other? Let alone for younger employees to enter our world as each year goes by. Have any of you tried to get into the mind of your so-called superiors? Have you ever pondered what their opinions are of you, rather us, really are?

We never think of this, and it is for a reason. Is this what we all went to college for? Looking back, it's not such a radical suggestion that schools could place a warning in their curricula. College will never prepare anyone for what they really should be prepared for. There is no Boss' Ego 101, or required psychology classes to be prepared for a megalomaniac who remorselessly fires an employee who disagreed with her. Brooke could not quit, that would mean Brooke wins. This cannot be allowed.

But I digress. Was it because Brooke was younger than Miriam and should have known her place? We may not ever know, but that suggestion is by no means outside the realm of plausibility. There is a major gap, in both access to wealth, and to perception; between the older generation, the baby boomers, and all those who came after. It's so easy to identify a superior in this conflict. After all, age is all the basis of power we seem to need. I dare to suggest that before criticizing the young, consider who raised them into existence. This did not come about without origin. This is ageism at its finest. More so it is acceptable ageism. I can say now that I will never accept it, and make a promise to you now that I never will.

What is more remarkable is that Brooke's departure did not even affect me directly that much. I was not close with her, though I enjoyed working with her. She was a good person and valuable employee here. Generally, we all are. We are all simply beholden to the agenda set by those above us, and fear them all the same for the sake of our very livelihood; we share this in solidarity. Yet, I know right and I know wrong. This was wrong. Brooke being fired the way she was is hardly my only reason for resigning now. Yet, isn't it reason enough?

I personally find it amazing; the things we could do and the better people we could become if we could ever re-channel the tremendous (and limitless) amount of energy it takes to spend lying, denying, covering our own asses, and saving the face of our own reputations around others who behave precisely in the same manner.

I ask you to stop for even just a moment to take a real look are where we are at; and yes "we," not just "me." We are at the very mercy of our own manager, our "superior," we are at the mercy of her discretions, whatever she so chooses them to be. Does she have our interests at heart; or more likely hers?

Have any of you ever noticed that Miriam was never promoted into the Senior Leadership Team despite her being here for so many years? I see no real conclusion that this is a statement on our manager's abilities per se, only that of her personality. I take no pleasure in pointing this out. I could gloat (not a fan of that behavior) and point out that this lack of a promotion is well deserved for her questionable if not egregious behavior, yet I find myself more sullen in the knowledge that this only shows how much even our superior's "superiors" do not seem to be at all concerned whom Miriam stands over; only that she does not stand among them. The peasants be damned.

They know what she is, and they do not care about what we are, or the daily tribulations of a group of people that they have been elevated above for far too long. This is how things are, certainly, yet I ask whom does this system benefit? This is our sin as much as theirs, perhaps more so. If you do not like the word "sin" then I will use "mistaken." We are so easily mistaken that the interests of those in power; the upper crust, high management, the rich; we presume that their interests are aligned with our own. They are not.

Those in such power are in their own world, a much different world. It's their own club, which you are not in. We want that world; we want to be rich. Hell, I want that. There actually should be nothing wrong with that, but unfortunately, there is. Why would they want you? Your success may not be their failure, but the less we have, the more they do. I hate to boil down to simple numbers but there is all the reason to do so. I'm sorry. Well, I'm not.

What is more astounding is that we never talk about any of this; the very subject of wealth inequality is off limits; and we are encouraged to not talk about this even when not actually being told that. I cannot think of one such instance where I or anyone was instructed otherwise yet we all seem to understand this rule; and we abide by it well. Who really benefits from this silence?

I have come to admit it to myself, even if none of you can, although I don't believe it true of most of you. I am convinced that our director is not our superior. No human being will earn my respect while behaving in a manner in direct contradiction to that very word. Should

Brooke have spoken as she did? Did her punishment fit her evident crime? Is any of this at least questionable? Why give up the very sovereignty of inquiry? Why abandon that feeling which is in our own hearts, or would be there if we allowed it? Are we really so evil? What I am certain of, and have no need of an answer for, is that the superiority as we know it is not there. We just may want it to be, sadly for our own selfish motives. Lest we rise above our own sins.

Is it not a lonely existence to be unable to say what is really on one's mind, to say what we think; as Brooke did? This is idiotic bliss at best. Is denial really so enjoyable? Again, to whom does our denial benefit? It does have value, sadly. We cannot keep this up. No matter how well we are at our jobs of denial, we can ultimately never shirk the responsibility we have always had in the first place. That is to admit that as a thinking people, as a community of adults, that we must finally concede to ourselves that there is nothing to gain from what we have done. There is no authoritarian solution to life's problems. They are not of this community, and they do not want to be.

We have to solve these problems ourselves. We cannot do so by pretending to get ahead in life. We cannot do so by emulating the behavior of those we perceive to be superior. If the boss is so infallible, if we accept this, we all but become them. There is hardly any such profit to be gained, save for them, and to be fed by us.

This is a responsibility we need no longer shirk or ignore. We can begin by forsaking all such ideas; to repudiate all such behavior; even in its very face if necessary. They behave this way only because we consistently allow them to. We often refer to "they;" and they are often only one, perhaps a few; yet we are many. Respect is something special in life, it's wanted and needed by all of us, and respect must be earned in any and all cases; for respect is not at all compulsory. It cannot be given freely.

We have no need for leaders such as this. We stand here inferior to an imposter, and the anguish of their supporters, many of whom we unfortunately are. I have committed sins here, and I admit this openly to all of you, even if you are indifferent, or have any such opinion. What is we and what are they? Whatever the answer, I realize that my own actions, my own sins, and indeed this very letter are less than trivial in transgression by comparison; and themselves barely worth a fret. If my leaving here and in this way really changes anything, then perhaps those willing to ponder other possibilities will. Perhaps now that I am gone, everything I have said, and indeed my very existence, may be forgotten. This is all of course entirely up to you. I will think on you and what has transpired here. It's important to know what not to do. The first step in solving any problem is admitting that there is one. If I can do so, then there is no reason you cannot. Thank you, and fare all thee well.

With honesty and the resilient spirt of friendship,
Din Swift

That was the end of that. My heart may have jumped when I actually hit the send button but my resolve never shaken. It was done. I just didn't know what the hell I was to do next. At least I followed thorough, and did what I said I was going to do. It has to count for something, I want to believe that. I do.

To my knowledge, they just accepted that resignation, they accepted what I had to say, doubtful any of it was ever really taken to heart by anyone, that's not what or who we are as a people; we are just not there, not yet. Growing is a slow process, though times do change, every empire has had its day, and then its history.

I never saw or heard from any of them again. I accept that. Though my heart will never be the same for the loss of a friend. Nor should it be. Indirectly, I actually did hear from more than one of them again. I have not entirely been excommunicated from my former place of employment. Though I know my name must never be spoken within those walls ever again. How could it be otherwise?

It was Joey LeMari who reached out to her, and let her know what had happened, what I had said; that I stood up for her even well after her dubious dismissal. He also told her that I was out of work and could use at least something to get by. That's how this all came to pass. Joey got in touch directly with Brooke Mesa after tracking her down for which reason I would never know. Maybe even after I was gone, he still remembered I was his friend to. It was Brooke herself who got in touch with me after sending that letter. It was a bit surreal, but very good to see and speak to her again. It was she who turned out to be most crucial to what lay beyond; and she who showed me what a lucky son of a bitch I really am.

Chapter Nineteen

fear

THE WORST THING ONE person can do to another is figure out their bullshit. That's something I do exceptionally well. I never wanted to hurt anyone, not even their feelings, though that is remarkably easy to do. I'm not a good liar. I am rather inept at that. There are worse things to be; though it's been rather difficult to think of any over the past month. That's about how long it's been since I sent that letter. I admit I wrote it not having any idea what would come after; knowing, yet not knowing that I would be out of a job. It's not a good situation to be in; it's largely why I backed out the first time. Yet I accept that no one really knows what will happen next after now; we just like to think that we do.

I do not regret what I have done. I just have to learn how to live with it; an ongoing process at the moment. The good news, if there ever is any of late, is that I did hear back from Kevin Roberts. That is, I got a reply from him of a sort. Essentially right after I sent that letter and resigned, I did email Kevin to ask him the status of my application. It was an email sent directly to him, yet he decided to reply with a copy and paste boiler plate "your skills are impressive, however, we decided not to offer you a position at this time" type response, and nothing else.

I wonder if he's annoyed with me for even taking some of his time away. If he is, he will forget soon enough. No consequences. What did I expect? In Kevin's case, I walked away from the argument. Sadly, this was probably all I could do. What could I say to him? I guess that's the whole point. Deniability. That, and I was still a bit freaked out from the epic resignation letter everyone was reading right about then. It still scares me. I just care.

There is a lot that is gone, maybe too much for me to handle. I don't know. I am out of full-time work, no real friends to hang out with; not a word from Dave, not that I should expect any. It's all been cleared away. What comes next is the larger question. I don't know that either. It's frustrating and scary all at the same time. Today, I leave my apartment again, and, despite everything, nothing has really changed. No, there is something. It's this strangely profound feeling that letting go of everything is the best idea I ever had.

For nearly a month, I was out of work entirely. I just hung around at home, mostly. I spent time looking for jobs, and even more time pining away as to what the next one will be, if there will be a next one at all. The rest of my life would do well to start as soon as possible. I can't move on if I can't move. Being out of work is not just they lack of the paycheck coming in. There is a loss of dignity, of purpose, and of community. Not just the money. I can live without the company I parted ways with but that was my job, I didn't own it, but it was mine. Now it isn't. At least it was my choice. My gut still wrenches in knots when I don't want it to. I think in copious amounts and details. It all keeps going, doubtful it will all truly stop.

Today I'm going to work for a few hours, my new part time job working with Brooke Mesa's tech team at a medical device production company. For the first couple of days, I was able to work remotely from my apartment. They want me there from time to time, and I need to get out more, so off I go. The job itself is mostly writing up report summaries on market research statistics. It's all, as Brooke promised me, quite technical in nature, but at this point as in others, I can't really choose where I work. I'm happy to have it, even when not really liking it. A part time job is still work; and that is good, though it's hardly enough. Even when Joey was hiring just a part time writer, it meant something. It was someone else's life; it was their future, whatever it may have been. I wonder if he and management in general will ever realize that. Unlikely, I suppose.

I'm glad Joey got in touch with Brooke on my account; somehow, I don't think he is too happy with me. I doubt his current opinions are at all positive. I will likely never know. I have no idea if he ever even hired someone like he was evidently going to. If so, I hope it's working out, for him at least, and for the new hire even more. Joey is no doubt still of his frame of mind on the subject. He's not changing. I guess he doesn't have to. I miss having him around all the same.

Brooke had been working the same job since she was "fired." She must have gotten my number from Joey directly, and asked me to meet her for a drink, coffee actually; well away from any of the haunts our former employers may be at. Free country but both Brooke and myself would just as soon never want to rub elbows with any of them ever again. Neither would they. I often wonder what would happen if I randomly ran into Miriam at a coffee shop or anywhere for that matter. That would be awkward, yet not at all an impossibility.

I sometimes think of how that would play out. What if I ran into Miriam, say in line at a coffee shop like this one? Would we say anything to each other? She didn't get the last word with me, so that would be an opportunity. Would she leave, not wanting to even be within five yards of me? Would I? How does a manager deal with bumping into someone whose lives they have ruined? They know they made a decision to let their subordinate go, but they are still human. They are still alive. I wonder if not being held, or even being in the position of being held accountable is the whole idea. It can't work all the time. It's okay if they don't win. That kind of loss should happen more often.

This particular coffee shop was better, none of them were there, just Brooke and myself and a couple of employees behind the counter. Brooke was always good to me, even though we were not close friends, just affable; back when she was working under Miriam. Maybe we should have been closer. Not everyone there had the mutual agenda. Brooke did not, and that is a pleasant thought. Pleasant is exactly what I could use right now, and I have it.

I never really took notice of Brooke before that coffee date, (not a date, however); I think she may be just a little younger than me. Yet she's more though, she is adult looking. More so than most even by the way she carries herself. It's real confidence, with less the ego. In other words, an actual adult. Brooke has well-kept skin, a dress that's long but not too long to hide anything, a lovely smile, and long black hair about her shoulders; and the best is the glasses. She's not like her former boss at all, though to be fair that is a low bar to pass. No, Brooke wears her glasses smart, which is the right way; and smart is sexy, no one talks about that enough.

After sitting down and quickly passing the hello and how are you reels, she said she could set me up with the part time job as they needed the help, and this was most welcome. We somehow became fast friends and I will not question any of it. It ultimately doesn't take very long to sign me up and get us going. But hardly to my surprise, Brooke did have a thing or two to say about where we used to work, and what we have become; and she was right.

"There is no winning with people like Miriam, Din. They have been given too much in life, they think they earned it and they think we did not work hard enough. Most of them kiss the boss' ass because they believe they are not actually doing that, and they believe it will help them get ahead. It won't. It creates nothing but divides. It's all bullshit. Still, what can anyone do? I could have created an uproar when I left, as you did, and I certainly had every reason to. I was leaving anyway; and Miriam saw her chance so she fired me. Petty, but it worked. I don't let her get me down, no matter what she might think. What hurts is there is no sign of this type of economy getting better; no sign of anything even getting close to being what it was, what it should be. That's another reason I left. I wanted no more part of it. We can only be superior by not behaving this way; by changing things when they are wrong. Doesn't work for them. Changing is admitting you are wrong; and that is one thing not a single one of those idiots is ever going to do.

"I admire you for at least calling them all out. Joey didn't mention anything to me about the aftermath of your resignation. I very much got the impression that he did not want to talk about it. Who knows what would happen, no one ever does what you at least tried to do, Din. They are all scared, and rightly so; their job is on the line. It should not have to be, I know it. But not all of them, in fact hardly any of them will be there as the months and years go by. A bad job is like a bad relationship, you wish you never had them, you wish things had gone probably completely different than they did; but the past can only be learned from. It's sad to say it; but our skills have little to do with any of it. It's not about what you did right, or what you evidently did wrong. It's all about them. The good news is you are still you. They lost."

She doesn't know I lost a great friend. I don't expect her to. Yet there's something to be said for someone who got fired the way Brooke did, yet still sits here with me with her head held high, as least compared to some; and certainly compared to me. I wish I was that resilient. Maybe I can be. It will likely take a lot more time.

Brooke deserved better than what she had suffered. She is better than that. She earned it, even if they do not think so. She is above all of this and it shows. I have to remind myself that there are many well above this behavior. This is yet another pleasant thought. Perhaps I have finally become at ease, and I thank her for that. Maybe everything would have turned out better for everyone if Brooke had never left; maybe things would have played out differently if she was around. It would have been better with her at least being there. Maybe it's lucky her that she wasn't.

Brooke didn't have to endure Chris' meltdown, something I would do all over again if a friend was in need. More than once, he would go on his tirades about the so called "lost generation." Chris may not be feeling so lost himself now but he's not wrong, just incomplete. What upset me more than anything whenever he would bring this issue to light was that in time, we, whatever we are, could become the "forgotten" generation. Worse, yet, we accept it without any real acknowledgement. Such ignorance is bliss; though to overlook for pure comfort can often be a debilitating disease. Sometimes I wish I could, yet I rarely forget a thing.

That rendezvous with Brooke was fairly quick, we continued to talk about how goofy some of those people on staff were, and wondered if Joey would ever trim his nose hairs, Brooke also implied Cathy is headed for a divorce, but could never say it to her face. Not that it would do any good if she had. Brooke and I have been working together for just a little while now, I don't know how long I can simply keep up part time work, and I will have to make time for interviews if any more come about. Brooke says she understands. She actually asked if I was up for going out for a drink this coming weekend. I said I was. I most certainly was.

Here we all are. What will become of us? We all have reason to at least ask. Perhaps more employees than just myself and Brooke will get sick of this train we have been on. Perhaps more of us will speak our minds. We are long overdue for a new renaissance; and more of us are seeing that the track we are on does not seem to go anywhere, and we lose more than we gain. It was not always like this. We saw it ourselves growing up.

Loss is common. I've been losing myself for far too long; I've lost money, jobs, good people; I may not be able to pay my rent in the long run, and the part time job won't be enough. I've sank money and time into cars that probably lay in a junkyard somewhere now. I have had bad dates, heartbreaks, and failed ventures. I've lost a great deal, to be sure. Worse yet, I have lost friends, and that's what hurt the most. It all goes somewhere. The only hope is all this loss can be checked, that the damage it inflicts upon our own mental and social landscape can be minimized somehow. It's damn near impossible, yet like a fool, I keep trying; for as long as I can.

I finally think I know what I want in life. I want what everyone wants; even if not admitting it is in their immediate interest. I want my future back. We were told to work hard, do good in school; at the very least we would have access to the wealth our own parents had before us, when they raised us as kids. We do not have to be rich, but at the least as well off or stable as what was already there. That was to be our future. What do our parents think of us now? Do they really want us to have less than they did? I doubt many of them believe that, at least not of their own. Yet, I sense more than just a small amount of survivor's guilt involved; or a noticeable lack thereof. Ideas like that can make us quite uncomfortable, particularly when we question why. For the boomers, we would never complain if we had what you had at least.

I don't see a need for apologies; we only wanted to go home. What is that? It's not just a house to indulge in real estate; it's not just a couch to relax upon (or for a friend to pass out on). There is something else. I say this word to myself: "adults." I use that word with caution, as much as I do "home." That all goes away when they leave; or leave us with next to nothing but longing for what is gone.

A home is more important than work; than making money, than making the boss look good; than failing in any of the above; of this much I am certain. It's all visibly within the past; and all of it was theirs, and not ours.

Modern humans should simply care more about each other more than we do; sappy sentiment maybe, but this is more elusive than we realize. It's even more elusive than my good friend realized. Why did we become so much less than we were? Is it so wrong to want this? Is wanting itself wrong? What is the proper consequence for issuing a question? I'll stop asking; though only for now.

I have to get to work. It's rude to be late. I walk out onto the street from my place. I can take the train to work, I even have a new book to read that Brooke lent me. That's even another pleasant turn. It would almost make me believe that things are changing. That would be good.

Then I stop walking, dead in my tracks, even for fear of missing my train. I am now reminded of an unfortunate truth. Nothing has changed. The milk crates are here, again, lying on the street as always, placed just far apart to reserve a parking spot for a certain SUV. It's not as cold as it was that morning, when my neighbor committed this crime right in front of me and all but succeeded in making me feel guilty for it. She is not here, and she's not here to make a disappointing face at me, to shake her head off her shoulders at the indignity of even the implication of wrongdoing. That's a bit of a disappointment; a small part of me wants her to be here. It's just as well. The sun is not completely out but it's a beautiful day. Too bad I spend some of it walking to a dumpster nearby.

I take them. It's ridiculous but I'm carrying two milk crates with me as I walk on. I will have to wash my hands after this, these things really are filthy. I feel like a bit of an idiot walking around with them, but I'm not scared. That parking spot is open now. It's a public space, and anyone can use it. That's how it should be. That is how it is. I toss the crates into the dumpster; they make a very pleasing clanging noise, loud enough to matter; to me anyway. I don't feel bad. I will do this again if needs be, and I see that as likely. After all, we are, everyone, all the better for it.

I can't fool myself, not everything is actually that great. I'm off to work again but I still feel like it's all wrong; that warning in my heart that things can and will get worse. It's possible, and given everything that has happened; seems probable. I've never been a glass is half empty, or a glass is half full kind of person. It's more than obvious to me that my glass is neither. It is right in front of me, I can see it. My glass is one sixteenth full. No more at the moment. Sorry to everyone for any and all negativity; yet if it's in my defense, I am honest. I don't like lying to anyone, nor to be lied to. Crazy.

Maybe I am a man out of my own time, from some different by-gone era that is never to return. I just have to accept time even if unable to. Yes, that should be easy. I wonder what it is all worth. I know that I miss everyone, and think about them all the time. I probably always will, if it's right or wrong. And those I miss; all of them, I wish them well. As well, I wish they were more like the memories I have, and not what they came to be; and where they ended up; out of my life. I'll always remember my friend, even though the pain of losing that will never really go away. I'm glad he was at least there, even if it was only for a short while. All friendships are extraordinary. I remember always; they were not our family, but the family we found. It's something else. It always will be. I'm still here, for whatever and to whomever that is worth. I am still here, and still alive. Even well rested.

Last night, I had a dream. I was flying, not very high though, like in a helicopter. I had next to no fuel was the truth of it; as if I was running life on fumes, and could not keep the engine going for long. Not to mention, the ground below me was on fire. Flaming trees and burning ground beyond all reason. There were maniacs running about everywhere; who would drink my blood if they felt so inclined to, and more so if it benefited them. That's who they often are. Then I started to fall, and they liked that I was descending. Then I woke up still afraid, actually shaking. Cold.

Now the dream is over, but I can remember. I could come crashing down right now. I could be consumed by those fires myself. Gone. I could run again. I don't know what to do next, or what is to come. It may very well fall apart all over again. It may. But that is alright.

Acknowledgements

Many thanks to the friends and colleagues who helped me along the way in life, and shared the many experiences that inspired this book. Special thanks to Sanjay for believing this book was a great idea; and to Colin for rescuing me from all the warzones I fell into (far more than one); and to his wife, Lisa, for being a true friend and great mother to their daughter, Hannah; who was the only human being on this earth who could get me to smile when it was otherwise impossible. Friends matter. If there is nothing else I have learned in this world, it's that. This book is also made possible by my niece, Brooke Denshuick, who always remains a positive light in my life and is bound for greatness no matter what. There are so many others to thank, trust me, you are not forgotten and I am a bad liar; even when that was to my detriment. Living in memory, I want to thank my grandfather, Francis Swift, for the time he shared with me in my own era, however long ago. There is far more than just something to be said of the past. Everyone: ask questions, especially if they don't want you to; and you are not causing any real peril to yourself; especially when considering the basis of comparison.

9 781735 891705